CW01429724

Nobody
Loves a
BIGFOOT
Like a
BIGFOOT
Babe

Simon Okill

C|M Christopher
Matthews
Publishing

www.christophermatthewspub.com
Bozeman, Montana

Nobody Loves a Bigfoot Like a Bigfoot Babe

Copyright © 2013 by Christopher Matthews Publishing

Editor: Jeremy Soldevilla
Cover design: Armen Kojoyian
Typeface: Georgia

ISBN 978-1-938985-03-4

Published by
CHRISTOPHER MATTHEWS PUBLISHING
http://christophermatthewspub.com
Bozeman, Montana

Printed in the United States of America

Dedication

Without my lovely wife, Shirlee Anne, this novel would not have been written. She has been the driving force that has pushed me to new limits.

Acknowledgements

I would like to add a big thank you to my editor and publisher, Jeremy Soldevilla, for believing in our novel. I would also like to thank Stephen King's *Salem's Lot* and *The Shining* for inspiring me to write.

THE SMALL NORTHERN CALIFORNIA town of Big Beaver in the Shasta Cascade Region has for a long time been a thriving tourist trap for those searching for Bigfoot. And for some Beaverites there seemed to be endless opportunities to create havoc during the tourist season with imaginative practical jokes.

On the northern edge of the township nestled the Whittleberry's small ranch-style house made of rough cut timber and river stones. The house was silent and as dark as the night. Two furry figures emerged from the forest, edging the property. They paused and listened for danger signs. The moon emerged from a dark cloud briefly illuminating both Bigfoot as they skipped across the lawn and entered the house by the unlocked back door.

The smaller of the Bigfoot opened a fridge with large, hairy hands and rifled through it, tossing food all over the kitchen floor. The Bigfoot grinned as it removed a doughnut like a ring on its finger.

The larger Bigfoot grinned back, licking its mouth.

In the time it took for both Bigfoot to find the downstairs bathroom, the Whittleberrys had staggered, somewhat worse the wear from the locally brewed beer up at Abe's Bar and Grill, to the front door and entered their home.

Barbie Whittleberry heard a splashing sound as if someone was using the shower. She rushed across the living area to the rear of the house and out of sight of Lance, without any thought to her safety.

An overly-excited Barbie returned and grabbed Lance's hand. She placed a finger to his lips to be quiet.

Lance Whittleberry frowned as he was dragged across the living area to the bathroom.

Lance and Barbie stood in the open doorway of their bathroom staring wide-eyed and open-mouthed at the weird scene before them. They were so amazed neither Whittleberry had the foresight to switch on the light. Enough moonlight cascaded through the window to show one Bigfoot scrubbing the lower regions of another in the double shower cubicle. Clumps of fur clung to the shower cubicle side and the floor was a disgusting, gooey dark mess.

Barbie also noticed the toilet seat was left up. She was about to berate her husband for this foul deed when she saw an uneaten doughnut on the rim. She wrinkled her nose at the thought of eating while using the facilities. She then gagged on the awful stink that invaded her nostrils. The smell reminded her of skunk spray and the gut-churning farts her father's dog would always leave hanging in the air during dinner.

One of the Bigfoot reached for something. An intense flash of light blinded both Whittleberrys. When their eyes became accustomed to the semi-darkness once more the bathroom was empty of Bigfoot and the stink was now contaminated with bleach. In the Whittleberrys' drunken state it was decided aliens had abducted both Bigfoot. Cool!

❧   ❧   ❧

SHERIFF LOUISE JESSOP'S office was neat and tidy. Nothing looked out of place, not even the fine old oak desk amongst the shining metal filing cabinets. A gun rack displayed various pump-action shotguns and massive revolvers. A board displayed lurid crime scene photos courtesy of the Bigfoot Bather. A flat screen monitor lay squarely in the middle of the desk, concealing the woman scrutinizing it.

There was not a single item of clutter on the highly polished desk. Lou's personal life was also clutter-free—free from a man who would appreciate her womanly charms. She had a fling or two, but none could rekindle the love she felt for *him*, nor the hurt.

Lou knew she was one hot cop. She had just turned thirty and still maintained her firm body and smooth skin from her teen years. Her blond hair was cut boyishly short. She wore very little make-up—didn't have to as she was a natural beauty. Her athletically slim, long legs accentuated her firm rear end and her ample breasts would often cause her shirt to pull a little too snugly across her chest, testing the buttons to the extreme.

And her uniform sure suited Lou—it really did. She was, however, a paradox, for there were occasions when she'd slip on a sexy, low-cut, black dress and actually put on some minimal make-up, the kind that glosses her lips. This she would do to raise the temperatures of the men at the local bar in town.

But getting all slutty didn't mean she was ready to "put out." It was in her nature to do a little cock-teasing now and again.

Sheriff Lou sat at her desk reading the local newspaper. The Busy Beaverite's report on the Phantom Bigfoot Bather Case—aptly named by ace reporter, Mocking Bird—was causing her hangover to go into overdrive.

"The Phantom Bigfoot Bather Strikes Again.

This is the third such incident to embarrass the sheriff's department. Local Beaverites, including Lance and Barbie Whittleberry, the Bigfoot's latest victims, are coming to the conclusion that real Bigfoot are responsible for the home invasions. The Whittleberrys were also witness to both Bigfoot being abducted by aliens. Many Beaverites have also seen strange lights above Little Beaver Picnic Area and are convinced Big Beaver is becoming the new Roswell. After thorough investigations into this heinous crime by Herb Herbert, our local medical examiner and yours truly, MB, local crypto-zoologist and expert on Bigfoot, Sheriff Louise Jessop is no nearer to discovering the identity of the perps."

Lou blew out her cheeks, sighed irritably and dropped the newspaper in a trash bin. She saw her worst nightmare on the computer screen. It was the DNA result for the Phantom Bigfoot Bather Case, a somewhat lengthy document by the irritated sounds coming from her lips—the irritation was more due to the annoying fact of the Bigfoot prank itself causing the entire department to become laughing stocks. Lou clicked the mouse with impatience. A printer sitting on a filing cabinet whirred into action, spewing forth the report.

As Lou sipped her black, extra sweet coffee to lift the pervading tequila fog, she thought of her best friend and number one suspect. *Damn you, Duane Dexter, why did you have to be such a lame brain,* she mused. She also pondered the fact that Duane knew full well she loved him like a brother and wouldn't arrest him. She blew out her cheeks in exasperation. She rubbed her throbbing right temple. The fog was gradually lifting. She moaned as last night's casual fling filtered through her brain mist. Why did she do it, she wondered? *Because of him—that's why.*

Yet again, it had been Brad who had plucked up enough courage to shower her with the usual compliments and had poured enough tequila down her throat to drown a million worms. He had done the gentlemanly thing and walked her home. Did he kiss her goodnight? Lou vaguely remembered with regret Brad giving her tonsils a taste of his tongue. To her shame she had reciprocated quite eagerly. But she had stopped Brad as his fumbling hand slid under her satin blouse and managed to fondle her breasts. That was as far as Brad got . . . she hoped. Yes, she was certain Brad had not gone to third base.

The phone rang on Lou's desk, breaking the monotony. She looked away from the screen and picked up the receiver.

Lou listened for a moment, sighing irritably and muttering, "Damn it . . . what is it now? Yeah . . . okay, thanks for telling me. Bye."

Lou replaced the receiver and blew out her cheeks with exasperation. A shadow suddenly engulfed the sheriff and her desk. She glanced towards the open door to see an overweight deputy briefly pausing.

The deputy gave her a sweet smile before flitting past her office carrying a tray crammed with doughnuts and a steaming hot mug of coffee.

Lou called out, "Dwight, get in here. We've got another one!"

The instant the words were out of her mouth her head began to throb. Shouldn't have raised her voice like that, not while that helluva mother of a hangover had shrunk her brains to the size of a peanut.

The outer office of the sheriff's department was almost empty of employees, except for Deputy Dwight, the most dietetically-challenged deputy in town. He was in his mid-twenties, not too tall which made him all the more fat, clean-shaven with a rosy-cheeked, round face that told everyone he was stupid.

The only other occupant was Noreen, the department secretary and general gopher. She sat at her dispatcher's desk casually reading a magazine while chewing gum. She was young, quite attractive, a little on the plump side with a profusion of blond hair. Her desk was not neat and tidy— clutter was the order of every day for Noreen, who loved cute, cuddly things. These cute, cuddly things were scattered all over her desk. There wasn't much space to actually do any work, which was perfectly fine with Noreen.

Hearing the sheriff's voice caused Deputy Dwight to halt in mid-stride. He looked wide-eyed across the office at Noreen, who looked up from her magazine. There was a look of horror on their faces; a look that said—we might have to do some work.

Dwight glanced down at the tray of doughnuts and coffee. He blew out his cheeks and gave a loud moan. He placed the beautifully laden tray down on his desk, picked up a doughnut and stuffed the whole thing in his mouth, washing it down with a mouthful of hot coffee. He dropped the mug, fanning his scalded mouth as bits of doughnut dropped all over the office floor.

Noreen shook her head with dismay and resumed reading her magazine.

"You better not be doing what I think you're doing, Deputy Dwight," Sheriff Lou called out.

Dwight gulped down the confection as he walked slowly into the sheriff's office.

Lou gave her deputy an annoyed look with raised eyebrows as he frantically wiped sugar dusting from his tunic, all the while swallowing down the doughnut in her presence. "How you can eat at a time like this beats the hell out of me, Dwight."

Dwight paused in mid-gulp and looked at the sugary coating on his chubby fingers. He quickly wiped them on his trousers.

"I'd rather eat before I visit the crime scene, if you don't mind," he grimaced. "'Cause afterwards I never seem to have any appetite at all."

And was it her imagination, or had he gained some weight? Lou noticed an extra wobble to the underneath of Dwight's chin and perhaps the smallest of rubber tires developing amongst the others. Yeah, it sure looked like Dwight had been feasting instead of fasting.

Lou's hangover kicked into another gear. She wanted to haul his ass over the coals, but decided not to as Dwight was apt to burst into tears if she berated him. But still, the sugar dumpling of a deputy had his uses. What they were, she could not remember at that exact moment.

And Dwight wasn't the only one of her deputies who could do with losing a few pounds. There was just one problem— Annie's Diner, which happened to be next door. Annie gave the sheriff's department staff—including the sheriff, an ample supply of all-they-could-eat-breakfasts. But unlike her chubby deputies, Lou worked off the ample intake of food with regular exercise.

"No throwing up . . . got that, chubby?"

Dwight didn't reply as he was busy using his tongue to fish out the last of the doughnut that had become wedged in his teeth before swallowing it down.

"Come on, Lou, you know I can take it. Haven't puked yet . . . just get a bit queasy, is all." He rubbed his rounded stomach and looked ill. Loud gurgling could be heard from Dwight's ever-hungry gut. He belched. "Sorry Lou." He belched again. "Are you coming to the crime scene? I mean . . . you ought to, don't you think?"

Lou blew out her cheeks and sighed. "Yeah, I guess so."

Dwight turned to leave the office. As he reached the door, he hovered a moment with sagging shoulders. He turned around and looked at his boss. He had a hurt look on his face.

"That's the 16th time you've called me chubby this week and its only Wednesday morning."

Lou stared at Dwight's cherubic face and smiled apologetically.

"Sorry about that . . . chubby," she said, feigning remorse at Dwight's discomfort. "Come on, lighten up . . . don't be so sensitive." With those words, she got up from her chair and gave a chuckle. "Only kidding, Dwight . . . there hasn't been another bather."

Dwight looked immensely relieved. He blew out his wobbly cheeks as he saw Lou's mischievous smile. "You really got me going there." The deputy paused as if in thought.

"Then who was that on the phone just now, if you don't mind me asking?"

Lou shrugged, "Just some concerned Beaverite informing me that our town welcome sign has been defiled, yet again." And yet again she thought of Duane, as this juvenile prank was right up his alley. "Thought I'd check it out, unless you want to go and take a look?" She smirked. "You don't look that busy."

Dwight looked positively crestfallen. He stood fidgeting and shuffling his feet like a naughty little boy.

Lou knew the answer to her question even before the words had left her mouth—he was looking forward to having a late breakfast with her other deputies, courtesy of Annie's Diner. Lou didn't want to spoil his fun. After all, it was Dwight's birthday and besides, nothing serious ever happened in Big Beaver.

But most of all, Lou felt like some fresh air as it might clear her head of the tequila overdose.

"Go on, chubby, gain a few pounds."

Dwight nodded to the sheriff and left in a rush.

MAJESTIC DOUGLAS FIR TREES lined both sides of the narrow two-lane highway that led into Big Beaver. On the incoming side of the road was the town welcome sign.

Sheriff Lou stood by the side of her patrol car with the two-way radio in her hand gazing up at the sign—"You're Welcome To My Big Furry Beaver." She smiled despite her hangover, thinking it just never gets old, although "Furry" was a little lame. Even she had come up with better stuff than that in her teen years. More fool the idiot who named the town in the first place. She decided not to dwell on that. Which led her thoughts straight back to Duane. *Damn it to bloody hell.*

It was late morning and the air felt brisk and invigorating with the strong scent of pine. She breathed in the rejuvenating freshness in the hope that it would help clear her head of tequila fog.

"Nope, that's not gonna cut it," she mumbled to herself, thinking, more coffee, that's what she needed. Lou fished around in the car and removed a silver thermos flask.

It was at that moment she remembered the busload of Japanese tourists arriving in town later that day. The silly suckers were hoping to get a glimpse of Bigfoot . . . perhaps be famous with a snapshot of Bigfoot taking a crap or whatever Bigfoot might do to get its picture taken—not thinking that if Bigfoot really wanted its picture taken there would be thousands of snapshots all over the place by now.

But Bigfoot was the last thing on Lou's fuzzy mind right then, for the last thing she needed was to explain what the graffiti meant to a busload of snap-happy Japanese.

"Fuck it," she muttered. Lou clicked the two-way radio, "Dwight, come in." She clicked again. "Will, come in." Lou clicked again. "Bill, come in." And finally, "Heidi, come in, damn it."

Not one deputy replied, and why should they? Nothing ever happened in Big Beaver.

"Damn it!" Lou clicked on to speak to Noreen.

"I can't get any of my deputies on their two-ways. Get one of the boys out here and clean up the sign." She paused then added, "Like now."

Noreen's faint voice came over the radio, "They're at Annie's having birthday breakfast."

Lou knew damned well where her deputies were. And it didn't take any guesswork on her part to figure out that her deputies had switched off their two-ways to have a quiet breakfast. It wouldn't be the first time nor would it be the last. "Yeah, I kinda know that, Noreen," she said in an irritated voice. "Tell me something new."

Lou listened to the thump-thump of her throbbing headache and longed to be back in bed sleeping it off. She gave the town welcome sign another glance and thought if Duane was responsible she'd kick his no brain ass so hard he'd come back with snow on his boots.

"Well, you know what to do, Noreen. Go next door and tell them to switch their two-ways on, or I'll be real pissed with them and put them all on report."

"But Annie's baked a special cake for Dwight with lots of frosting and whipped cream and stuff."

"Isn't that so nice for Dwight," Lou replied sarcastically. She warned herself not to raise her voice realizing it would only give her headache further reasons to get more pissed than it already was.

"Well . . . seeing as it's Dwight's special birthday with his special birthday cake, I won't ask the sweet thing to come out here and clean the sign. So tell Will or Bill to move their good-for-nothing butts, right the hell now!"

Shit . . . that did it. Now Lou's hangover had jumped into overdrive. The hammers were pounding the back of her head.

"Okay, Sheriff," Noreen answered timidly.

Lou hooked the radio back into the patrol car and stared at the sign.

"Shit," she muttered, opening her flask and pouring black coffee into a silver plastic cup. She sipped her lifesaver and sighed as the caffeine rush kicked in. Out of the corner of her eye, the sheriff noticed a bush quivering across the road. She smiled as she drank her coffee.

CONCEALED BY THE QUIVERING BUSH squatted Chief Mocking Bird. The 30-year-old bachelor was better known to his friends—and some not so close to him—as MB. His shimmering, raven-black hair was tied back in a ponytail, giving him the desired appearance of a local Native American. There were some who said he was good-looking, and he would have to agree.

He was perfectly concealed in the undergrowth covertly watching the sheriff. His lean face was camouflaged with streaks of mud and dark green facial paint. He wore his usual camouflage fatigues that gave the desired effect of the local flora. MB was a wannabe member of the BFRO-Bigfoot Field Research Organization. He wished that one day he'd become a fully-fledged member, but after his last attempt they declared him a raving lunatic.

MB aimed his directional microphone at Sheriff Lou and listened intently. So far all he had was a boring conversation between the sheriff and Noreen over those dumpling deputies. He was tempted to go across the road and say hello to his friend, hence the quivering bush.

But MB guessed quite correctly that Lou was in a particularly bad mood because of what those mischievous teenagers had done to the town welcome sign, and let's not forget that humungous hangover due to the amount of tequila she'd drunk at Abe's Bar and Grill the previous night with himself, and his best friend, good ol' Duane-o.

MB chuckled quietly, and mused, she'd never find out who was responsible for defiling the sign. The law hardly ever did find out those responsible for scribbling on the town welcome sign. It just wasn't a priority—not that there were any priorities in Big Beaver.

MB regarded himself as a stand-up, law-abiding citizen and knew he should tell the sheriff who was responsible, but he—Chief Mocking Bird—was no snitch. And besides, he didn't want to give himself away, not just yet.

As for that Chief thing, well, Mocking Bird liked to stretch the truth for the tourists, for Old Indian legend tells us that man is judged by his nickname, and if he gains respect from nickname, then he is a fortunate man to be sure. Not to mention, said tourists were always ready to buy him a beer or two or three, and have their photo taken with the Big Brave Chief.

MB smiled to himself when he thought back a few years ago—fifteen years to be exact—to when he'd been just a mere pup. He'd been hiding in the undergrowth in this exact spot—something he often liked to do, and had watched Lou magic-marker the sign with something lewd. She had done it on a dare—dared by Duane, and as far as he knew, she had only done it the once. It was something that he would never let her forget and would often tease her about.

MB turned his attention away from Sheriff Lou to look at a yellow VW camper heading towards Big Beaver. It was those mischievous kids again—the very same ones that had defiled the town welcome sign the previous night. He hoped they wouldn't give the game away if Lou decided to stop them for no apparent reason, except for being guilty of something as all kids were.

SHERIFF LOU WATCHED the VW camper's approach and decided to let it pass. She recognized the van as belonging to Beau Flucker. It suddenly occurred to her that Beau might very well be responsible for this crime. He was always up to something stupid, but if he didn't do it, probably one of his friends did. Perhaps Duane wasn't responsible after all.

Lou stared at the approaching VW. She could make out three individuals sitting in the front of the camper—Chad the driver, Naomi and Debbie. No Beau. He was probably sleeping off the excesses of the night in the back of the van.

To the sheriff's surprise, the camper stopped suddenly by her patrol car with a screech of rubber, skewing alarmingly, stopping just two inches from the car's rear bumper.

The sheriff raised a curious eyebrow, folded her arms and half wished the teenagers had wrecked her car. It would have made this trip worthwhile.

MB FROWNED and wondered what the teenagers wanted to say to the sheriff. It wasn't normal, getting the law's attention like that. Something was up. He eagerly listened in. He watched Lou put a hand on her hip and indicate with a come-here hand.

The three teenagers frantically bundled out of the camper, gesticulating down the road. The kids bombarded the sheriff with a cacophony of jumbled words, not making any sense at all, except it had something to do with Beau Flucker as his name kept cropping up.

They sure seemed upset about something, the chief thought. And where was Beau? What if he'd had an accident? A brief look of angst flicked across MB's face. He watched and listened.

Sheriff Lou put up her hands and shouted as loud as she dared, "Shut the hell up!"

The three teenagers faltered for a moment with over-excited faces.

Sheriff Lou nodded, "That's better." She pointed to the road sign. "You kids do that?"

MB waited for the obviously guilty teenagers to answer as they gawped at the sign with blank, innocent looks.

Naomi, a petite, pretty-faced, reddish-haired seventeen-year-old, glanced at the sign and shook her head no.

"Beau's gone missing. He's been missing all night."

MB's first instinct was to shrug with a sad understanding at hearing Beau had gone missing, but Old Indian legend tells us man who eavesdrops should wait until the fat lady has sung. MB gave a mischievous grin as a thought struck him. Beau hadn't really gone missing. He was just fooling around again. This wouldn't be the first time he'd faked his disappearance, nor was it the second time either.

MB tried to remember how many times Beau had gone missing in the woods, claiming Bigfoot had abducted him. The answer eluded him. No matter. Yeah, sure, Bigfoot abducted him, *as if,* thought MB.

SHERIFF LOU LOOKED dubiously at Naomi. She glanced over at the other two fidgeting teenagers then back to the emotional teenager. The sheriff's instincts told her they were fooling around, as usual.

Twice she'd actually fallen for Beau's antics and had mounted time-consuming search parties into the woods for the idiot, only to call off the search as Beau had miraculously shown up in town telling everyone, who was dumb enough to listen, that Bigfoot had abducted him.

How Beau managed to escape the clutches of Bigfoot was never determined, for not even Beau could come up with an adequate explanation. Small wonder then that no one believed Beau no matter how much he insisted he was telling the truth.

Pretending to be abducted by Bigfoot was a well-worn practical joke, realized Lou. It was getting old. Many Beaverites and tourists alike had claimed Bigfoot had abducted them, some even going so far as to say they were sexually abused by Bigfoot. A certain member of Beau's family, namely his father, Walt Flucker, claimed he'd also been regularly abducted by Bigfoot, not to mention *regularly* taken by tall, blond aliens from the planet Abba.

"Oh yeah . . . gone missing has he? Spent the night in the woods again, have we?" Lou asked sarcastically.

She sniffed Naomi's filthy T-shirt. It stank of wacky tobaccy. The sheriff shook her head warily, unable to summon up the tiniest amount of concern for Beau's whereabouts.

"Hope you told your parents where you were last night?" she warned with raised eyebrows.

Chad, a pimply-faced, scrawny, seventeen-year-old with a mop of black hair, jumped nervously up and down on the spot. He pointed into the woods, directly at MB.

"Beau went to take a piss behind a tree and that was the last we saw of him . . . honest."

Lou tilted her head and folded her arms as she looked at Chad. She gave him a dubious look. She wagged her finger.

"Better not be messing with me, Chad, I'm not in the best of moods right now."

"You gotta believe us, Sheriff," Debbie interrupted. She was an overweight, bespectacled seventeen-year-old with short, spiky black hair.

They were certainly putting on a good act, thought Lou. They seemed genuine for once.

"I suppose you're going to tell me Bigfoot took Beau . . . again?"

"Well, yeah? I guess ... Maybe ... I don't know." Chad said. "It obviously wasn't aliens."

Naomi nudged Chad in his guts with her elbow, beseeching, "Chad's right . . . it wasn't the aliens . . . we don't know who or what took Beau, but it's the truth . . . he's gone missing . . . and for real this time."

Lou rubbed her throbbing temple and sighed. Well this was a new slant on things. Beau's friends always claimed they knew what had abducted Beau—a Bigfoot. She sighed heavily. What if they were telling the truth this time? Lou doubted it, but what if they were? What a fucked-up start to the day.

But Sheriff Lou had her job to do and that meant to serve the community to the best of her abilities. And that meant if someone, especially some snot-nosed kid went missing she had to take it seriously. But how seriously? That was the all-important question.

Well, that depended on the circumstances and the person who had gone missing. How could she take Beau Flucker's disappearance seriously with his past history of fake abductions? But she knew she'd at least have to go through the motions and look like an interested sheriff doing her honor-bound duty.

Lou blew out her cheeks and sighed heavily, "Okay . . . where exactly were you when Beau supposedly disappeared."

Naomi pointed in the direction they had come from, a ways up the road. "In the clearing . . . up at Little Beaver."

Little Beaver! That place is becoming a tourist trap for alien abductions and Bigfoot sightings. She was reminded of last year's incident when two locals went missing for almost two days. She was on the verge of contacting the FBI when Walt turned up with both of them, claiming to have been abducted by aliens and experimented upon. All three would not divulge what these experiments were.

Better take a look, thought Lou. She scanned from one innocent face to the next and knew beyond all doubt she should have stayed in bed this morning. Nothing ever happened in Big Beaver. She walked up to the VW van and peered in the back to see a mess of camping gear, but no Beau.

"One of you had better come back with me. That's you, Chad."

Chad perked up and looked ready to go with a wide grin.

"You two kids had better get back to town." She gave the two girls a questioning look. "I don't suppose you've been drinking and puffing on the magic dragon?"

Debbie and Naomi shook their heads, no, and tried to look like two little schoolgirls. They failed miserably.

Lou smiled knowingly, "What the heck . . . I was your age, once." She looked at Chad. "Come on, dufus, you can show me where you were last night."

"Right on, Sheriff!"

Lou turned towards the woods on the other side of the road and called out, "See you later, MB." She waved to the quivering bush.

FROM HIS HIDING PLACE, deep in the undergrowth, MB the eternal voyeur, watched Chad hurry round the sheriff's patrol car and get into the passenger side. He dropped his directional microphone when Lou called out and waved to him.

"Shit!" MB prided himself on being invisible for Old Indian legend tells us that man who is invisible cannot be seen.

MB watched the sheriff drive off for Little Beaver. Girlish giggling drew his attention back to the two teenage girls. Now what were those kids up to? Beau taken by Bigfoot! That's impossible. Most likely ol' Duane-o put them up to it. Yeah, that's it. Hold on though, Duane wouldn't be that dumb. So what if Bigfoot had taken Beau? Nah, there were no such creatures as Bigfoot, thought MB, even though as a crypto-zoologist it would have been his sworn duty to believe in such things.

He watched the tail lights of the sheriff's patrol car disappear round a bend in the road. A moment later the VW camper started up and sputtered off towards town.

MB's thoughts returned to Bigfoot. Suppose, just suppose, Bigfoot had taken Beau? That would be fucking amazing. At that very moment, he felt an overwhelming excitement at the prospect of Beau being kidnapped by Bigfoot. A new sense of purpose overwhelmed him, but it was only fleeting. He quickly told himself to get a grip on reality—there were no such creatures as Bigfoot. With a woeful sigh, MB removed his headphones and started to pack all his covert listening gear into a camouflaged rucksack.

4

AT THE SAME TIME Sheriff Lou was en-route to Little Beaver, Duane Dexter sat at a table eating breakfast at Annie's Diner. He was two years older than Lou, tall with straggly, shoulder length, blond hair. By no means unattractive, but due to his shabby appearance—scuffed jeans and beer-stained shirt, and being in need of a good shave, his Nordic good looks were well-hidden from all but those who had seen Duane looking better. Not that Duane gave two flying farts what anyone thought about his appearance.

Duane looked around Annie's rustic—and proud of it— diner and smiled at the chintzy curtains, the chintzy tablecloths, the chintzy napkins, all clashing hideously with the bare, rough-hewn wooden walls, adorned with photos of—you guessed it—Bigfoot.

He stared at one blow up and thought long and hard. Where was he that day? Nothing came to him. Fuck it! It'll come to him when he least expected it, which was basically how Duane went through life—never knowing what was around the next corner—for one of MB's Old Indian legends tells us that man who always knows what's around the next corner is one dull dude.

Duane was in the middle of eating a cooked breakfast of thick-sliced ham, three eggs over easy, beans, hash browns and blueberry buckwheat pancakes, accompanied with a large prune juice and several cups of strong black coffee—a breakfast of champions.

Someone shouted out, "Hey, Duane-o, why don't you scrub my furry ass clean?"

Several customers sniggered.

Many Beaverites regarded Duane as the prime suspect in the much-discussed, topic number one serial bather case. The case in question—though not injurious to individuals, had forced the sheriff's department to investigate this most mischievous of crimes when they could have been spending time and effort dealing with genuine crimes in town, of which there were none.

Annie Bumgardner—who happened to be born on the same day as Duane—was the excessively buxom, blond-haired owner of Annie's Diner. She stood behind the counter of her establishment serving breakfast to her customers. Annie was quite attractive and relished showing off her Grand Canyon cleavage as she leaned over the counter top for her male customers to ogle. By now, Annie had gained quite a few pounds, but wore it well.

Sheriff Lou's four deputies, including Deputy Heidi, Annie's identical twin sister, were seated at the counter eating their large breakfasts mainly consisting of Dwight's birthday cake, the remains of which were scattered over the counter top. Of course, Heidi was not fixated on Annie's breasts bursting forth from her deliberately undersized shirt, the buttons of which strained to keep them from spilling onto the counter top.

There was barely a seat to spare at the tables or at the counter of the diner. Annie's wasn't the only diner in town, but what made her place so popular with the locals and tourists alike was the best and cheapest food in town with plenty of bosom to go with it. Her "All-you-can-eat breakfast days" were a spectacular success and particular favorite of those horny men who chose to eat at her establishment.

Locals and tourists loved breakfast time at Annie's. And she loved them back, usually with a big hug—the lucky ones receiving a face-full of her breasts. It had to be said that Annie was a giving, nurturing woman, whose one aim in life was to get hitched and push out a couple of kids before nature took its inevitable course. Duane was her number one choice for supplying the necessary man juice. Unfortunately for Annie, he was also her twin sister's first choice for the necessary man juice needed to produce the required baby bump.

Duane was well aware what the sisters—known affectionately as the Bumsen Sisters, wanted from him, but so far, he was playing hard to get, and wasn't ready to donate the required man juice for that reason. He was quite happy to keep things just the way they were with both sisters, that being, Annie and Heidi would oblige him whenever they wanted some booty, Bigfoot-style. Five times a week with both sisters equaled to ten fucks a week minimum, more than enough to keep him happy.

Annie opened the counter top flap and sauntered over to Duane's table with a steaming pot of coffee.

Duane slowly munched on the last slice of pancake, noisily savoring it.

"Yummy," Duane exclaimed, rolling his eyes.

He re-focused his eyes, noticing the sarcastic smirks on Bob and Chuck—two grizzled slackers in their mid-forties—seated in a corner. It had to be Chuck who made that bather comment, thought Duane. He ignored the asswipe hunters, not because he didn't like them, but simply because they were hunters.

With a cheeky smile on her face, Annie topped up his coffee and asked, "You want some more?"

Duane stared into Annie's wobbling bosom then into the come-and-get-it look on her face. He was drained after last night.

"I've had enough, Annie."

"Aw, don't be like that . . . you must still be hungry after last night?" She gave a naughty little chuckle and nudged him with an elbow, sloshing coffee. "Come on, my Bigfoot boy."

"No can do," he said with that amiable smile of his.

Annie sat down on the vinyl seat next to Duane. She nestled up close and put her hand on his knee and gave a squeeze, wrinkling her nose at his pungent body odor.

"How's your sweet, lovely head, my big, bad Bigfoot boy?"

Duane lifted a cheek to scratch his butt and thought for a moment about which head she was referring to. He decided she was referring to his upper head. He lightly tapped his temple. No pain. "Not a twinge."

Annie pursed her lips together and pouted. Her hand rummaged Duane's goods. "That head, silly."

Duane realized he hadn't been much company last night—sex-wise, due to having over-indulged on beer and whisky at Abe's Bar and Grill.

"Sorry about last night. But you know how it is." He looked down at his groin being massaged by Annie's hand. "It just wasn't in me to oblige both you girls."

Annie gave an exaggerated sigh, "Don't fret, hon . . . it was my fault for letting Heidi get to you first." She shook her head and stared coolly at Heidi's back. "That one sure knows how to drain a guy."

Duane shrugged an apology for he was so easily duped by one of the sisters pretending to be the other one. It was impossible to know which one was which because they truly were identical twins. But he didn't mind being duped, for it only added to the sexual experience.

Sadly though, last night he'd had too much to drink and when Annie told him of his mistake, he just didn't have the energy or the inclination to do her. The real reason for his guilt—though he never made it obvious to the sisters—was that he had a softer spot in his heart for Annie than for Heidi. Annie was more easy-going, not unlike himself.

Heidi liked to boss him around, probably because she was in law enforcement. She often liked to tell him exactly what to do while lovemaking, which gave Duane the feeling of being a love monkey. That's why he could be fooled by the sisters—they knew each other's little preferences so well they could switch whenever they felt like it, leaving poor Duane none the wiser.

Duane dreaded the day when he'd have to choose between them. He hoped that day would never come.

Annie gave his groin a light squeeze then stood up. "I know you'll make it up to me next time, hon. My bed is always waiting for you. And my heart just yearns for you, Duane, my wondrous Bigfoot boy."

Duane smiled affectionately, despite knowing that Annie's bed wasn't just waiting for him, nor did her heart just yearn for him. Sad to say, but eligible men were in short supply, and Annie liked to play the field, as did her sister.

"What would I do without you, Annie?" He smiled that amiable smile of his.

"You'd do alright . . . you always do." Annie's face went serious, "Last night I dreamt Willis came back to town just for me." She looked a little sad. "I would've done anything for that guy, but he never cared for me. I'm glad he left the way he did . . . for it sure knocked him right outta my heart."

Duane thought about his best friend—the town's all-American hero, who had had every girl's heart fluttering after him. He gave a sad sigh.

"You have such a big heart Annie . . . I'd like to bury my face in it."

Annie gave another sigh as she kissed Duane's forehead. She almost choked on his body stench.

"I don't want to hurt your feelings, hon . . . but you stink real bad. Why didn't you let us give you a scrub down last night?"

Duane shrugged, sniffing his armpits, "I don't think I smell that bad."

"Believe me, hon . . . you're ripe!"

Annie glanced over to the counter where the deputies were finishing off their excessively large breakfasts, which in all probability would render them useless for the rest of the day. Good job nothing ever happened in Big Beaver. She looked back at Duane and blew him a kiss as she sauntered off.

Duane grinned and caught the kiss. He kept an eager eye on Annie's curvaceous hips and rump as she sauntered from table to table, topping up empty coffee mugs. He sighed with contentment and thought life was pretty damned good. He had a nice comfortable home. He had a very healthy bank balance.

In fact, he was the most loaded bachelor in Big Beaver, having inherited a small fortune from a distant relative, proving that fairytale dreams do happen. But the most important things in Duane's view were his good friends and an ample supply of booty call. What more in life was there?

Duane gave another contented sigh as he took a sip of coffee. He closed his eyes for a moment then opened them slowly. He felt relaxed. He had a nice warm feeling in his tummy and not just because he'd eaten his fill. His only concern at that moment was that he had something important to do in town, and for the life of him, he couldn't remember what it was.

Duane's attention was drawn away from Annie and the deputies when Noreen came into the diner in a rush. He watched her make a beeline over to the deputies.

She stopped by twin deputies Bill and Will.

They were both chubby with rosy faces. Both were twenty-nine years old. That's where the similarities ended. Bill was a good six inches taller with short curly blond hair. Will was six inches shorter with a blond buzz cut. When they were born, their parents named them both William. Don't ask.

Duane was mildly curious what Noreen said to the two deputies. Perhaps it had something to do with him, he wondered. Perhaps they'd had the DNA results back from Sacramento? Not that the results would tell them anything. He made absolutely sure he had thoroughly contaminated the evidence.

"Why me?" Deputy Bill pleaded, in a high-pitched, feminine voice.

Everyone in the diner turned to look at the deputy.

More sniggers drifted from Chuck and Bob.

Deputy Bill whirled around and glared at the hunters with a hurt look on his chubby face.

Duane listened in. He guessed that Lou wanted Deputy Bill to do something, something that didn't involve eating. How could Lou be so mean on Dwight's birthday? It crossed Duane's mind that he should go over to Deputy Dwight to wish him a happy birthday. He thought about it some more, casually scratching his butt, and decided he'd sip his coffee instead and just sit quietly at his table until he was ready to make a move to do that all-important thing.

Ah, home sweet home, Duane mused. Still scratching his butt, he thought of his log cabin in the woods, where life was perfectly peaceful, where he could enjoy the serenity of nature and his own easy-going company. There was just one thing wrong with that scenario—his best friend Willis wasn't a part of his life anymore. Thirteen years it had been. He really needed to see him for there was something important they had to discuss, something so important that he couldn't think what the fuck it was.

5

AS SHERIFF LOU was en-route to Little Beaver, and Duane was having his breakfast, two FBI agents sat on a red leather sofa in the outer office of the Sacramento Bureau shrink, Doctor Ramón Fernandez, awaiting his arrival.

Agent Candice Merlot, a stunning African-American in her late twenties, scrutinized the contents of a magazine. She casually twisted a finger around a stray curl of her fashionably straightened hair. She was not overly tall, but she sure made up for that with her lithe, muscular body that fit snugly into her gray suit.

Sometimes she liked to be just Merlot, and like the wine, she was smooth, lively on the tongue and full of velvety textures that lingered well beyond the first tantalizing sip. As Candi, she liked to be slowly unwrapped and savored for her sweet taste, something she had picked up during her modeling days for *Sports Illustrated*. She adored Latin American music, loved to salsa and liked her food spicy—the hotter the better. But, most of all, Agent Merlot liked the guys and the guys sure liked her.

Merlot glanced at her partner, Agent Willis Johnson. He was a few years older, taller and fit looking, with a lean, somewhat chiseled, but attractive face with short auburn hair. She knew he never missed his daily work outs. That he never ate anything unhealthy. He ate tons of fiber. He liked country and western music, and as for the ladies, well, only Agent

Johnson knew what he liked. He would never kiss and tell, keeping everything bottled up, which was the reason they were waiting for the shrink.

They sat together on the long comfy sofa, but at either end, as far apart as possible. Agent Merlot looked casual with legs crossed while Agent Johnson sat straight-backed, serious-faced and looked uptight.

Merlot glanced at her wristwatch and noted the time. She scrutinized her taciturn partner. Ten minutes had elapsed since they had entered Doctor Fernandez's cozy outer office. Neither had spoken a word to one another in all that time. That was just how Agent Johnson liked it these days—as silent as Clint Eastwood in a spaghetti western.

The small fan on the black desk at their feet gently oscillated, thus providing a therapeutic white noise that made the silence bearable, thought Merlot. She guessed it had been intentionally left switched on by the good doctor.

Merlot cast a familiar eye around the very feminine outer office. Normally she would have concluded the shrink was on the same team, but she knew better, as did all her female colleagues. Pink was the order of the day to match the flaming red sofa. Both colors were used deliberately to elicit a response. There were three scatter cushions on the sofa, but one was now being throttled in the vice-like grip of Agent Johnson's clenched hands.

The door of the outer office opened and in walked Doctor Ramón Fernandez. *Wow!*

Merlot stared at the man of her dreams. Ramón was a gorgeous Latin American in his early thirties. His shining black hair, dark brown eyes and olive skin were perfectly encased within the confines of his dark gray suit that seemed to Merlot to be a size too small. She ogled his tight buttocks and muscular thighs as he walked past her.

Merlot stared agog at the breathtaking sight before her, licking her lips suggestively. *Way too sexy for a shrink*, she thought. She shifted on the sofa as her juices started to flow. She had nicknamed Ramón "Doctor Sluice" and had been severely reprimanded by her anal boss and Agent Johnson for blurting it out on occasion.

"Agents," Doctor Fernandez said, nodding as he entered his private domain.

Merlot looked for approval from her partner. She got nothing but an icy glare. She nodded her head with dismay and entered the consultation room.

Agent Johnson sighed heavily and jumped from the sofa like a coiled spring. He followed Merlot into the office and slammed the door.

MERLOT RECALLED THE FIRST TIME she'd been in Doctor Fernandez's consultation room which was even cozier than the outer office. Pale blue was the order of the day with dark blue chenille armchairs. The walls were festooned with Doctor Fernandez's psychiatric accomplishments. On his desk was a computer and photos of his family—no wife.

Merlot was there to explain her partner's condition. She informed the shrink that they'd been partners for nearly a year and a good friendship had grown between them. Without warning, he had gone completely insane. He had become distant and offensive. And not just to her, but to other FBI agents as well. The once super-cool Agent Johnson had become easy to provoke into bouts of anger. On two occasions, he had warned Merlot to shut her big mouth. And on more occasions than that, Agent Tightass had used very insulting comments to describe Agent Merlot's happy-go-lucky attitude. There had also been several complaints of civilian harassment aimed at Agent Johnson.

During this initial consultation, Doctor Fernandez asked Merlot a lot of personal questions about her partner. Was he seeing someone?—*don't know*. Was he regular?—*don't know*. Was he sleeping?-*don't know*. Have you had a sexual relationship with Willis?—*that's sick* . . . he was more like a brother to her.

It was soon established that Agent Merlot knew nothing about her partner. But Merlot did however tell Doctor Fernandez that she suspected whatever was troubling Johnson had something to do with his home town, and perhaps a certain woman residing there.

Merlot recalled removing a folded magazine page from her jacket pocket and handing it to Doctor Fernandez. The picture displayed Annie Bumgardner in all her luscious glory. The mention of the home town caused Merlot to erupt into laughter throughout the consultation. Apparently, in an interview, Annie mentioned how her heart had been broken by a certain young man who had left town unexpectedly, the upshot of which was she was prompted to up and leave Big Beaver as well to pursue a modeling career.

Agent Merlot also recalled her partner receiving a letter from Big Beaver. After reading it, he went berserk and had been that way ever since. She couldn't be absolutely sure Annie was the reason for her partner's troubles, as he was so tight-lipped on the subject.

Merlot snapped out of her recollection as Doctor Fernandez sat in his armchair opposite her and deliberately sat with legs apart, revealing a sizeable piece of luggage. Merlot shifted uncomfortably in her armchair as south of the border became activated at the sight of such good wood—mature hard mahogany on her woodometer scale.

She cleared her throat and smiled at the stunning Doctor Ramón who had obviously noticed the effect he was having on her by the increased bulge between his legs. Merlot gazed into his luscious eyes with a look of wanton abandon. She decided to be the first to speak—no choice really.

"I forgive you for calling me a puck bunny and a twinkie, Agent Johnson," she said in a friendly tone of voice.

Agent Johnson remained silent, his expression grimly serious. His jaw muscles were clenched so tight Merlot could hear his teeth grinding.

She thought that if her partner wasn't careful the Bureau would insist he took more than just counseling—a prolonged leave of absence. Merlot didn't want that to happen. She would have to break in a new partner.

"Don't suppose I can buy you a coffee later?" Merlot offered.

No reply from her anal partner.

Merlot shrugged. What more could she do? She returned her attention to the awesome Dr. Ramón. He sure was a gorgeous specimen of hardwood. She wavered as the doctor shifted to accommodate his erection. Merlot was surely gratified.

"Sorry I'm late," Ramón casually offered. He smiled just for Merlot. "Good morning, agents." He averted his gaze from Merlot's overtly intense sexual come-on look.

Merlot knew from that moment that her luck was in. She smiled ever so briefly, licking her red lips with a tongue that begged for more. She wondered if he had any tan lines. Her fervent imagination ran riot with thoughts of the exquisite Ramón lying naked on a beach while she massaged sun lotion into the glorious skin of his firm buns.

Doctor Fernandez gave a warning cough.

Merlot apologized with a furtive smile and settled back into her chair, looking serious.

"Good morning to you, Doctor Fernandez."

"You can call me Ramón, if you wish."

"Ramón it is then."   The female agent knew beyond all doubt Ramón wanted her as much as she wanted him.

Ramón focused his attention on the dour Agent Johnson. He pursed his full lips in thought.

"Don't you think it's a good morning, Agent Johnson?"

Agent Johnson seemed immune to the doctor's charm. His expression remained serious. He didn't speak right away, rather allowing the silence to maintain his serious stance.

"What's so good about it? It's just another shitty morning like any other shitty morning."   Agent Johnson scowled with menace.

"I see," the good doctor said, with eyebrows raised. "Well now, what do you want us to talk about, Agent Johnson, or can I call you Willis?"

Willis fixed the doctor with a steely look, "Whatever. Can I go now?"   He started to get up.

"No you cannot, Willis."   Ramón pointed to Willis' chair to remain seated.

"Quack," Willis whispered under his breath as he sat back down.

Merlot's eyes almost popped out of their sockets, thinking now you've done it, Agent Tightass.

Ramón had good hearing, apparently. "I heard that."

Willis shrugged his shoulders as if he didn't care.

Ramón persisted with the good doctor routine. "Come, come, Willis, something is bugging you. You want to know what I think is the root cause of your sudden behavior?"

Willis didn't reply. He looked around the room seemingly uninterested.

Merlot gave her partner a concerned look.

"I think your hometown of Big Beaver has a lot to do with what's troubling you, and perhaps you still hold a torch for an old girlfriend there. Am I right about the letter you received two months ago?" Dr Fernandez waited for a reply with an expectant look.

Merlot bit her hand to stop the giggles as Big Beaver filled her mind with images of trim. Those thoughts soon vanished as she imagined Ramón's luscious lips pleasuring her.

Willis narrowed his eyes and turned his attention upon his partner, "Bitch! Trust you to put two and two together, and come up with nothing."

"Prick!"

"Okay girls, that's quite enough." Ramón started to write something out on a notepad.

Willis stood and was about to leave.

Ramón lifted a finger to halt Willis. "I haven't finished." He ripped off a sheet from the notepad and handed it to Willis. "Your prescription, and adhere to it or you will be placed on suspension."

Willis snatched the piece of paper from Ramón's hand without reading it and left the office.

Merlot waited in her armchair for Ramón to declare his undying love for her.

The gorgeous doctor gave Merlot an inquisitive look, "Is there anything more, Agent Merlot?" He smiled.

Oh yes, there was more, but Merlot knew now was not the time.

6

SHERIFF LOU LISTENED to nature's masterpiece filling the air with a mix of blue jays, mountain chickadees, yellow-headed and red-winged blackbirds. The pleasing symphony soothed her hangover. She smiled as she heard a red fox yelping, a bobcat yowling and the distinct bugling of an elk. The calls reminded her of why she never moved away from Big Beaver.

Chad pointed to the tree where Beau had taken a piss.

Lou carefully walked around the tree and noticed several different kinds of sneaker prints in the dry earth at the base of the trunk and what looked like deer print or some other large mammal.

"Let's see your sneakers, Chad."

Chad looked down at his sneakers and lifted a foot for Lou to take a closer look.

"Stop being a dufus, Chad. Take one of them off so I can get a close look."

Chad shrugged as he removed his right sneaker and handed it to Lou, hopping on his left foot.

"We kinda thought Beau might still be here . . . you know, like hiding from us, like he often does."

Lou placed a sneaker carefully over a print. It matched, but the other prints had to be Beau's and the other teenagers' as the tread marks were different. She sniffed the sneaker in her hand and wished she hadn't. Her nostrils detected the strong smell of animal musk that pervaded the surrounding area. She coughed.

"Smells like some animal's been marking its territory," Lou said with watery eyes.

Chad held his nose as he took the sneaker from Lou's hand.

"Jeez . . . that smells real gross, like skunk and cooked grizzly turds," he said as he slipped on his sneaker.

Lou nodded in agreement and wondered what kind of animal had been spraying around the base of the Douglas fir. She frowned as the smell seemed not too dissimilar to the serial bather case.

Chad glanced warily at the surrounding trees and thickets. He heard a rustling and shivered.

"Maybe it was a grizzly?"

"Maybe," Lou said with a troubled look on her face.

Chad pointed out, "But if a grizzly got him, where's Beau's body parts . . . and I don't see blood all over the place." He glanced around with a mix of horror and glee on his face. "Maybe the grizzly's buried him and plans to eat him later?" The teenager looked wide-eyed at Lou. "They do that, you know." Chad searched the area with a keen eye. "But there should be some blood, don't you think, Sheriff?" He grimaced, delighting in the gruesome scenario. "Yeah, lots of blood all over the place."

Yeah, there surely would have been some sign of Beau being taken by a grizzly, thought Lou. She gave Chad a disparaging look for reveling in what might have happened to his friend. It wasn't a joking matter, anymore. She surely had to take Beau's disappearance seriously now. But something didn't quite sit right with her. She felt it in her gut. Something was off-center about the whole thing.

She gave Chad a questioning look. A part of her was hoping Beau and his friends had concocted this little charade to catch her and her deputies for the third time. The alternative that Beau had actually been taken by a grizzly or even by some nut job was a very disturbing thought indeed. Her stomach started to churn over. Of course, Beau could simply have run away.

"If this is some kind of prank, it's time to call it quits, right now," Lou demanded in a stern voice. She softened her tone. "You and the others won't get into trouble . . . I'll let you off with a warning, is all."

Chad shook his head vehemently. "It's not a prank, Sheriff, honest to God. Someone or something really has taken Beau this time."

Well, thought Lou, if Chad was messing with her, he was putting on a good act. He seemed genuine by the look on his face. Her head began to throb again. She felt a little queasy at the prospect of finding a mauled, possibly half-eaten Beau in a bear dig. She instinctively put her hand to her sensitive stomach in an attempt to quell her urge to puke. She sniffed. The musky animal spray didn't help matters.

She sighed and shook her head. She knew when she first took this job that there would be a distinct possibility of gruesome scenes where hunters had shot each other by mistake or got mauled by a bear, but thankfully, up until now she'd had it easy. Nothing much ever happened in Big Beaver, and that was fine with Sheriff Lou.

Sure, her town had its fair share of trouble, especially Saturday nights when the locals would get rowdy with tourists. But a few knocks and bruises was all that amounted to. And there was the occasional breaking and entry, car thefts by drunken teenagers, family squabbles that ended in makeup tears, juvenile trouble and last, but not least, the practical jokers—but no major crimes. Lou was kinda proud of that.

Her town was a nice amiable place to live in or to just take a vacation in. Some people in town still kept their doors unlocked at night. Her town was a good place to raise kids. It was a place where tourists came by the bus load to do some sightseeing, get a glimpse of Bigfoot, or do some hunting and fishing.

Sheriff Lou heard the approach of a vehicle's engine not far away. It was the sound of a four-wheel jeep. Who could it be? It sounded like MB's Cherokee. *Could be wrong though*, thought Lou. If so, the last thing she needed was someone coming to Little Beaver for a nice picnic only to find Beau's dismembered body. What would that say about her town?

She knew she'd better go and see who'd arrived. If it was just someone out for a picnic she didn't want them trampling about the place, messing up the crime scene, if there *was* a crime scene. She heard the vehicle's engine stop and a door slam shut.

"You think maybe some axe-wielding nut's got him?" Chad asked excitedly. "Maybe we'll find Beau's head stuck on a branch . . . that would be awesome."

Lou didn't reply. She gave Chad a quick, disparaging look then turned to leave and headed for the clearing.

Chad looked around at the vast forest with a hint of fear. He quickly followed after the sheriff.

7

AS DUANE SIPPED HIS COFFEE at Annie's Diner, it suddenly dawned on him in a rare moment of clarity what he had forgotten he had to do in town that day. That's it—he had to go to the salon for a trim. He finished off his coffee as quickly as possible before he forgot the trim. He rushed up to the counter and slipped a ten dollar bill between Annie's enormous breasts.

Annie waved Duane goodbye as he exited the diner.

He sauntered off down the main street to his left as if he had all the time in the world, passing Bert's Sporting Goods, Gerry's Hardware Store, The Busy Beaverite office and Sally's Sew What Shop.

Duane came to a stop outside Colette's Head Job. For some unknown reason, he looked back the way he came at the sheriff's department next to Annie's Diner.

He noticed that Lou's patrol car was missing from its allocated spot. *What could she be up to?* He scratched his butt as he thought. Nothing came to mind.

Duane peered through the window of the salon. He could make out Colette, the glamorous salon owner, and her spiky, purple-haired young female assistant tending to two early forty-something women undergoing various stages of hair treatment.

The women being tended to were very familiar to Duane and he knew each one of them enjoyed a good gossip. He shrugged his shoulders and thought—*so what if it'll give them something to gossip about.* So he entered Colette's establishment.

Colette was a friend of Duane's; a really close friend of his, though not as regularly close a friend as Annie or her sister. But close enough for Duane to call on Colette from time to time for some extra-extra booty call.

But, unlike the Bumsen Sisters, Colette wasn't looking for a husband and definitely no kids. She was already married and had three teenage kids, but her husband, Pete, and she had what was known as an understanding.

Pete was a roadie for a female heavy metal band—The Crap Suzettes. It was reliably rumored around town that he had a second wife somewhere. It was also rumored Pete had a third wife somewhere else and possibly married to the entire band. It was also rumored that Pete was a bit of a womanizer. But they were only rumors.

Duane was immediately struck by the heavy odor of perfume and hair sprays sucking the air out of his lungs. He coughed.

All attention focused on him.

"Hello, ladies."

Everyone greeted him with a friendly hello and a sweet smile as Duane was a likable character and most women took to him in one way or another. They either lusted after him, or they simply liked him as a friend. All in all, Duane had a strong effect on women, but as yet, he couldn't understand why. And he had no inclination to find out, either.

Duane focused his stinging eyes on Colette. "It's time for my trim."

Colette covertly looked at her client before nodding her head and pointing with scissors towards the hallway door.

"Be just a minute," she told her customer. "What trim . . . oh, right . . . that trim . . . out back in the storeroom." She sauntered off from the salon.

Duane smiled a little sheepishly at the clients as his foggy brain cleared enough to remind him just how stupid he really was. Not a trim, you dumbass—he was there for some trim—Colette's pertly shaved trim to be precise. He nodded his head and walked casually with his hands in his jean pockets and followed Colette from the salon.

THE ASSISTANT AND THE TWO gossipy women watched Duane and Colette disappear into the hallway. Chatter went into overdrive.

"What kind of trim does he need?"

"The only trim Duane gets is south of the border."

"What . . . you mean Colette and Duane?"

"Why not Colette and Duane?"

"He's doing me . . . that's why."

"And me."

"You? No fucking way."

"Why not me . . . I'm just as much a looker as you?"

"For fuck's sake . . . he's doing everyone in town who wants it."

"Really . . . even Sheriff Lou?"

"She ain't that desperate."

"Well, you were."

"So were you, bitch."

Squabbles ensue.

THE STOREROOM SHELVES WERE STACKED with various hair products and hair styling devices. Duane was pushed against the shelves.

Colette pounced on him like a sex-starved sex kitten, "Give it to me real hard, my Bigfoot boy." She backed off, wrinkling her nose in disgust. "You stink!"

"So I've been told."

"What the hell." Colette pounced on Duane for the second time. She grabbed his goods and squeezed a little too hard for Duane's liking.

Duane was caught completely off guard and flinched in pain. "Sorry Colette, but I'm just not in the mood anymore."

"Since when?"

"Since last night with Annie and Heidi."

"Damn . . . those two are a menace."

"Don't I know it . . . still a tad tender down there."

Colette regained her composure. She bent down and picked up several boxes of hair colorant scattered all over the place. She started to restack them. She frowned.

"Hey . . . what the hell did you want with all that hair colorant I gave you last month?"

Duane looked at her with a twinkle in his blue eyes and grinned. He touched the tip of his nose and winked.

"No questions, we agreed." He gave another grin.

She gave Duane a keen look. "You're up to something weird with all that blond hair dye, I just know it." She grinned. "You've gotta prank on the go, haven't you?"

Well, to be exact, thought Duane, he wasn't up to anything mischievous, not really. He had merely done something special for some friends of his.

Colette finished stacking the boxes. "Pete's away all week, so don't be a stranger."

As Duane thought for a moment as to when he could drop in on Colette for some sex, his butt itched for a good scratch from his thinking finger. When could he fit her in—the Bumsen Sisters were selfishly taking up all of his time; okay he was spoiling them a tad too much, but he hated the thought of having to say no to them. But they were getting greedy for his man juice. So when could he fit Colette in?

"I'll see when I can fit you in," he offered.

Colette suggestively moistened her lips with her tongue and kissed him full on. "There's more of that, so make it soon, my Bigfoot boy."

Will do, thought Duane, with a naughty glint in his eye.

ONCE OUTSIDE COLETTE'S hair salon, Duane walked back up the main street to his Harley motorcycle parked outside Annie's Diner. He glanced next door at the sheriff's department and saw that the sheriff's patrol car was still absent from its parking spot. Shame about that, he would have liked to have called in on Lou on the pretext of saying hello, when in fact his real motive would have been to find out if she'd had the DNA results back from the lab in Sacramento on the Phantom Bigfoot Bather Case.

For, if there was one thing Duane really liked to do, it was to gloat upon his mischievous deeds and the effect they had on others. It was just harmless fun in his eyes. To others, namely the sheriff's department, it was a downright nuisance.

Duane knew that most people in town didn't mind the thought that someone was entering their homes and making use of their bathroom facilities. And though the sheriff's department was taking the case of the Phantom Bigfoot Bather serious enough, not even they were too eager to catch the perp red-handed, so to speak.

Duane grinned to himself and gave a nod. It was for the best that she wasn't in. Best get home. He kicked his bike into action with a roar. He slipped his Bigfoot helmet on and kicked into first gear. As if on cue, the music emanating from his speaker system was *Born To Be Wild* by Steppenwolf.

8

MB PULLED HIS GEAR OUT of the back of the Cherokee jeep. He glanced over his shoulder at Sheriff Lou and Chad as they approached.

"Hey, Sheriff," MB called out.

"How long were you listening back at the sign?" Lou looked irritated. She faltered and glared at him.

MB grinned disarmingly. "Yeah, well, you know how it is." He winked and tapped his directional microphone. "I saw and heard the whole thing."

Lou gave him an annoyed look. "You were hiding there all that time?"

MB apologetically shrugged his shoulders. "Yeah I was . . . so what?"

MB smiled in the hope that his geniality would assuage Lou. It sometimes did. Sometimes it didn't. Depended on what sort of mood she was in. He had a hunch the sheriff was in no mood to be messed around. She seemed cranky and looked hungover from Abe's last night. "Sorry, I know I should have made my presence known. But..."

Lou shook her head in despair. "I could confiscate that device."

MB laughed. "Old Indian legend tells us that man who doesn't listen in on other people's conversations, will never find out what bad things are being said about him."

Lou didn't reply, she just put her hands on her hips and looked un-amused at MB's smiling face.

Yeah, Lou sure wasn't in a good mood, thought MB. He figured he'd better put on a serious face.

"You'd better show me the spot where Beau went to take a piss then."

Lou and Chad trudged back to the infamous leaky tree with MB in tow.

MB knelt down and sniffed the ground around the offending tree. Offending was the right word—real stinky, he thought—not unlike that found at each crime scene left by the Phantom Bigfoot. He ran his fingertips over the dry earth and then put his fingers up against his nostrils and took a good sniff. It was a familiar smell.

"Smells like grizzly piss mixed with human piss, and . . ." MB sniffed and grimaced with a cough. ". . . Definitely some skunk in there, too."

Lou and Chad stood back and watched expectantly as the amiable crypto-zoologist picked up a broken branch, inspected it, sniffed it then tossed it away. It was just a broken branch.

MB noted the dry ground around the base of the tree was strewn with loose undergrowth that had been trampled down by several different feet, including Lou's. He closely scrutinized the shoe prints.

MB pointed out animal tracks, "Mostly white-tailed deer, badger, fox and bobcat, nothing that would be harmful to a human. There's no sign of a grizzly print, but that doesn't mean a grizzly hadn't taken Beau . . . but. . ."

MB inspected the trunk of the leaky tree. There were no telltale signs of clawing that always accompanied a bear attack.

He pointed to the bark, ". . . See? . . . no claw marks. Bears always like to scratch up a tree when they piss on it." MB pointed to the ground, "I suppose these prints around the tree belong to you and the other kids as well as Beau's?"

Chad opened his mouth to reply but Lou answered before he could.

"I've already ascertained those prints belong to Chad and his friends."

Chad beamed proudly, "It's true, dude . . . those are our prints."

Lou heaved a weary sigh and pointed to a set of particular prints. "Those must belong to Beau, see where they are deeper. That's where he stood to take a pee." She pointed to the damp bark of the tree and looked at Chad. "No-brainer here doesn't have a clue what took Beau this time."

Chad looked indignant, "Who's calling who a no-brainer?"

Sheriff Lou glared at Chad, "I am . . . dufus."

Chad agreed with a resigned nod, "Well, that's okay, I guess."

MB sniffed the bark of the tree. He nodded his head and wrinkled his nose.

"That's one really bad mother of a smell!"

"Could that be grizzly sign?" Lou asked, gagging on the stink.

"No way, dude . . . I'm betting it's Bigfoot got him," Chad butted in over-excitedly.

MB shrugged to Chad. Well, that was the million dollar question. No, make that a two million dollar question. Had a grizzly taken Beau? The signs said otherwise. But what if a Bigfoot had taken Beau? The notion was too fanciful to think seriously about, but the thought that Bigfoot had indeed taken

Beau struck a chord in MB's delirious mind, for it amused MB to once more think upon such a notion as the existence of the elusive Bigfoot.

Thump! Back on planet earth, MB could find no sign of Bigfoot prints, real or fake, no Bigfoot hair, or any other sign to indicate that the non-existent creature had been here. MB sighed inwardly with the thought that, yet again, he had failed to find conclusive evidence that Bigfoot existed.

Without evidence to support what had happened to Beau, who or what had taken him was anybody's guess. If indeed anything untoward had happened to Beau. He was more than likely just fooling around, thought MB. The lack of evidence certainly confirmed that hypothesis.

"Doubtful it was a grizzly," MB mused. "I don't see anything to support that scenario here. There's no sign of a struggle. See? No blood. No torn clothing. Sure, there are several different sets of human footprints and some animal prints, but nothing to indicate anything bad happened here."

Lou peered down at the ground and looked thoughtful. "My gut tells me Beau's just fooling around, as usual."

"Can I quote you on that?" MB said.

"No way, man . . . something took him. If it's Bigfoot . . . I wonder what it's doing with him," Chad said, eyes wide with excitement. "Hey, dude . . . do Bigfoot eat people, like in that movie, *Abominable*?" Chad chuckled, "That was so awesome!"

Lou asked, "You're the expert, make a guess?"

MB sighed heavily, "What . . . whether Bigfoot eat people or not?" He saw the look on Lou's face. She was beginning to lose it. What the fuck. "Old Indian legend tells us that man who makes a guess sometimes guesses wrong."

Chad chuckled at MB's remark.

"Yeah, I guess you're right," Lou agreed with a sigh.

"Hey . . . I just had a thought . . ." Chad exclaimed.

"Don't tax your brain, Chad," Lou teased.

"You don't think Duane-o's got anything to do with this?" Chad looked really pleased. "Well, you know . . . he likes to go about dressed up as Bigfoot."

MB and Lou exchanged glances. MB knew they were both thinking the same thing—Duane-o wouldn't be daft enough to get involved in Beau's abduction prank. The dumbass would know it would get him into trouble with the law—not that Lou would arrest him, but the Mayor would insist that Duane be held accountable for complicity in Beau's abduction prank, if it was found out he was involved in it.

"Leave the thinking to me, Chad," Lou remarked in a weary voice.

Chad shrugged his shoulders and looked disgruntled at Lou. "Okay, I get it . . . but if a grizzly or Bigfoot hasn't taken Beau then it has to be Duane-o or some evil, axe-wielding cannibal . . . maybe he's being barbecued right now."

MB stood up and folded his arms across his chest. He gave Chad a sharp look.

Chad stirred uneasily beneath Chief Mocking Bird's condescending gaze.

"What I say now, dude?"

"Old Indian legend tells us that if all the stupid dudes in the world thought at once they wouldn't release enough energy to light one bulb."

Chad looked hurt. "That really hurts, dude." He perked up. "But, like honest, MB, I'm telling the truth."

Either the kid was a good liar or he was telling the truth, thought MB. Nah, the kid had to be a good liar for the alternative was too unpleasant to think about.

MB nodded his head and smiled amiably at Chad. "Old Indian legend tells us that kids with something to hide make bad liars."

Chad casually shrugged his shoulders, "Have it your own way."

MB and Lou exchanged dubious glances at one another. They were thinking the same thing—had Beau really gone missing? Fool me once, fool me twice, but fool me three times just ain't so nice.

9

EARLIER THAT SAME DAY, the bright moon reflected from two large eyes within the forest. The eyes stared at the strange yellow four-legged thing resting at Little Beaver picnic area. Large tufted ears twitched to the sound of happy voices emanating from the young pale ones sitting around the campfire drinking and having a good time.

From behind a nearby tree, something hairy watched the four pale ones. It was something of sufficient weight to cause the undergrowth to rustle and for twigs to crack beneath its heavy feet. Shiny, big, deep blue eyes, watched the fun-loving youngsters with an envious look. For the eyes were young too and wanted to join in. The hairy creature stepped from behind the tree.

Olaaa, the young female Bigfoot was small for a Bigfoot and when fully standing was no more than one and half strides high, but she was very strong, as displayed by her immense hands snapping a hefty branch as she wooed her soon-to-be play thing-the pretty blond pale one.

Her lustrous hair was a light fawn, but dappled with patches of dark reddish-brown, here and there. She had a pair of golden circles around her eyes, giving the appearance of spectacles. Her face was quite pretty in a Bigfoot way, with fine hairs barely covering her light, golden brown skin. Her cute little snout twitched with every scent it detected. Her suckle-bumps were just beginning to show through her luxuriant chest hair which covered her all the way down to her nether regions, where the hair hung in long damp tufts.

She moved slowly and as carefully as she could towards the sound of laughter. She was very mindful to keep well-hidden amongst the brush and thickets. From her vantage point behind another tree, she watched and listened.

Olaaa's chosen one sat by the fire enjoying his friends' antics, slurping what she hoped was happy juice. She watched the plump dark-haired female with rings on her face point a strange box at the others. At first, Olaaa was alarmed. She thought it was a fire stick, but the strange box seemed to attract them in some way.

The dark-haired male with the spotty face started to act in a very peculiar way, sending frightened signals to Olaaa's ears.

"Oooooh," he laughed. He started to remove his upper covering.

The female giggled, "That's my boy . . . take it all off."

Although the words were broken up, Olaaa could understand the gist of what was said, recognizing familiar words spoken by the pale ones. She truly wished she could speak to them. She grinned, showing her big yellow teeth as the pimply male stripped almost to his thruster, revealing a lean chest. She chortled as the male threw the body top into the fire.

The other pale ones egged him on by clapping and wolf-whistling.

Olaaa's big eyes widened with delight and arousal at the sight of the dark-haired male's naked and lean upper body. She licked her dark brown lips wantonly with her long, pink tongue.

"Wooo-wooo wooo-weee," she bleated quietly to herself.

Beneath her right big foot there was a twig of a tree. *Snap* went the twig beneath her clumsy big foot.

She looked down at her clumsy big foot and cursed quietly by snorting air nasally, "Ftftftft." The nasal snorting was a general term used by Bigfoot to describe something unpleasant from smells to feelings.

Olaaa was alarmed to see and hear sounds of distress coming from the pale ones. She thought she might have given herself away. She was desperate for them to stay and not run off.

The red-haired smaller female pointed in Olaaa's direction and spoke, "Did any of you hear that? Something's out there! Something's moving about over there."

Olaaa sensed amusement rather than terror from that pale one.

"It's just old Duane-o up to his usual tricks," the beautiful blond one said. He drank some happy juice.

Olaaa perked up at hearing Duane's name spoken by her plaything.

Olaaa's binocular vision allowed her to see the tiny pictures displayed on the strange box held by the plump female. Her chosen mate, the blond male pointed to the heavens in a scary way.

"I know . . . it's those aliens come to take us. It's my old man you want, not me," he shouted out, laughing.

Olaaa looked up to see nothing but the stars.

Olaaa frowned for a moment. Were these pale ones waiting for the bright lights to take them away? If so, they were in the right place.

Olaaa knew what she should do now, when the pale ones were close by who might get a glimpse of a Bigfoot. She knew she must leave quickly. Hide. But Olaaa sometimes didn't do as she was told to do by her elders. After all, she was still considered a baby by her tribe, but Olaaa was growing up fast and couldn't wait for what wondrous things nature had waiting for her.

She remained perfectly still. She wanted to stay and watch the teenagers. In fact, she wanted to join in the fun. She warned herself not to tread on anything that might give her presence away.

Olaaa's blond plaything took a long gulp of happy juice.

Olaaa licked her lips as her nostrils detected the distinct smell of happy juice. She ached all over to join in their fun, for Olaaa sensed that these pale ones were a lot like her.

The pubescent Bigfoot cocked her head as the dark-haired female started to shake the picture-box in her hand as if frightened.

The dark-haired male squealed in terror. "Oooooh, Bigfoot."

The red-haired female stared right at Olaaa with a terrified look—genuine fear.

Olaaa wondered if they could see her.

The pale ones looked expectantly into the pitch-black darkness of the forest.

Olaaa's chosen one playfully punched the red-haired female in the shoulder as he got up. He wobbled as if he'd had too much happy juice.

Olaaa's big blue eyes rounded as she looked at the delectably gorgeous, blond pale one. Her heart fluttered then raced wildly.

She watched him stagger off towards the edge of the clearing and disappear behind the tree out of sight of his friends. But Olaaa could still see him standing at the base of the tree.

With almost unbearable excitement, she stared at him unzipping his jeans to urinate. She saw the steady flow of his pee on the ground and against the tree. The smell of his manly essence and muskiness aroused her.

She swished her hips suggestively, cooing, "Woooo-woooo-woooo."

Behind the cover of the thickets, Olaaa placed each big foot to the ground with extreme care and walked towards her unsuspecting plaything. She stopped behind the leak tree and listened to him zip up his fly. Olaaa breathed heavily with excitement. She licked her lips.

An owl screeched, as if to alert Olaaa's pale one, but the plaything was a little too happy on the juice to heed the warning of the wise old owl. He belched.

The chosen one called out. Olaaa thought he was calling to her. Olaaa sighed on hearing the pretty pale one's voice. She sniffed the night air then sniffed her own pungent odor. She sniffed her very hairy, excessively damp armpits.

She snorted nasally with disgust. She smelled like a raccoon's behind. She needed a good dowsing in the river if she was going to attract her pretty boy.

"Woooooo-wooooooo," she called her plaintive mating call excitedly into the night.

The unfamiliar calling sound—which was so loud it seemed to be inches from his ear—which it actually was, suddenly warned the plaything. He reacted as if in danger. Before he could cry out, a big hairy hand, pink and calloused, came up to his face and covered his mouth, stifling his scream.

Olaaa was so excited she let out her mating call.

THE TEENAGERS STOPPED THEIR merry-making and listened. All eyes were focused on the spot at the edge of the clearing where Beau had gone to take a leak.

"Weeeeoooooeeeeeoooo."

"Shit, did you hear that?" Chad exclaimed. "What if it's those aliens who keep abducting Beau's old man ... maybe they've come for Beau?" Chad looked up to the sky. "Beau says those aliens are up to something weird." Chad saw nothing unusual.

"It's just gotta be Bigfoot," Naomi whimpered. She grabbed hold of Chad's arm and shivered with fright. "It's come to have its way with us."

Chad pushed Naomi away, laughing, "Yeah, with you, not me." He chuckled, "I bet it's real hung . . . like down to its knees."

Naomi punched Chad in the arm, "That's so gross, you pig."

Debbie directed the camcorder to the spot where Beau had gone to take a leak. "It's only Beau pissing around as usual."

Naomi jumped to her feet and looked frantically into the dark woods. "Beau . . . you there?" she shouted. "Beau!"

OH, HE WAS THERE alright. It occurred to Olaaa that the pale ones were calling out for her plaything. She mouthed the word Boo! She connected this word to her chosen one. He fainted with pure terror as Olaaa swiftly lifted him before he collapsed and slung him over her shoulder, fireman-style.

A moment later, Boo threw up over Olaaa's back. A moment after that Boo passed out again.

Olaaa didn't mind him throwing up down her back. She was excited and eager to take him back to her lair to play with.

But a voice inside her told her she was doing wrong. Alas, Olaaa was too young to take heed of her conscience, as all young Bigfoot are apt to do. She just knew she wanted Boo to be her special plaything.

With all the jostling Boo came around. All he could see was Olaaa's hairy rear end.

"Help me," Boo whispered in terror, somewhat croakily with a dry mouth as he was carried into the deep forest.

Boo's weight caused Olaaa to rip off a fart. The noxious fumes caused him to pass out once again.

❧   ❧   ❧

IT WAS NOW DAWN. The campfire embers smoldered. Thin wisps of smoke swirled up into the cool morning air. Golden rays of sunshine filtered through the trees and the ground-hugging mist. A white-tailed deer munched on the thin grass at the edge of the clearing. It looked at the disheveled heap of humanity and continued to eat, unconcerned.

Beau's friends had collapsed in a drunken heap around the fire. Their cozy tents hadn't been used. Second by second, the forest became alive with birdsong and the awakening of its resident fauna.

One by one the teenagers started to stir. They were hungover and aching from sleeping on the damp grass. They stretched and breathed in the fresh morning smells of the pine forest surrounding them.

Debbie yawned widely, noticing that Beau had not returned.

She called out, "Beau, where are you?" She watched the deer skip away with a look of concern.

DEEP WITHIN THE FOREST, the shrill sounds of birds accompanied Olaaa on her trek back to her lair. She crashed effortlessly through damp and misty undergrowth with an unconscious Boo slung over her shoulder.

Olaaa merrily called out to her brethren, "Wooooo-eeeee-wooooooo-eeeee."

Several wooooo-weeeee-wooooooos replied. Olaaa increased her speed through the thick undergrowth. She stopped suddenly. Something told her that her family would not approve of what she had done. They would say she had contaminated their secret hideaway deep in the forest where only one pale one had ever gone before.

10

BY MIDDAY, MOST BEAVERITES knew what had happened to Beau Flucker, thanks to Beau's friends who had spread the word quickly around town that he'd gone missing, yet again. His parents already knew the complete unabridged version before Sheriff Lou showed up on their doorstep.

Walt Flucker opened the door with a grimace and allowed the sheriff to enter the Flucker household. He was a huge bear of a man, in his early forties with salt and pepper, close-cropped hair. He had a ruddy complexion from spending a lot of time outdoors.

Sheriff Lou took a seat on the sofa with Beau's less-than-distraught mother, Rose, a petite woman in her mid-forties.

She was a sweet-natured woman, but it was well-known she wore the pants in the Flucker home. Her bullish husband, Walt, was putty in her hands.

Lou and Rose sipped coffee from delicate porcelain cups on saucers; all very gentile.

"He'll show up, and when he does, I'll give him a good telling off, Sheriff," Rose said. "He's a good boy at heart . . . just likes to get up to mischief, is all." Rose looked at Walt's dour face. "He takes after that one . . . monkey see, monkey do."

Lou wasn't surprised by Rose's reaction on hearing her son had gone missing. The poor woman must be fed up with his antics by now. Lou sipped her coffee.

"It's no laughing matter spending the town's taxes on a pointless search party."

Rose nodded her head in agreement and patted Lou's knee in consolation. "I know, my dear. I don't know what to say."

Walt stood by the fireplace with a permanent grimace on his ruddy face. Above the fireplace was a Sharps rifle, and above that monstrous gun was a stuffed head of a deer that had obviously been shot by Walt. The rest of the living room walls were dotted with Walt's hunting trophies strangely mixed with sweet paintings of flowers that Rose had painted herself.

Walt flexed his manly biceps protruding from his red-checked shirt with sleeves rolled up. His jeans had two inch turn ups, making him look like a perfect effigy of Paul Bunyan, except for the massive beer belly and the fact that Walt had never in his life chopped down a tree with an axe.

Like so many in town, Lou had often thought that Rose and Walt were ill-suited. Walt was a fervid hunter and a collector of antique guns, not to mention a fanatical Elvis Presley fan. Rose had a passion for the finer things in life, classical music, ballet, painting pretty flowers and landscape scenes. The Fluckers seemed to have very little in common except the conception of their son, but to those who knew them, Walt and Rose were as much in love as the day they were married.

"Wait till he gets home, I'll give him more than a good talking to this time," Walt said with real menace. "This is the millionth time he's pulled this prank."

Walt was also a fisherman, which explained his penchant for exaggeration, as proved by the smallest steelhead ever to be mounted and displayed for all to see next to the deer's head.

"It's all your fault he likes to pretend to be abducted," Rose accused, wagging her tiny finger at her husband.

Walt grunted his disapproval at being reprimanded by his wife in front of Sheriff Lou. He clenched his fists.

"The problem with the world today is that parents have got to be ever so nice to their kids. In my day my father wouldn't stand for half the crap that Beau has put us through," Walt stated with a glare.

Rose placed her coffee cup and saucer on a side table and jumped to her feet. She marched up and stood facing her husband. She started to prod him forcefully in his excessively hairy chest with her tiny finger.

Walt didn't raise a hand to stop his wife; he just grimaced and took it like a bowl of quivering jelly.

Everyone, including Sheriff Lou, knew he had never raised a hand to his wife and never would, but she had listened many times to Walt bragging at Abe's Bar and Grill how he wore the trousers in his home.

"Now, now mother, you know how I feel about you prodding your finger into my chest," Walt said with a nervous smile.

Rose continued to prod, exclaiming, "Don't you now-now-mother me, Walt Flucker, you useless good-for-nothing. Beau is only taking after you. How many times have you claimed to be abducted by Bigfoot?" She stood back a pace with hands on hips.

"Can't rightly say offhand . . . but I was," Walt replied indignantly. He pleaded to Lou with hand on heart. "I was genuinely abducted by Bigfoot, not to mention these tall, blond aliens from the planet Abba."

"Yeah, yeah . . . so you've said as often as I dared to listen." Lou sounded irritated.

"I know you don't believe me sheriff, but it's the God's honest truth . . . I was abducted by aliens. The females had long blond hair . . . very Swedish in appearance. They were slender, young and beautiful, with soft hands and supple bodies with perky breasts with upright nipples. And there was this one overweight male alien who looked exactly like Elvis, who told me he actually was Elvis, and that they had sent Elvis' clone back to earth so nobody would notice his abduction." Walt paused and looked thoughtful for a moment or two. "The females would do anything I wanted them to do, sex-wise." He started to grin at the lewd thoughts invading his mind. "Their sexual parts were right where they should have been, and like the saying goes, if the hat fits—wear it."

Rose punched him in the arm. "Jesus, Walt . . . is that all you can think about . . . S. E. X.?"

Walt gave a snigger. "Not all the time, Rose, darling, love bud of my life . . . sometimes, as you know, I ponder the fate of mankind and the consequences of global warming."

Lou had spent just about enough time as she dared with Beau's parents, realizing they were not taking his disappearance seriously. She handed her empty cup and saucer to Rose as she got up from the sofa.

"Well, the FBI has been contacted. If Beau hasn't turned up by tomorrow, they'll be sending two agents from the Sacramento Field Office to help us with our investigations."

"Shit," Walt said, mimicking awe. "The FBI are coming." He shook his head with dismay. "Whoever they'll send won't be able to find the whereabouts of a missing toilet roll even if it was shoved up their tight asses."

Lou didn't reply to Walt's crude remark. "I'll keep you both informed of my investigations."

Rose nodded her head politely, "Thank you, dear."

Walt shook his head and grimaced. "F-B-I," he slowly sounded the letters with a disgusted snarl on his lips. "Feeble-Brained Idiots. Shit, that's all we need."

It was no secret to Lou that Walt had a strong contempt for the FBI, mainly due to the Bureau's reluctance to believe he had been abducted by aliens. She hoped that there would be no reason for FBI agents to come to Big Beaver. That Beau would show up before they did.

"Talking of idiots, that reminds me—you had the DNA results back on the Phantom Bigfoot Bather Case yet?" Walt asked.

Oh yeah, she had the results back, thought Lou. And as expected the analysis of the hairs left by the Phantom Bigfoot—the third such incident in less than two months—could not be ascertained because, once again, they had been contaminated with bleach. As for the pungent odor, it was determined to be caused by various animal extracts, skunk urine and sulfur oxide for that extra lingering noxious smell. It was confirmed by all involved that the perp was a class "A" nut job.

Whoever was responsible for the practical joke—and she was pretty damned sure it had to be Duane—had cleverly manufactured each crime scene to prevent it from being properly analyzed. One thing though—and everyone in Sacramento was in agreement, it could not be a Bigfoot, because Bigfoot was a myth.

"Yeah, I've got the results of the DNA," Lou replied. "The same . . . as usual."

Walt looked disgusted. "I hope no one's going to blame me for contaminating the evidence this time. I merely help extract the evidence from the scene as requested by you, ASAP, with the utmost of care, I might add." Walt folded his muscular arms with pride in his plumber's job. "Not my fault I had to take a piss at the wrong moment."

"Like I said, as soon as I know something, you'll know." Lou nodded to the Fluckers.

Rose led Lou from the living room, down the hall to the front porch. "Please don't mind Walt, his bark is worse than his bite." Rose smiled sweetly, "And don't worry your pretty head about Beau, he's probably laughing right now."

Lou smiled at the poor woman, "Speak to you soon, Rose."

11

OLAAA SAT UP AND YAWNED. She stretched hairy arms and looked about her little home.

The cave was small, dark and decorated with flowers and leaves of every color. The walls were adorned with crude drawings of tall men with pale hair floating into a massive doughnut with what looked like rays beaming down. The entrance to the cave was covered by bushes and undergrowth and was barely big enough for an adult Bigfoot to squeeze through.

Olaaa sat on her haunches, watching a sleeping Boo from a dark corner of the cave. She slowly rocked back and forth, mewing pathetically.

A shaft of sunlight filtered through the entrance onto her plaything as he lay comfortably on a bed of leaves and grass. He was trussed up with thin vines to prevent him from escaping. A piece of cloth torn from his t-shirt was tied around his mouth to muffle any sounds he made which might attract the other Bigfoot to his whereabouts.

Olaaa looked lovingly at her plaything. If wishes could come true she wished he would reciprocate her love. But such a love between a Bigfoot and a pale one was forbidden.

She sighed woefully then gave a whimper, "Weeeewooooeeee."

Olaaa crept closer to Boo and stroked his fine blond hair. More than anything right then, Olaaa wanted to be blond like her plaything.

"Weeeooooweeeeeooooo."

12

IT WAS 8:30 IN THE EVENING of the first day of Beau's disappearance, and still no one took it seriously. But Beaverites did take seriously Wednesday nights at Abe's Bar and Grill. And this was Wednesday night.

Abe's was located on the western edge of town, at the top of Main Street. At the back of the building was a micro brewery, delivering four distinctive beers to the locals and tourists alike. Little Beaver Light at 3.4%—Big Beaver Bitter at 4.9%—Bigfoot ESB at 5.6% and last but not least, for those Beaverites who wanted to fall down real quick—Sasquatch Ale at 7.2%.

Several Beaverites entered the large log and stone cabin with a red sign stating this was Abe's Bar & Grill.

The place was fit to burst with locals and tourists, including the newly arrived Japanese sightseers. Live entertainment and dancing added ambiance to the beer-guzzling, shoe-tapping rowdy atmosphere. The walls were rough-hewn logs and the floor consisted of sawdust-covered planks of pine. All in all, a very rustic, but friendly place to get your brain totaled.

SHERIFF LOU SAT ON A swivel stool at the bar savoring the last mouthful of her tequila on the rocks. She was casually dressed in figure-hugging jeans and a tight t-shirt which accentuated her glorious figure. The only makeup adorning her face was bright pink lip-gloss. Her short-cropped hair was spiked with gel and somehow it suited her.

Behind the bustling bar stood the six-feet-three inch tall Abe, a well-fed, red-faced, jovial man in his early sixties. He laughed as he served drinks and chatted to his customers. Like Annie's Diner, Abe dished out the freebies, and Wednesdays and Mondays were all-you-could-eat-steak-and-fries night, accompanied with one free beer—a pitcher of Bigfoot ESB.

The sheriff's department also received extra freebies in the shape of all-you-could-eat-steak-and-fries night, six nights a week, excluding Sundays.

Abe watched Lou as she emptied her glass. He had a concerned look on his otherwise cheery face.

"You sure you want another one, Lou? I don't want you shutting me down for serving drunks."

Lou thought about that for a brief moment and frowned—if she happened to be the drunk then how could she shut Abe down?

"Fuck it, Abe . . . fill her up," Lou ordered as she pushed her empty glass across the bar.

Abe deftly caught the glass, dropped in some crushed ice and tipped an ample quantity of twelve year old tequila into it.

"Heard Beau's gone missing . . . yet again," he mused with a chuckle. "Also heard, you had the dogs out looking for him, yet again." He looked cheekily at her as he slid the glass back to Lou.

Lou nodded and sighed wearily as she caught her glass. She took a hefty sip and pondered her situation.

"Yeah, well, the dogs couldn't track him—too much stink. Beau probably backtracked his way from the spot where he'd gone to take a leak." She shook her head with dismay. "I betcha all the money in the world he was lying in the back of the van, hiding under all their camping gear." Lou took a hefty gulp.

"Damn it to hell . . . should've searched the van." She blew out her cheeks. "What's done is done, I guess."

They were all in on the charade, thought Lou. By now, Beau was probably hiding out somewhere in town having a big laugh at her expense. Of course, she was just guessing, but her gut was telling her nothing bad had happened to Beau. He'd probably show up tomorrow, if he didn't show up tonight. And he'd probably say Bigfoot took him—like father like son.

Abe shook his head. "He's just messing with you, Lou . . . you know that."

She nodded her head. "Yeah . . . I guess so."

As Lou took another sip of her tequila her face contorted at the dreadful pong of rotten eggs and stale sweat. She gagged on her drink, and turned to see Duane standing next to her.

Duane was dressed in his Bigfoot duds, minus the furry head. He smiled amiably at her. His eyes twinkled mischievously.

Lou smiled and looked at him with a mixture of affection and revulsion. She sniffed his manly odor and got a quick reminder of the crime scenes. She'd often remarked—not just to Duane, but to other Beaverite's that if only he'd get a haircut, shave off that beard and wore some decent clothes and not his faded, tatty jeans and "I'm a Bigfoot" t-shirt, or that stinky Bigfoot outfit of his, he'd pass for not half-bad, quite acceptable, even attractive. Not that she could ever be actually attracted to him. It was just an observation on her part. Besides, Duane was more like a brother to her. He was her best friend.

She knew damned well Duane wasn't concerned in keeping up appearances. Neither was he that bothered in attracting the fairer sex. So why was he so popular with the ladies? One reason—Duane was loaded.

He had been left a considerable amount of money by a distant relative who had no family except his distant cousin, Duane. The distant relative, Cousin Wilbur, Duane's grandfather's cousin had bought a parcel of land in Florida in the late '50s. The land was your basic swampland full of gators and such, but Wilbur knew a deal when he saw one. He sold the land to a devious developer who built condominiums— mostly retirement condominiums on the land once it had been drained. And like Duane, Cousin Wilbur was a loner.

But unlike Duane, Cousin Wilbur had business acumen. He went from dubious deal to dubious deal.

Lou was well-aware—in fact anyone who knew Duane was well aware, that Duane sadly lacked the skill or desire to make his mark in life.

Lou knew that Duane was content to meander along life's highway, bonking his brains out, performing at hen parties, singing and playing his guitar at Abe's Bar and Grill. Not to mention pranking the shit out of her.

There was also another factor to take into account for Duane's popularity with the ladies—he was real good in bed. But Lou didn't want to dwell on such a lewd thought—because he was like a brother to her, and such a thought seemed indecent.

It had to be said that most Beaverites liked Duane. Though there were some that thought him a little too weird, living all alone in that cabin of his in the woods.

Yeah, he sure was one weird son-of-a-bitch, agreed Lou.

Duane nodded to a Japanese tourist sitting next to Lou, who was giving her an amorous, all be it drunken look. The tourist got the meaning right away and sauntered off his stool.

Duane sat down at the vacant barstool next to Lou and put his arm around her shoulder. He gave her a big Bigfoot hug. He looked concerned, but the mischievous twinkle in his blue eyes gave his true feelings away.

"Aw, what's bothering my gal? Come on, you can tell ol' Duane-o."

Lou narrowed her eyes as she looked at the feigned look of concern on his face. "Two things are bothering me, right now."

"Heard Beau's gone missing again," Duane said.

"Oh yeah . . . that's one of them."

"He'll show up when he has a mind to . . . so hang loose."

Lou nodded her head and sighed, "Yeah, I guess."

Duane gave Lou a pensive look, "The results from the Phantom Bigfoot Bather Case back yet?" He scratched his butt with his thinking finger.

"Had the same conversation with Walt earlier today . . . and yes, they have."

"DNA give anything away?"

"Nope."

Duane nodded his head and said, "Shame about that . . . a real shame."

Lou saw the concern on his face, but she was quick to notice the twinkle of humor in his eyes. She gave a long, weary sigh. She loved Duane and knew the feeling was mutual. But he sure knew how to yank her chain with his practical jokes. Lou looked away from his face and gazed miserably into her glass of tequila. She gave another sigh.

"I dunno . . . what is the world coming to?"

Duane solemnly nodded his head and agreed. "Yeah, what is the world coming to? You gotta admit there's a lot of weird shit going on." His tone was mockingly serious.

Lou wasn't fooled by his tone of voice. She took a sip of her tequila as Abe came over to them with a refill of beer for Duane. She gave Duane a withering glance.

Abe placed the full glass of beer on the bar in front of the amiable Bigfoot and walked away to serve some other customers that were eagerly jostling for a prime position at the bar.

"Shit, Lou, I've told you, it ain't me," Duane pleaded. "It has to be some other sicko in town responsible for clogging up Beaverite's pipe works." He took another mouthful of beer and grinned. He scratched his butt again. "You wanna know who I think it is?" He paused for a moment and smiled. "That shit-for-brains Walt. He loves drains . . . loves the smell of them . . . wouldn't surprise me if he bathes in drainage." As an afterthought, "Sure smells as though he does."

Sad to say, some of what Duane said made sense, but Lou didn't really think the town plumber was the Phantom Bigfoot. Everyone knew that Duane loved to play practical jokes. How many times had he been caught red-handed by MB and tourists alike in his tailor-made Bigfoot feet stomping up the ground in the woods somewhere?

And how many times had someone photographed or got Duane on a camcorder in his Bigfoot duds, only for him to take off his Bigfoot head just before it got blown off by some excited hunter? Of course, there had been countless occasions when a hunter had actually shot at Duane mistaking him for a grizzly or Bigfoot. He had the scars to prove it. That Duane sure was one stupid fucker.

Lou lifted her gaze from her glass of tequila and looked keenly at her best friend. He had to be the Beaver Bigfoot, for he sure as hell was dressed for the part.

Duane ran his fingertips over his unshaven chin and looked thoughtful for a moment or two, then gave a grin, scratching his butt with his thinking finger.

"One thing you got to admit though, your deputies sure have lost a few pounds recently. Guess their delicate stomachs can't take that phantom stink." He sniffed his armpits, "Smells worse than me." Duane gave another grin. "And as for the good people of Big Beaver, well hey, not many seem to mind there's a Phantom Bigfoot in town." He chuckled, "He's becoming quite a celebrity."

A look of exasperation darkened Lou's face. She had to admit Duane was right about her deputies. They had lost a few pounds, apart from Dwight—another reason she had not arrested Duane. As for most people in town, they didn't take the antics of the Phantom Bigfoot too seriously. In fact, there were some who hoped the prankster would pay their home a visit. It was deemed an honor.

Lou sighed inwardly knowing that if she did find out Duane was the culprit he'd place her in a moral dilemma. Could she actually have him arrested and convicted?

Duane shook his head solemnly and raised his beer glass to his lips. He took a mouthful of Bigfoot ESB, licked the froth from his stubbly chin and moustache, then started to chuckle.

"Lighten up Lou. No one's being harmed." Duane scratched his ass. "Oh yeah, what was the other thing bothering you?"

She was the town sheriff, a person with responsibilities, someone who enforced the law—she had no one to love—that was the fucking problem. And it was thirteen years to this very day that heartless bastard left her without a word. Okay, so Beau had gone missing. How could she lighten up? Lou gave Duane a withering look.

FROM HIS VANTAGE POINT seated at a table close to the bar, MB sipped his beer and watched Duane and Lou talking. He was not alone.

Two very attractive, early twenty something females sat at his table. They were keen fans of the singing duo that consisted of MB and Duane and their adoration of them knew no bounds.

MB hoped he was going to get lucky that night—lucky with both females in tandem.

As MB watched Lou and Duane, he saw his furry friend give the sheriff a peck on the cheek. If he didn't know any better it could look like the sheriff and Duane had a thing going, but MB knew all the affectionate stuff that went on between them was purely platonic.

MB often thought it was a shame Duane and Lou couldn't hit it off with each other, it would sure help Lou's disposition. MB was reminded of an Old Indian legend that said opposites attract. But in Lou and Duane's case they were far too opposite.

"Excuse me, ladies," MB said as he got up from his chair. "I think I'm needed at the bar."

The two adoring fans waved at MB as he left their company. "Don't be too long, Chiefy, baby."

MB quietly approached Lou and Duane like an Indian on the prowl. Neither sensed his approach until he placed a hand on their shoulders.

"You're not taking advantage of the law are you, Duane-o, my good buddy?"

Both Lou and Duane swung round on their bar stools to look at MB's grinning face.

"You two look as though you could do with a . . . stiff . . . drink?" MB teased.

MB knew that despite being loaded with money, Duane never turned down a freebie of beer.

"Sure thing, MB," Duane nodded.

Lou took a sip of tequila and shook her head. "Uh-uh, this is my last."

MB nodded and caught the attention of Abe as he served drinks to some customers at the bar. He returned his attention back to Duane. "Heard the scoop on the poop yet?"

"Oh yeah." Duane shrugged, "No luck again . . . go figure . . . too contaminated, so Lou tells me . . . just like the other two." He sniggered, "Shame about that." He shook his head woefully.

MB noticed the look on Lou's face as she stared at Duane and came to the conclusion she was thinking the same thing he was—Duane-o had to be the Phantom Bigfoot.

13

IT WAS THE START OF A NEW DAY. The sheriff's patrol car sped down the narrow highway. It turned off onto a small, bumpy logging road that led to Little Beaver then made another turn right before entering the picnic area. Sunlight dappled the windscreen as the car passed a never ending line of firs.

Lou drove with a grim determination for she had hoped with the start of the new day Beau would have shown up. She had no choice but to treat him as a missing person and continue with her investigations, though her gut told her he was still messing around.

The sheriff slowed down and turned onto a tiny logging road, no wider than her car. Branches swished and scratched the sides of the cruiser as a ramshackle log cabin came into view.

Dense woods surrounded Duane's isolated homestead consisting of a cabin with ivy creeping all over it. The sheriff's patrol car stopped right in front of the main door of the cabin in a cloud of dust. Lou stepped out of her cruiser and surveyed the wilderness that crept right up to the porch.

Two other vehicles were also parked outside the cabin— Duane's Harley Davidson and a shiny, new, blue Winnebago campervan gaily painted with large white Bigfoot footprints. *Bigfoot Mobile* was written on both sides of the camper van. The camper was scratched all over.

Lou stepped onto the porch and tapped the screen door. The floor beneath her feet creaked alarmingly. She kept moving in case she went through the floor.

A sudden creak of the screen door exposed Duane's beaming, unshaven face. He prompted Lou inside with a wave of his hand and a scratch of his ass.

Lou followed Duane into the main living area. Not that anyone could call the room a decent place to live in. *Even pigs had better homes than this,* thought Lou.

She rather gingerly sat in a beaten up, threadbare armchair that smelled real bad. In fact it smelled quite similar to the crime scenes—most curious. She was trying not to pay too much attention to the cluttered living room, but it wasn't easy. Her concentration started to waver with thoughts of tiny livestock finding a new home on her body. She touched an arm of the chair and instantly regretted it.

Something sticky and quite pungent stained her hand yellow. She sniffed the goo and almost choked on the smell of rotten eggs and stale garlic. She was again reminded of the Phantom Bigfoot. She wiped her hand on the chair, now thoroughly distracted from her task.

Surely with Duane's money, he could afford a luxury cabin, furniture to match, nothing but the best, and yet he chose to live in such a shabby home. She'd often commented upon this fact, but he'd never done anything about it.

He was—and there was no doubt in her mind—an incurable eccentric. Money was of no real use to Duane. Keeping up appearances didn't bother him. He didn't care what people said or thought about him.

She focused her attention on a recumbent Duane as he lay comfortably on the sofa. She couldn't help but notice clumps of cushion and springs poking through the woven material of the collapsed sofa.

Duane was casually dressed in a faded t-shirt covered in food stains and threadbare, red and navy check long johns. On his feet were disgustingly grubby Bigfoot slippers.

Lou fidgeted in the gross-smelling armchair. She wondered what that stink was, and worse, what was that yellow stuff. Lou gave Duane a quizzical look.

Duane sat bolt upright as something dawned on him.

"Where are my manners today?"

He sprang to his feet. The sofa gave an audible squeal as fresh springs popped anew through the rotting material. He shuffled off to the kitchen, out of sight.

The sounds of coffee making could be heard.

Lou got up and made a quick search of the rest of the living room. She had to admit that some areas of the living room smelled real nice, despite its clutter. She faltered, wondering what that nice, flowery smell was. Her keen eye detected several air freshener wands dotted about the room giving off a sweet fragrance.

Suddenly something nipped her bare arm. She started to itch, thinking the armchair was flea—infested. She furiously scratched her lower arm. She wondered if Duane had fleas, but she hadn't noticed him scratching before—unless he was thinking with his butt-finger. The little nipper had progressed to her back. *Damn it Duane!*

Lou shouted out, "What the hell's been in that armchair, Duane?"

Duane entered the living room with two mugs of steaming coffee. "Why d'ya wanna know?"

"I think I've picked up some miniature guests."

"Oh . . . sorry about that," Duane said with a shrug, handing the mug to Lou. As an afterthought he explained, "Some hunters' hounds chased a raccoon through here, not long back . . . they were all over that armchair like fleas on a Bigfoot."

Lou sipped her coffee. Not bad.

"Beau has never stayed missing for more than nine hours," she said, sounding troubled.

"He'll show up," Duane replied with an unconcerned shrug.

If Beau knew what was good for him he'd better show up soon, thought Lou. She decided not to return to the armchair and remained on her feet.

"Something I should've asked you last night at Abe's . . . have you seen any strangers in the woods in the last two days?"

Duane looked thoughtful for a moment and idly scratched his butt. He shrugged as he sat back down on the creaking sofa.

"Duh—I'm always seeing strangers in the woods . . . you know, hikers, campers, hunters and such . . . just the usual crowd hoping to get a glimpse of Bigfoot or bag a specimen." As a little added touch, he said, "No alien shit though."

Duane shook his head and eased himself away from a spring that was trying to ream his butt hole, but no matter where he sat another spring was waiting. He gave up.

"But Lou, this isn't the first time he's gone missing nor will it be the last."

Before she could reply, Lou felt a sharp nip on her backside. She twitched and involuntarily scratched her butt. She stood looking at Duane, scratching her backside frantically while trying not to spill her coffee.

"Don't I know it," she agreed irritably.

Her gaze held onto the stinky armchair. She had an irresistible urge to blow it away with her Magnum .44.

"I don't want to ask this . . . but are you involved in Beau's disappearance?" Lou immediately felt ashamed.

Duane looked genuinely aghast at Sheriff Lou. "Me! You think I'm hiding Beau?"

Lou gave Duane a keen look. He seemed genuinely shocked by what she had just asked. Of course, he could be putting on a good act, but her gut told her that her friend didn't have anything to do with Beau's disappearance. And that was fine with her.

"Sorry about that, Duane, but I'd be remiss in my duty if I hadn't asked what was on everyone's mind."

"If you like, you can take a look around the place," Duane offered. "You don't need a search warrant." He suddenly went stiff, "Who's *everyone*, Lou?" Duane sighed, "No, don't tell me . . . that shit-for-brains, Walt!"

Lou nodded yes and had to agree, Walt Flucker surely was a real shit-for-brains. Should she take him up on his offer of a search? She hesitated for a moment.

"No need for a search, Duane . . . I believe you had nothing to do with Beau's disappearance."

She looked at her best friend—the guy who'd saved her all those miserable years ago, and could see the relief on his face. She glanced at a fading photo in a wooden frame above the fireplace. It was of her, Duane and *him* displaying a massive steelhead. A twinge of sadness tugged at her heart. Her thoughts wandered back to her surroundings.

"You're not much for housekeeping are you?"

"Can't say that I am," Duane said with a shrug. He watched Lou scratch her behind with a smirk. "Don't scratch, it just makes them bite all the more."

Lou gave the armchair a look of disgust then looked back at her amiable host. "That armchair stinks more than just dog. What the hell made that smell?" It sure as hell reminded her of each crime scene, but not as pungent.

Duane was slow to reply as he gave the matter some thought while scratching his butt with his thinking finger. He blew out his cheeks and shook his head.

"Search me, Lou. You know I never lock my door . . . guess some critter nested there while I was away . . . a skunk maybe."

She loved Duane, but why couldn't he take more pride in himself and his home? "You know it wouldn't hurt to get a haircut and put on some decent clothes and give this place a dusting." She thought the only thing this place needed was a bulldozer.

Duane didn't reply for a minute. He gave Lou one of his amiable smiles before he spoke. "I'm happy the way things are."

Most times she found that amiable smile of his hard to resist, like now. She smiled affectionately at him.

"Love you, Duane, you scruffy, lazy bastard."

Duane didn't take offense at her remark. He just continued to smile that amiable smile of his as he watched her place her mug on the floor then walk over to the door.

DUANE STOOD ON THE PORCH and watched Sheriff Lou's patrol car drive away down the dirt road. He smiled as he waved goodbye.

As soon as the cruiser had turned a corner in the dirt road, he called out, "Teeelaaa!" He gave the safe whistle several times.

He scanned the perimeter of the forest that surrounded the cabin. From behind a fir tree stepped a stunning, six and a half foot, foxy red Bigfoot with gold-colored streaks in her hair. Teeelaaa had a bright yellow streak running down her forehead to her pert little snout that twitched incessantly seeking signs of danger. Her suckle-bumps were fully developed and quite overly-sized for a female Bigfoot. Her snout told her she was indeed safe.

Duane smiled, and beckoned her to come to him with a wave of his hand and a come-hither whistle.

Teeelaaa sniffed the air again as if to make sure no other pale ones were nearby, stepping into the clearing.

She skipped up to Duane, squealing with joy, "Weeeeooooeeee."

"I don't know about you, but I'm hungrier than a grizzly after winter," Duane said with a smile, rubbing his stomach and licking his lips, "Teeelaaa hungry?"

Teeelaaa nodded yes.

Duane nodded his head as he entered his cabin to make them something to eat in the kitchen.

Teeelaaa eagerly watched Duane preparing her favorite—canned tuna on toast with melted cheese topping. And for a special treat he plopped a big dollop of mayonnaise on top. Bigfoot went nuts for mayonnaise, especially the garlic variety.

Many times Duane had blissfully watched Teeelaaa and her hairy friends scavenge for food as nature intended. With her powerful hands she would rip from the earth bunches of wild garlic and devour them with relish. She also went nuts for nuts of all kinds and bonkers for berries.

Berries held a special meaning to Bigfoot, but more on that later.

14

EARLY THE FOLLOWING MORNING, a shiny, black FBI Sedan drove at the regulation steady pace—well within the speed limit, down the narrow two-lane highway towards the town of Big Beaver.

Agent Willis Johnson sat in the passenger seat irately tapping his fingertips on both knees. He was tight-lipped as he looked out of the window at the endless row of trees passing by. It was clearly evident he was not in the best of moods. The closer he got to Big Beaver the worse his nerves jangled—nerves of guilt—nerves due to *her*.

Agent Merlot was at the wheel. Occasionally she would smile to herself at the sight of such pleasing scenery, or a red-tailed hawk soaring above; it made a welcome change to concrete gray.

Coming into view was a road sign—"Bigfoot Bend—please slow down for Bigfoot crossing the road."

Merlot chuckled out loud and pointed to the sign. She dutifully slowed down and scanned the forest for Bigfoot, calling out in a cute voice, "Here, Bigfoot."

Willis stared at the sign as it flashed by and grimaced. He was aware that his pulse rate had increased and his palms felt clammy. He had a bad feeling in the pit of his stomach, like a nest of snakes squirming out of control. And his throat felt dry. He wondered if this is what a panic attack felt like.

Willis recalled telling his FBI supervisor that it was a pointless waste of time reassigning him to a missing person case and sending him to Big Beaver to investigate the disappearance of Beau Flucker, someone well-known for claiming he'd been abducted by Bigfoot. He had pointed out to his FBI supervisor that his area of expertise was audio and visual surveillance.

His supervisor had told him in no uncertain terms that it was on Doctor Fernandez's prescription that Willis be sent to his hometown to sort out his personal problems.

It was just dumb luck that this abduction case should occur at the wrong moment, and a perfect excuse to be psychologically evaluated to see how he'd react on returning to his hometown, a place he had expressed negative feelings about and was possibly the root cause of his recent antagonistic behavior. *Shrinks! What do they know*, thought Willis. Problem is, deep down, Willis knew the shrink was spot on.

Willis looked askance at his partner and saw her take her eye off the road to admire her reflection in the rear view mirror, and inspect her exceptionally white teeth.

The vain bitch will kill us both, thought Willis, as he looked back out of the passenger window.

"Eyes on the road!"

The Big Beaver welcome sign loomed up in front of them like something out of his nightmares.

Willis swallowed nervously. His pulse rate went up a notch. He ran his clammy hands down the legs of his trousers. The bad feeling in the pit of his stomach had started to give him the cramps. Sweat broke out on his brow. He started once again to tap his fingertips on both knees.

The woman he once loved was so close his guilt was ready to explode in his head—guilt at dumping her without saying anything. He just up and left.

The sign read "Welcome to Big Shaved Beaver."

At first, Willis wasn't at all amused at what was emblazoned on the sign for all to see. *Disgusting*, he thought. But inwardly, the juvenile reference caused him to smile at distant memories—fond memories of *her*. Outwardly, he was a rock.

Merlot looked at the sign and chuckled. She slammed on the brakes with a squeal of rubber, and peered up at the town welcome sign through the front window.

"Welcome to Big Shaved Beaver!" Merlot took a snapshot of the sign with her cell phone and sniggered.

Willis turned to look at his partner and gave her an irritated look. "It's juvenile and it's disgusting." He desperately wanted to laugh, but his stoic manner wouldn't allow him to let his guard down. He would be vulnerable then.

Merlot continued to look up at the sign. She chuckled. She started fiddling with her cell phone.

"What the hell are you doing now?"

Merlot grinned and pressed a key, "There."

"You sent that to the guys back in Sacramento, didn't you?"

"You betcha," Merlot said, bursting out laughing.

Willis clenched his fists in anger. Didn't his partner realize what a pain in the butt she was? And just like the idiot who had defiled the town welcome sign, Merlot was a juvenile with a disgusting mind. Willis would give anything right now to see the looks on his comrades' faces back at the field office. But there was that rock again.

"Are you going to stay here all day admiring such vulgarity?"

Merlot couldn't stop giggling. "Lighten up . . . don't you think Big Shaved Beaver is a good one?" She sniggered. "But I can think of a few better ones - such as Big Furry Beaver or Big Trimmed Beaver."

Willis' thin lip curled into a vicious snarl.

"Zip it!"

Merlot looked askance at her partner. The smile left her face as she judged the nasty look Willis was giving her.

"You really mean that don't you?"

"What do you think?" Willis showed his partner the grimmest grimace he could muster. He was gratified to see Merlot's unsmiling face. "That's better. Now let's keep it that way before I do something you'll regret."

"Okay, I get it, Dirty Harry, keep your gun holstered." With those words Merlot put the car in gear and drove off.

Several moments of zip it passed until Merlot began to chatter, like she always did when she was nervous.

"I'm looking forward to seeing your hometown and meeting the people you grew up with." Merlot grinned, showing her perfect white teeth. "Come on, Willis . . . should be fun."

Willis didn't reply. His gaze remained focused on the endless row of trees. He began to fidget. The thought of returning to Big Beaver, meeting the people he grew up with, seeing old friends and one friend in particular, filled him with dread. He hadn't seen or spoken to her for thirteen years. He'd thought when he left Big Beaver that he'd never return. That his life could only get better. He'd been planning to join the FBI and leave his hometown since his mid-teens. One thing he hadn't planned on was falling in love with the most gorgeous girl in town, though at the time he'd thought his love for her was just young love and that he'd get over her.

With mounting unease he wondered how she'd react to him coming back into her life, after ditching her the way he did. She'd probably knock out a few teeth. He couldn't blame her if she did. He truly regretted leaving her that way. He felt guilty for not saying goodbye.

But Willis knew the real reason why he'd left without saying anything. He wouldn't have been able to handle the tears and hurt. His resolve would have weakened and he would have probably ended up staying in Big Beaver for the rest of his life. And if he had stayed, what would he have done with his life? Become a deputy, maybe even sheriff? That was not how he planned to live his life.

Over the years he'd dwelled more and more on his reason for leaving her. Had he made a mistake in leaving? No, he didn't think so. He had his life to get on with—*his* life.

But these past couple of months, she had been on his mind more and more, ever since that damned letter—the letter that crushed his cold heart. He was still waiting for the right woman to come along, but none could cause sparks to fly like she could.

Had she been the right woman, perhaps the only woman? Willis didn't know the answer. What he did know, was that deep down, Doctor Fernandez was right, he did have unresolved issues in Big Beaver—issues that had fucked him up real good.

"You suppose we'll catch a glimpse of Bigfoot while we're here?" Merlot asked, suppressing a fit of the giggles.

Willis only half heard his partner speaking.

"What was that? Catch a glimpse of . . . what?"

Merlot repeated herself in an obvious way, "Catch a glimpse of Bigfoot while we're here."

Jesus Christ! Was his partner kidding? *Only idiots believed Bigfoot existed*, thought Willis, which confirmed his suspicions about Merlot. He didn't reply. He continued to look out of the passenger window, hoping Merlot would shut up.

"Hey, Willis . . . you ever seen Bigfoot?"

Willis didn't reply.

"Well . . . have you?"

Willis gritted his teeth. His partner was irritating the crap out of him. "No I haven't," he replied tersely.

"Wouldn't you like to see Bigfoot?"

Willis turned to look at his partner and wondered if she was being annoying on purpose or was she completely unaware of how much of a mind-blowing, brain-destroying irritant she was these days?

Once they got back to Sacramento, Willis promised himself he was going to insist on another partner, one that was less of a blabber mouth of humungous proportions.

"I'd like to see Bigfoot," Merlot said as she glanced in the rear view mirror and saw a solitary figure on a motorcycle coming down the road behind them. Her eyes opened wide in amazement.

"I didn't know Bigfoot knew how to ride a motorcycle," she commented with a smile.

Willis glanced in the passenger side mirror and saw his old friend Duane approaching on his bike, wearing his Bigfoot duds and his Bigfoot helmet. Bigfoot's furry party head was attached to the back of the Harley Davidson, along with his guitar.

"Fuck . . . it would have to be triple D, that dumbass, Duane Dexter," Willis muttered. He watched Duane come alongside their car and wave frantically.

Willis didn't return the gesture. His expression was serious, not even a glimmer of a smile for his oldest and one-time best friend. Deep down, Willis wanted to cry for ditching him too. But the rock remained just that—a rock.

Merlot waved back, "Hey, Mister Bigfoot!"

With a wave of his hand, Duane drove past the FBI car and sped off down the road in front of them, entering the outer limits of Big Beaver.

"Does everyone you know have to be an asshole or a dumbass?" Merlot asked. "You know it takes one to know one."

Yeah, he knew the guy. Willis remembered what good friends he and Duane had been. He had brief recollections of their glorious fishing trips for steelhead. They went back a long way. They'd grown up together in Big Beaver. They'd been like brothers, no, more like blood brothers. But that was then.

This was now. Willis hadn't seen or spoken to Duane for exactly thirteen years, along with everyone else in Big Beaver—everyone being *her*. And here he was returning to his shitty hometown to help solve a shitty case so some shitty nut doctor could declare Willis fit for shitty duty. The nightmare was about to begin. Shit! Shit! Shit!

15

MERLOT DROVE DOWN the main street of Big Beaver. She noted with a smile, Big Beaver's bustling thoroughfare lined with the usual kind of shops and businesses one would expect in a thriving tourist trap.

Beaverites and tourists alike sauntered happily along the boardwalks, going about their day-to-day business.

Willis pointed to the sheriff's department next door to Annie's Diner.

Merlot saw Annie's Diner and grinned mischievously as she pulled up next to a patrol car. She got out and stretched aching muscles.

So this is Big Beaver. Cool!

"I'm having a David Lynch moment." She thought the town looked as though, at any moment, a miniature truck, laden with logs would drive through the town of Twin Peaks. She looked at Willis and sniggered at the scowl on her partner's face.

Willis started walking towards the sheriff's building.

Merlot frowned, "Hey, don't you want to see Annie?" She indicated Annie's Diner.

WILLIS GRUNTED. Nothing had changed. He was in a shitty time warp. Shit! Why should his partner think he'd want to see Annie Bumgardner? She was the furthest thing from his mind. He didn't acknowledge Merlot as he entered the sheriff's department. His stomach was in overdrive. He wanted to puke.

LOU SAT AT HER DESK going over some paperwork. She looked up when Deputy Dwight knocked on her open door and showed the two FBI agents into her office. She'd been expecting their arrival, but she definitely hadn't expected to see Willis Johnson, the heartless bastard.

The sudden, heart-stopping shock caused Lou's hand to crunch up a piece of a report. She dropped it into a wastebasket without another thought as her mouth dropped open in surprise. She swallowed nervously. He had finally come back after all these years—after countless unreturned phone calls and letters.

Lou could feel her cheeks flushing with embarrassment. Was she blushing? Oh God, no, she hoped not. The last thing she wanted was to go all girlish and weak-kneed. *Get a hold of yourself. You're the town sheriff, not some sweet, innocent high school kid.* But that's exactly how she felt and that's exactly where her heart had been left—on the high school prom altar of love.

Lou shifted uncomfortably in her chair. She and Willis made uneasy eye contact. An eternity stretched into seconds.

Deputy Dwight hovered by the door waiting for his orders.

"Agents Johnson and Merlot," he announced. He cleared his throat and paused by the door.

MERLOT WATCHED Lou and Willis continue to stare uneasily at each other. Merlot, the incurable romantic, knew this day would get better, and came to the conclusion she had made a big mistake. No—make that a huge mistake, for Annie wasn't the reason for her partner's behavior. How could she be so far out of whack? To take her mind off things she eyed up Dwight with her woodometer.

Dwight noticed the curious glance from the delectable Merlot and flushed with embarrassment.

Hmm . . . haven't had chubby sex in a long time. Nice piece of softwood, Merlot thought.

Dwight cleared his throat, "Anyone for coffee and doughnuts?"

Merlot looked knowingly at the sheriff and her partner, thinking—go on kiss her, you idiot.

"Agent Johnson?" Dwight prompted. Dwight waited for a respectable moment. "Agent Johnson?"

"Yeah, whatever," Willis replied, obviously distracted.

The female agent correctly ascertained that Willis' well ordered world was spinning out of his control by the beads of sweat bursting on his forehead.

Dwight turned to his boss. "Coffee and doughnuts, Sheriff?"

LOU'S ATTENTION was so focused on her old flame she didn't hear her deputy ask if she wanted doughnuts and coffee. Her head had exploded with the music of love. Willis had changed. He was leaner. His handsome face was more chiseled. He looked older. She noticed a few flecks of silver in his auburn hair. The suit and tie looked good on him, but she remembered nostalgically how gorgeous he looked in tight jeans and a T-shirt. Good enough to eat.

"Sheriff," Dwight persisted in an impatient way.

Finally Lou spoke in an off-handed way, "Hold the doughnuts."

Deputy Dwight nodded and left the office, closing the door.

Lou couldn't tell what Willis was thinking. He looked so cold and indifferent. He was all business. He was FBI right down to his regulation shiny shoes.

"It's been a long time, Willis," Lou said in her serious voice, but one that lacked its usual authority. She remembered him being the decent, clean-cut and all-round honest guy, someone who took things a little too seriously but could laugh when called for. Above all he had been her best friend and first love.

She had sworn if she ever saw him again she'd take a swipe at him. She could never forgive him for ditching her without saying goodbye. So what if his parents were moving to San Francisco. He could have at least said goodbye. It had been left to Duane to break the bad news.

Suddenly all the pent-up anger and heartbreak hit Lou in a rush. Her eyes grew cold as she looked at the heartless bastard. She indicated to the two chairs in front of her desk.

"Please, take a load off."

The FBI agents sat down in the chairs.

Willis sat stiff-backed and serious-faced—the rock.

Merlot sat more casually in her chair with a leg crossed over her knee. She was the first one to get the ball rolling.

"We'll need to appraise the area where Beau was last seen, ASAP."

"Yeah, I guessed as much."

Willis and Sheriff Lou made eye contact again. It couldn't be helped.

Merlot looked from her partner to the sheriff, then back to her partner.

Willis broke eye contact for the second time. "Has the area been sealed off?"

"Of course," Lou snapped. "We're not hicks, you know."

His voice was different, thought Lou. There was so much about him that had changed. She could plainly see he wasn't the man she'd fallen in love with. Her heart sank with that realization.

"We've scoured the area, along with as much of the woods as we could." She sighed, "Pointless really." She shrugged, "Can't see the woods for the trees."

"Do you think it possible Beau has faked this abduction?" Willis asked.

"Oh yeah," Lou nodded. "His friends are probably in on the little charade."

"So we don't take his disappearance seriously, then?" Merlot said.

"This isn't the first time Beau has gone missing. Two months back he did the same thing. When he did show up he claimed he'd been abducted by Bigfoot." She told them this knowing full well the agents already knew as much as she did. It was something to say to get her mind off Willis.

"Yeah, we know," Merlot agreed. "Kids!"

"Yeah, kids!" Lou sighed. She glanced at the heartless bastard. She remembered the time he and Duane had pulled the same prank, claiming that a harem of Bigfoot babes had abducted them and had forced them to do certain things of a sexual nature. Willis could have fun back then, but what about now? Deep down in her heart, Lou wanted to know.

Deputy Dwight knocked on the door and entered with a tray of coffee and doughnuts. He placed the tray on the desk.

"Annie's finest. You won't find better doughnuts anywhere." With that, Dwight left the office with a doughnut in his pudgy hand.

"Hey, Dwight, what have I told you?" Lou warned.

Dwight briskly walked away unable to answer with a mouth full of doughnut.

"If Beau Flucker doesn't show up soon we're going to have to take his disappearance seriously. It could be for real this time," Merlot insisted. She chuckled. "Flucker . . . I'd run away with a name like that."

Sure this could be for real, thought Lou, but her trusty gut was telling her that Beau's disappearance was just a hoax. Lou gave Merlot a thoughtful look. It was better than looking at Willis. She didn't trust herself.

"He'll show up and when he does he'll say Bigfoot took him." She shrugged her shoulders, "Or that aliens abducted him."

"You can be that sure?" Willis asked in his regulation, matter-of-fact voice.

"I'm one-hundred percent sure, Agent Johnson. This is just one of his many little hoaxes," Lou declared, giving him an icy stare.

"For now we tend to agree." Willis paused, looking thoughtful. "Does Duane still have that old cabin of his father's?"

Lou nodded yes. She frowned. She didn't like the way the conversation was going. Willis couldn't possibly think that Duane had kidnapped Beau.

"Lives there permanent now," Lou declared somewhat nervously.

"It's a perfect place to hide Beau."

Lou gave Willis a curious glance. *What was he up to?* Of course, he could be right in thinking that Duane was in on Beau's little joke. If there was one thing Duane liked it was a good prank, thought Lou. But nevertheless, she didn't think Duane was involved. This case seemed different somehow, especially now that the FBI was involved.

Merlot joined in on the conversation. "Your report states, there's a possibility Beau might have been attacked by a grizzly . . . but you haven't found any trace of an animal attack where he was last seen."

"That's correct. Mocking Bird did a thorough investigation of the area and found nothing to support that scenario."

"This Mocking Bird . . ." Merlot couldn't help grinning as she said his name. ". . . is the local crypto-zoologist? I take it he knows his business?"

"He's the best." Lou gave a furtive glance towards the man who had broken her heart. *Why did they have to send him? Damn it!* Her broken heart told her he was just as good looking as the day he left, he just needed to get out of those clothes, let the stubble grow a tad and loosen up a whole lot.

Get a grip on yourself, urged Lou. No, no, no, don't even think it. It's over. He broke your heart. You'd have fallen apart if Duane hadn't been there. Not like Willis Johnson, the heartless bastard. She more than ever felt like taking a swipe at him and knew if he stayed much longer in town, she'd do just that.

MERLOT FOUND HER GAZE wandering around the office to the board on the wall behind her partner's head. Pinned to the board were six color photographs. Three pairs of shots displayed a shower cubicle or bath completely fouled with clumps of fur. Two toilet rims displayed an uneaten doughnut. She grimaced at the crime scenes luridly on display, thinking, *how could anyone eat on the pan?*

Merlot was curious, "Uh . . . I'm curious about those photos."

Lou appeared relieved by the question. She blew out her cheeks as she looked at the crime scene photos on the board.

"They're evidence of a . . . serial case—the Phantom Bigfoot Bather Case. They're what you might call crime scene photos."

WILLIS TURNED SIDEWAYS to look at the photos. "Yuck . . . food on the toilet!"

He had a look of disgust on his face. And that's exactly how he felt—disgust at his leaving her without a word. He wondered when would be the right moment to broach the all-important subject—the real reason he was back in town—that damned letter. Who sent the letter and who was she thinking of marrying? Now was obviously not the time to ask.

"Precisely," Lou said. "Someone is entering Beaverites' homes . . ." She looked a little sheepish, ". . . which is kinda easy, as most don't lock up at night; and uses the facilities. There've been three such incidents so far. The perp leaves clumps of fur all over the place and remains of a doughnut . . . and a smell that's so bad . . . and when I say *bad* . . . I'm not joking. After every crime scene, we have to wash all our clothing in industrial-strength detergent and still it lingers; then shower using a strong solution of fresh lemon juice . . . but that doesn't really help . . . nothing does."

"Sounds like the sort of thing Duane would do," Willis said.

"Yeah, it sure does," Lou agreed.

"This Duane character is popping up like a red flag," Merlot commented. "Any proof it's him?"

"No proof and no witnesses," Lou replied with a sigh. "We've had the fur analyzed. It's not fur and it's not exactly human hair. It's been contaminated each time, but there are those who think they're Bigfoot hairs due to the large, muddy footprints found all about the place." She cleared her throat, "As for the smell . . . well it's not as if we can analyze that."

"No such thing as Bigfoot," Willis declared.

"Well, what we know so far is nothing—a big fat Bigfoot nothing." Lou paused for a moment then added, "We've searched Duane's cabin for anything to link him to the crime, but found nothing."

Willis shook his head. "Duane's smart for such a dumbass."

"How come no one's seen him do it?" Merlot had a fit of the giggles. ". . . Sorry . . . but this is just too much . . ." Merlot cleared her throat, ". . . What I mean is, why Phantom Bigfoot?"

"That's a good question, Agent Merlot," Lou replied seeming somewhat irritated at the question. "MB works for our local paper, The Busy Beaverite. He thought up the name . . . now it's stuck."

16

TO MOST PEOPLE, the only clear sign of the teenagers' camp at the Little Beaver clearing was the remnants of their campfire. But MB, with his keen, skilled eye, knew what else to look for. He noted the footprints left by the teenagers. Saw where they had pitched tent. Even knew where they had sat around the fire. With a chuckle, MB saw yellow crime scene tape, at the spot where Beau had gone to take a leak.

With the patience of someone who had spent a great deal of his time watching, listening and waiting for Bigfoot to show itself, MB was content to wait for the sheriff and the FBI agents to arrive at the crime scene.

He sat on his small camping stool, passing the time, listening to the sounds of the forest animals. He ate a couple of high fiber bars and drank strong black coffee from a thermos. MB was in his element as he identified the staccato calls of Bewick's wrens, blue jays and black-billed magpies.

In the far distance, MB recognized the booming bugle of elk, the roar of the bear and that strange sound which he could not put a name to—weeeeeeooooooweeeeeoooo. This last animal call echoed around the vast forest like native drums.

MB was a man content to bide his time. There was an Old Indian legend that he adhered to—it said that it is best to be patient with time, to ignore the ticking clock, and not to be in such a hurry to reach the end of one's life. He savored the simple things, no matter how trivial, no matter how humble. It was what life was all about.

MB looked up at the sound of two approaching vehicles, followed by the sound of doors slamming shut. He heard the sheriff and the two FBI agents approaching through the woods from the parking area of Little Beaver. He caught glimpses of them as they passed through dapples of sunlight. Moments later they emerged from the trees.

Nothing much ever surprised him these days, but the sight of Willis Johnson in his city duds—totally inappropriate for trekking in the woods, took MB by surprise. He, like almost everyone else in town, knew damned well about the agents' arrival, but not their identities. He almost choked on his coffee, spilling some down his fatigues.

"Shit," he muttered quietly to himself, brushing the stain into a larger stain. The hot coffee forced MB to jump upright as if coming to attention. "Hi, Sheriff," he said with a smile.

Lou forced a smile but didn't speak.

Willis was also grim-faced.

The stunning female agent beamed a wide smile.

MB wondered if she was an idiot, smiling like that, for Old Indian legend tells us that woman who smiles all the time should be in the nut house.

MB surmised correctly that Lou was more than a tad unsettled by her old flame suddenly showing up, unannounced, just like his departure. *Things could get real interesting,* he mused. Oh yeah, real interesting was an understatement to end all understatements.

The look on Lou's face said it all—she still had the hots for Willis, despite what she said to anyone who cared to listen. MB recalled Lou telling him—after she'd had a few too many tequilas at Abe's, that if Willis came back into her life, she'd first tell him what she thought of him for ditching her, then she'd either take her gun and blow his balls off or she'd cuff him to the bed and fuck him senseless. MB concluded that Sheriff Lou was a contradiction in terms.

The crypto-zoologist focused his full attention on Lou's old flame.

Willis Johnson looked older, but that was to be expected after thirteen years. The guy was still a well-chiseled figure of a man.

MB decided to lay off manly descriptions, for Old Indian legend tells us that man who dwells on such things is on the wrong team.

"Hi, Willis. Long time no see." MB smiled in his amiable way.

"MB," Willis nodded, in a so-fucking-what attitude.

Merlot introduced herself, "And I'm Agent Merlot." She gave MB a thorough once over. She giggled. "Nice piece of Redwood."

Willis flashed Merlot a warning look.

"Uh . . . hi there, Agent Merlot." MB wondered why this gorgeous female was giggling and what she meant by the Redwood remark?

Merlot shook MB's hand, "Just make it Merlot, okay?"

"Sure thing, Merlot." MB beamed a wide smile. "This way," he gestured with a hand as he walked over to the edge of the clearing to the spot where Beau went to take a leak. "That's where Beau took a piss and that was the last place he was seen. No doubt he'll show up and come up with that same lame excuse-Bigfoot, as if?" MB paused and shook his head. "Everyone with an ounce of sense knows Bigfoot doesn't exist."

"But, you're a crypto-zoologist?" Merlot asked incredulously.

"That I am, but Old Indian legend tells us that man who finds what he has always been looking for has no reason to go on."

"But I thought you guys . . . you know . . . really believed in Bigfoot."

Sure, MB wanted to believe in Bigfoot. His job—not that he got paid or anything, depended on it, but so far he had nothing to prove the creature existed. Okay, he had plenty of photographs, most of which were displayed on Annie's Diner walls, and a few good casts of Bigfoot's big feet, but none of it was for real. He and Duane knew that.

MB sighed heavily and thought it time for another of his gems of wisdom to impress the FBI agent. "Old Indian legend tells us that man who finds truth in all things is wise."

A puzzled look flittered over Merlot's face. "That's cool. I didn't know that."

"Why should you? Old Indian legend tells us that it is a wise man that admits he doesn't know everything."

Merlot's expression lightened on hearing MB's latest gem.

"You seem to have one of those for every occasion, MB."

MB studied the agent's openly smiling face and thought, here was someone worth knowing. She sure was hot even if she giggled too much.

MB nodded seriously, but didn't speak. That was enough chat for now.

Willis and Lou stood staring at MB and Merlot with impatient looks on their faces.

"Give it a rest with those Indian legends, MB. You wouldn't know one end of an arrow from the other," Willis said with a knowing smirk.

MB looked hurt as he watched Willis walk off towards the area marked with yellow crime scene tape indicating the spot where Beau had gone to take a leak. He gave Willis' back the bird.

Lou followed Willis, a few paces behind.

MB watched with shrewd eyes as Willis ducked under the yellow tape, followed by Sheriff Lou. He hoped Lou would hit it off with Willis, and so left them some breathing space.

BUT THE SHERIFF and Willis stood by the tree where Beau had taken a leak, looking more efficient than gooey-eyed. They kept their distance. Neither uttered a word. There was an uneasy silence between them that spoke volumes.

Lou sighed with relief when MB and Merlot joined them. She was glad of MB's company, for he acted like a buffer between her and Willis. She watched the female agent slip on disposable gloves to survey the area around the tree and wrinkle her nose at the disgusting stench, even though the smell had by now dissipated to minimal strength.

Lou commented, "No sign of anything out of the ordinary, apart from that God awful smell." The smell reminded her of the Phantom Bigfoot. *So, did Duane really have something to do with this?*

"I've never smelled anything so bad . . . what is it?" Merlot asked with a grimace and a brief bout of coughing. She wiped her watery eyes. She took extra care not to touch anything with her clothes.

"It's mostly deer musk mixed with Beau's piss, extract of skunk and something I can't quite put my finger on," MB said with authority.

With eyes trained to look at crime scenes, Merlot scanned the ground by the base of the tree and pointed at snapped twigs. "Agent Johnson, what do you think?"

Willis grimaced and grunted as he thought. "I still believe the kid's fooling around . . . but I could be wrong," Willis declared in his super efficient way.

Merlot remarked, sarcastically, "That's a first."

Willis glared at his partner with clenched fists.

Lou furtively glanced at her old boyfriend and thought it wouldn't be the first time you were wrong, Willis Johnson, you heartless bastard. It was wrong to ditch me like that, you heartless bastard.

"Like I said, Beau's done this before," Lou said with an edge of hostility to her voice.

She and Willis made eye contact.

The unease between them was plain for MB and Merlot to see.

Lou told herself to put aside her personal feelings and concentrate on the situation at hand. Was she wrong not to take Beau's disappearance seriously? She was reminded of the tale of the boy who cried wolf. What if the wolf in Beau's case was some grizzly or some sicko? No, she still didn't think that was the case. He was fooling around and she was sure of it. She knew Beau. Knew what sort of kid he was. Knew he liked to have the sheriff's department going out on wild goose chases looking for him, just like his old man.

"Yeah, but where is he now? That's what I'd like to know," Willis said.

A serious look settled on Lou's face, but she wasn't thinking about Beau. A thought had just occurred to her—*was Willis married? Divorced? Seeing someone in a serious relationship?*

"Wooooooeeeeeoooooeeeeeaaaaaa."

Merlot stood erect and looked wide-eyed at the surrounding impenetrable forest. "What the fuck was that?" She hugged MB like a frightened girl.

MB WAS MOMENTARILY taken aback as Merlot covertly squeezed his firm ass. He gently pushed the agent away, looking awkward.

Sheriff Lou looked seriously unsettled by the howling as she released the strap on her holster and placed a trembling hand on her trusty Magnum .44.

"Wooooooooooo-wooooooooooo-wooooooooooo."

MB sighed, knowing it was probably Duane. He watched with considerable amusement, as Lou and the FBI agents looked startled, scanning their surroundings with wide eyes. He had sent his recordings of those sounds for analysis. He got nothing.

"It's just Duane-o," he suggested, with the air of someone who knew what he was talking about.

"Are you sure that was human?" Merlot pondered out loud. Fear furrowed her brow. She grabbed MB's arm and held tight.

MB stared into Merlot's fearful eyes and smiled to placate her terror. "Nothing to worry about . . . he gets a kick out of making that weird noise when there's someone to hear it, like you three." MB chuckled.

"Have you actually seen him make that sound?" Merlot asked as she released MB's arm.

"Good question . . . and I have to admit I haven't caught him at it . . . but he has told me he likes to make those noises to spook hunters, and just for the sheer hell of it."

"It has to be Duane . . . he always was weird," Willis remarked.

In the not too distant distance that strange call could be heard again— "woooooeeeeeooooooeeeeaaaaaa."

A snapping of undergrowth could clearly be heard.

"Wooooeeeeaaaaaeeeeeooooo."

"Waaaaeeeeeoooooaaaaeeee."

"Sounds like more than just one person," Merlot said with an edge of fear. "You positive Bigfoot doesn't exist?"

MB placed a hand on his heart, "I'm as certain as a chief can be."

"Quit that chief shit," Willis warned.

"No I won't . . . so what you going to do about it?" MB looked ready for a fight then smiled.

"Give it a rest, you two." With that, Sheriff Lou left the crime scene and trudged back to her car.

MB blew a kiss at Willis and grinned.

Willis shook his head in annoyance. He raced after Lou and grabbed her by the arm.

She whirled around and stabbed Willis with a hard glare, "Let go."

Willis, thrown off by her gruffness, stammered, "I . . . I . . . was going to ask you about . . ." He stopped. "Never mind. We need to speak with Beau's parents. They still live off Mill Road?"

Lou nodded her head yes then shook her arm free.

17

ON THEIR RETURN to Big Beaver, Agents Johnson and Merlot parked their shiny black sedan outside the Flucker residence on Mill Road. The house was a white clapboard affair, replete with a white picket fence, and an avenue of rose bushes leading up to the porch.

Willis knocked on the door and waited with a look of trepidation on his face. He turned to Merlot, "Leave the questions to me."

Merlot saluted Willis.

Rose Flucker opened the front door to the FBI agents wearing a brightly colored floral kimono, and a shoulder length blond wig.

Agents Johnson and Merlot flashed their ID badges for Rose to get a good look at, which she did, making sure the faces matched the IDs.

"Willis Johnson, is that you?" Rose said with a smile on her face. "I'd heard the FBI were looking for our Beau."

Willis remained serious faced. His tone was strictly professional and to the point. "Indeed . . . we'd like to speak with you and Walt about Beau's disappearance."

A troubled look flittered across Rose's face. She looked somewhat dubiously at Willis, totally ignoring the female agent. "You really want to speak to Walt? Are you sure? I mean, you and he never did hit it off."

"Be that as it may, we need to speak to both of you in order to clear this mess up. The sooner we do that, the sooner we can leave."

Rose shrugged her shoulders and gave another smile. "Okay, come on in, but I can't be responsible for Walt."

Agents Johnson and Merlot stepped into the hallway of the Flucker residence.

Willis gave the décor a discerning look. On the walls were stuffed heads of animals and Rose's delicate paintings of flowers and local scenery.

Rose closed the door behind them. "This way," she said cheerfully as she led the way down the hallway.

From her cheerful manner Willis realized Rose Flucker wasn't taking her son's disappearance seriously, even though it had been a full two days.

As Rose walked down the hallway she informed her guests, "Walt is in his spaceship, don't you know."

The FBI agents stopped momentarily and exchanged questioning looks.

Merlot grinned and whispered, "His spaceship . . . this I gotta see." She drew out her cell phone in readiness.

Willis didn't respond. His expression was serious. They'd both read the report on Walt Flucker and his alleged alien abductions. The man was a major league nut job. Just like most people in Big Beaver.

"Oh yes . . . his spaceship. He spends a lot of time in there, these days. It's down in the basement."

Walt's make-believe spaceship was in the basement. *As good a place as any*, thought Willis. As they followed Rose Flucker, Willis recalled that as a teenager Walt used to watch a lot of sci-fi on TV, especially Star Trek. As he got older it was the X-Files. It figured that Walt would make up a story about aliens abducting him.

Rose reached the basement door first and opened it.

The light was already switched on allowing them to see into the depths below. They remained in the hallway and peered down the wooden stairs that led into the basement. There was a lot of clutter down there, noted Willis, but no sign of a spaceship.

"This way," Rose cheerfully said, as if calling to pets.

The FBI agents shrugged and followed Rose. At the foot of the steps Willis gave his surroundings a quick look. There was still no sign of a spaceship. But what did he really expect? Some crappy kid's model made out of tinfoil?

Rose pointed over to a closed, inconspicuous yellow wooden door. "It's in there." She walked over to the door.

The agents followed, not knowing what to expect.

Willis approached the closed door with trepidation at coming face to face with Walt Flucker. His pulse rate went up a notch.

The wooden door looked just like any other wooden door, thought Willis. He'd at least expected the door to Walt's "spaceship" to be made of some kind of metal and be gray in color.

Rose pressed the communication panel on the side of the door. It gave several loud clicks. She spoke into the communication panel.

"Greetings, Captain Flucker . . . Agents Johnson and Merlot are here."

There was no reply. A moment later the door automatically swung open accompanied with a swish noise, just like in Star Trek.

The FBI agents exchanged quizzical glances before stepping inside Walt's "spaceship."

The first thing Willis noticed was the steam, like a sauna. The second thing he noticed was Walt Flucker immersed in a hot tub, like a sauna. There was something different about Walt, but he couldn't quite put a finger on it?

Merlot suppressed a giggle. Her eyes were wide with amazement.

"Pinch me, Agent Johnson . . . am I seeing what you're seeing?"

Willis didn't reply, but gave Merlot a friendly punch in the arm as he followed Rose into Walt's "spaceship." The steamy heat of the room made an instant impression. He could feel beads of sweat on his brow.

Merlot pretended to rub her sore arm as she followed her partner.

The door closed behind the FBI agents with another swish.

Willis gave his surroundings a disdainfully quick glance. If he didn't know any better he would say that he was in a Swedish sauna room.

The walls, from floor to ceiling, were made of paneled cedar wood. There was even a massage table in a corner. And on one side of the room was a long wooden bench.

Seated on the wooded bench were six life-size female dummies with blond wigs dressed in kimonos, and standing to the side of them was a life-size plastic cutout of a pudgy Elvis Presley dressed in his white Las Vegas regalia.

Over in another corner of the room was a small glass-paneled room. Inside the room was a shower cubicle. The only other things that stuck out like sore thumbs—as did everything else, were several '70's-style, groovy, wax lava lamps. Very trippy indeed!

This is too weird, thought Willis, as he tugged on his tie to loosen it and allow some of his body heat out. The sweat on his brow trickled down his face. He could feel his shirt sticking to his back.

Walt remained in the hot tub and watched the two agents approach. His eyes narrowed as he focused all his attention on Willis. His lip curled into a snarl, just like Elvis.

"Shit, if it isn't Willis Johnson? I heard you'd joined the Feds."

Willis hadn't expected a warm welcome. "We'd like to ask you a few questions about Beau."

"What for . . . Beau is just fooling around." Walt looked pleased at Willis' discomfort. "You look a little hot under the collar, Willy boy. You and your hot partner fancy a dip?"

"No, we would definitely not fancy a dip," Willis said curtly, as if offended by the very suggestion of immersing himself in the hot tub with Walt Flucker.

Now, if it had been Lou in the tub . . . *no, don't go there you idiot. Get into character—the rock. That's better.*

"When did you last see Beau?" Willis demanded.

"Well . . . before he went missing," Rose said in a matter-of-fact obvious way.

"Uh-huh . . . did he seem . . . upset about anything?" Merlot asked, emphasizing upset.

Willis shot Merlot a look to keep quiet, but knew beyond all doubt she wouldn't be able to keep her big mouth shut.

Merlot poked out her tongue and shrugged.

Rose thought for a moment and smiled. "Beau's a fun-loving boy . . . why would he be upset if he's having fun? Always has a smile on his face."

Walt looked affectionately at his wife. "Have to admit, Beau sure takes after his sweet mother . . . wouldn't harm a fly."

Walt and Rose smiled lovingly at one another.

"So you don't think he could have run away?" Merlot asked, as she undid several buttons of her blouse, revealing cleavage.

Walt looked incredulously at Merlot. "Not our Beau . . . he'd have no cause to, would he, Mother?" Walt smiled at Rose who agreed with a nod.

Walt turned to Willis and asked, "Well . . . what do you think of my spaceship?"

Willis paused for an incredulous moment before he dared to reply. The asshole couldn't think he was actually in a spaceship, could he? If he did, he was all the way nuts.

"It's just a sauna," Willis sighed in an irritated way.

Rose gasped with shock and put a hand to her mouth.

Walt's face reddened with rage. He took in a deep intake of breath, repeating that rapidly to calm his anger down. He looked absolutely stunned by what Willis had just said. His eyes widened with indignation.

"Well, yeah . . . it is a fucking sauna, asshole . . . but it's much more than that. I'll have you know this is an exact replica of the room the aliens had me imprisoned in," Walt implored in an indignant tone of voice. "You see the massage table over there?"

Both agents glanced at the massage table then looked back at Walt.

"Don't tell me . . . it's Doc McCoy's surgical table," Merlot said with a chuckle.

Walt faltered, giving Merlot a condescending look before continuing, "No . . . it's just a massage table, little lady. These gorgeous female aliens massaged my entire body, and when I mean entire, I mean down there." He pointed to his genitals floating free in the hot tub. "And it was done on a table just like that. Not two or three female aliens, but a whole horde of them, and all at once. Their touch sent shivers down my spine. And they did strange things to me which I cannot go into detail about." Walt indicated with his eyes that Rose would be upset if he went into detail. "I lie awake at night thinking what they did to me."

"Still looks like a sauna to me," Willis insisted, knowing the lunatic might flip any moment now.

"You FBI got no imagination. I tell you they were Swedish-looking aliens, and they modeled the rooms of their spaceship from an IKEA catalog." Walt looked serious.

Merlot, trying desperately not to laugh, asked "Why do you think they were Swedish aliens, Mister Flucker?"

Walt groaned out loud, "I didn't say they was Swedish, just Swedish-looking . . . but FYI, their planet is called Abba, and they played Abba real loud all the time . . . their favorite tune was Super Trouper."

Merlot exploded with a fit of the giggles.

Rose could plainly see the rage on her husband's face. She tried to defuse the situation.

"Care for some sushi?" She smiled sweetly. "It's what the aliens gave Walt to eat. They told him he would remain healthy, and . . . you know . . . ready for you-know-what if he ate it all the time." She giggled like a schoolgirl on her first date. "My love bunny eats nothing else now."

Willis stared in disbelief at Walt for several moments. Didn't the asshole know that sushi was a Japanese meal? He knew the best thing to do was to leave without getting in too deep with Walt Flucker concerning his alleged alien abduction. However, he couldn't resist one more jab at the crazy coot.

Willis said, "I read your statement on your abduction. You say that you saw the real Elvis Presley on board the spaceship and that he had been replaced on earth by a clone."

Walt glared at Willis, with a mean look in his eye and shouted, "I know what you're doing—you're trying to piss me off, asshole."

Merlot gave her partner a discreet tap on the arm. "Enough said, Willis. Let's move on."

Willis didn't make any attempt to leave the room. He had upset Walt and it felt good. He gave Walt a thin smile.

But the smile soon left Willis' face when Walt stood up in the hot tub to reveal an extremely hairy body—so hairy it covered his goods. That's what was different about Walt!

Merlot looked away, holding her mouth as if to puke, "Hairy guys are so icky . . . that's so gross."

Walt started to chuckle at Willis' and Merlot's unease, "Before I was abducted, I barely had a hair on my body . . . now look at me . . . I think they're changing me into a Swedish Sasquatch."

Willis wrinkled his nose in disgust and looked askance at his partner who had started to snigger again. "I am surrounded by idiots."

Merlot continued to snigger. "I'm beginning to so love this town."

Willis didn't say another word. He turned and left the spaceship to the Fluckers.

Merlot faltered instead of hurrying after her partner, exclaiming, "Hey, I was having fun."   Before she left the spaceship, she turned and snapped Walt in all his glory with her phone.

WILLIS SAT BEHIND the wheel of their car, waiting for Merlot with clenched fists.

Merlot hopped into the passenger seat, fiddling with her phone.

Willis looked at the cell phone and up at Merlot's concentrating face, "What the hell you sending now?"

Willis leaned over to get a better look, but his partner covered the cell phone with her hand.

Merlot gave Willis a cheeky look and shrugged, "Couldn't help it . . . sorry."   She put her cell phone in her jacket pocket and turned to Willis, "You know something . . . if I was Beau, I would have run away a long time ago with parents as nuts as that."

Willis gave a weary sigh and nodded his head in agreement.

"Where to now, Massah?" she said in a *Roots* voice.

"What have I said about that slave shit?"   Willis started the engine and drove off down Mill Road and back to the sheriff's department.

18

IN A DARK ROOM, a large flat screen TV displayed Debbie's camcorder disc. The antics of the teenagers were there for all to see.

"Freeze that!" Willis ordered. "No, not that frame. Scan back." He shouted excitedly, "That's it!" He got up from his chair and walked up to the flat screen, pointing to a blurred image in the dark woods. "Zoom in on that." He hoped it was Duane dressed as a Bigfoot.

Deputy Dwight clicked the mouse of the laptop and squared off the area Willis had pointed at.

The image, although more blurred than ever, showed a furry shape lurking behind the offending tree.

Willis stepped back to get a better look, "Hello, Duane-o." He turned with a triumphant gleam in his eye.

Sheriff Lou shook her head with dismay, "You cannot expect me to believe that's Duane." She gave Willis a look of disdain. "That could be anything."

Merlot chuckled, "Yeah, Bigfoot."

Sheriff Lou got up and switched on the lights. She nodded to Dwight to stop the film.

She opened a door to a side interrogation room and beckoned, "Okay, you three, come on in."

Sheriff Lou, the two FBI agents, Beau's friends and Deputy Dwight—who was also there to take notes, sat around a circular table with the closed laptop on it and several mugs of stale coffee, and a plateful of stale doughnuts.

Debbie was adamant to Willis. "It's just like we told the sheriff. Beau went to . . . you know, take a pee behind a tree, and that was the last we saw of him."

Willis said in his regulation, matter-of-fact voice, "Look, Debbie, we've seen the evidence. Underage drinking and smoking joints is against the law."

Chad nervously giggled. "We'd never do anything like that, Agent Johnson . . . honest."

"Better put us on the top ten most wanted list," Naomi said with a snigger.

Willis regarded Chad with a cold, disparaging look. "Giggle all you like, but if all of you are involved in this charade, be warned, the FBI does not take kindly to having their precious time wasted."

Chad looked desperately to Sheriff Lou. He shook his head.

"Sheriff, I'm telling the truth. Beau's not fooling around this time."

LOU DIDN'T ANSWER Chad's comment. Her full attention was focused on Willis. She leaned forward to put her elbows on the table and rest her chin in her hands. Her thoughts were elsewhere, in another time, long, long, ago, when things had been so perfect between her and Willis.

Ever since she first saw Willis win the pennant for their high school football team, she knew he was the one. She remembered at the tender age of fifteen plucking up the courage to dance with him at the school celebration party. He dared to kiss her. She was in love. For the next two years she and Willis dated in secret as her father was the sheriff at the time and had a penchant for scaring away her boyfriends. Only Duane knew what was going on between them.

During their last summer break, she, Willis and Duane spent a night camping out in the woods. Whether it was the moonlight or sharing a tent together which sparked things off between them, she suspected the latter, but they ended up cuddling and kissing while Duane conveniently went off into the woods to see if he could spot a Bigfoot. And the inevitable almost happened. With a sigh of regret, Lou recalled frantically fumbling with Willis' jeans, but then something curious happened.

Strange animal howling echoed around the forest—howling that was now familiar. Lou was frightened and re-buttoned her blouse. Willis became alerted to the sound of heavy feet crunching through the undergrowth. They both scrambled from the tent to see what it was, but there was nothing to be seen, not even Duane. That was it, her chance with Willis had come and gone for he left town soon after.

Lou often wondered what would have happened if they'd have done it and she'd gotten pregnant, and how their lives would have changed. She would never have become sheriff and Willis would never have left Big Beaver and joined the FBI. Willis would have done the right thing and they would have gotten hitched.

She sighed inwardly at the thought of the domestic bliss she might have had then quickly brushed it aside. Her life had taken a different direction. She was the town sheriff. She wouldn't change her life for anything, not even for him. Or would she?

But here he was after all this time. She wondered if he still had feelings for her.

"You know what happened to the boy who cried wolf?" Willis warned in his stern voice.

Chad turned away from ogling Merlot's body. He was adamant, "So what? I'm telling you . . . Bigfoot or some nut job has taken Beau this time."

Merlot replied with a smirk, "I thought you told the sheriff you didn't know who or what had taken Beau?"

Chad sounded exasperated. "We can change our minds ... can't we?"

Willis raised his eyebrows. "Don't you kids realize how serious this is?"

"How serious can Bigfoot taking Beau get?" Naomi asked Merlot.

Willis asked the big one, "Is Duane in on this?"

Chad shook his head no, emphatically, "No way, man."

Throughout the questioning, Lou had allowed her thoughts to wander but she'd been aware of what had been said. She knew they would get nothing more out of Beau's friends.

She gave an exasperated shake of her head, "That's it . . . you can all leave now."

The teenagers were slow to make a move.

"Out!" Lou shouted with a finger pointed to the door.

The teenagers exchanged glances, shrugged their shoulders, got up and without another word leisurely left the room.

Willis nodded to Merlot, "Come on . . . time to pay a visit to an old friend."

19

AT ABOUT THE SAME TIME Willis and Merlot got nothing during the interrogation, Olaaa sat on her haunches at the edge of a small clearing in the woods, eating from a piece of bark full of wild berries. She allowed the afternoon sun to bathe her in its warmth, exaggerating the beautiful dapples of gold in her fine hair. Behind her right ear she wore a white dog rose indicating she was in love.

Olaaa bleated, "wooooooo—woooooo - wooooooo."

                                ớ   ớ   ớ

GRIZZLE-FACED BOB and Chuck, the two hunters last seen at Annie's Diner, were dressed in army fatigues and peaked caps and wore green face paint. They cautiously walked up to the edge of the same clearing with their rifles at the ready.

As yet, they were unaware that a Bigfoot was nearby. Their army fatigues were covered with foliage to further camouflage them, as if an animal wouldn't think it strange seeing a bush walking through the forest.

The hunters didn't speak to each other, only signaling with hand movements in a military style. They didn't want to be heard by any unsuspecting creature that might be within range of their rifles. Only the sound of undergrowth being snapped beneath their sturdy boots gave their presence away.

THE SOUND OF UNDERGROWTH snapping should have alerted Olaaa—she knew to be wary of pale ones, but Olaaa was distracted with her feast of berries and thoughts of her plaything.

She was in love for the first time in her life, and it had to be with a pale one. Poor Olaaa had no choice really for there was only one adult male to ten adult females in Olaaa's Bigfoot pride—of which, Olaaa would soon make an 11th adult female. Olaaa's desperate eye had strayed outside her own species, but to mate with a pale one was forbidden. She went about her business, happy in the knowledge that she had found her perfect mate in her beautiful Boo. The trick was to keep him a secret.

Olaaa mewed, "wooooooo—wooooooo—wooooooo."

BOB AND CHUCK stealthily avoided as many twigs as possible as they skirted the edge of the clearing, and homed in on the strange animal noise that sounded more like an eagle owl than anything else.

TEEELAAA SQUATTED on her haunches eating bright red berries, not too far from the same clearing.

She sniffed the air and giggled as only a Bigfoot could, "sfsfsfsfsfsfs."

Crouched out of sight was Maaawooo, a massive, muscular, seven-foot-tall, Bigfoot with greasy, slick black hair. It was quite apparent Maaawooo was rampant for Teeelaaa's ripeness, blatantly on offer. His overly eager thruster frantically twitched for the most beautiful of all Bigfoot babes. Maaawooo called out, "wooooooooo-wooooooo."

Teeelaaa heard the call and replied, "Wooooooeeeeeoooo." She excitedly rubbed a handful of berries over her moist lower regions.

Maaawooo grabbed a handful of berries from a bush and rushed off to Teeelaaa. He burst through the thickets and did a kind of Bigfoot Boogie around his mate—more like a salsa. Maaawooo held out a palm full of red berries and moved his hips from side to side in a provocative manner—thus revealing his rampantly large, bright pink thruster, indicating his desire to mate.

Teeelaaa looked at his chubby and giggled, "Sfsfsfsfsfsfsfsf."

She hesitated to accept his gift. Sometimes she liked to play hard to get, just to tease Maaawooo.

"Weeeeooooeeee," she bleated submissively.

Maaawooo began to push his groin forward, causing his thruster to swing slightly from side to side.

Teeelaaa smiled flirtatiously, taking the berries from his hand. She started to back slowly away, taunting him with her dark blue eyes. She shook her head no. She was still playing hard to get, slapping away Maaawooo's awkward grasps at her swinging suckle-bumps.

OLAAA FELT THE URGE to doodoo. She tossed the bark aside, dug a deep enough hole, and squatted over it. After a few strains of the hips, Olaaa had finished her business. She pushed the loose earth back over the two foot dropping then walked into the meadow. She sat down and slid across the grass to wipe her bottom from leftover doodoo. At that moment her nostrils began to twitch as her olfactory senses detected the foul stink of strange pale ones. She took a big sniff. It wasn't Duane. He had a familiar scent that she had become accustomed to, not unlike her own. This odor was unfamiliar and dangerous. She knew she was in danger.

She jumped to her feet, screeching, "Eeeeeeeeee!"

Her hair prickled and fluffed up, making her seem twice her size. In fear for her life, Olaaa ran from the edge of the clearing and back into the welcome embrace of the forest.

BOB AND CHUCK stood up in total surprise. They both knew what would happen if they bagged a Bigfoot—they'd be rich and famous.

The hunters opened fire at the sight of the fleeing Bigfoot, without any thought to the ramifications of depriving the scientific community of investigating a living example of a species hitherto deemed nonexistent. Thankfully, bullets splintered saplings all around the Bigfoot as it made good its escape.

OLAAA FELT A SHARP pain in her shoulder as a bullet found its mark. Olaaa gave a shrill cry, "Eeeeeeeeeeee."

She was very afraid now. Her heart pounded as she ran for her life. Tears filled her eyes. She didn't want to be shot at any more, but more bullets zinged past her.

"Eeeeeeee," Olaaa screamed, smashing through the forest, ignoring her injured shoulder and thorns from brambles that ripped clumps of hair from her body.

ಇ   ಇ   ಇ

TEEELAAA WAS FINALLY READY. She got down on all fours and put her face to the grass, lifting her buttocks for Maaawooo to get an eyeful of moist, red nether regions.

With wild abandonment, Maaawooo tossed his berries away then slammed his twitching pink, thruster deep into Teeelaaa's quivering ripeness.

"Wooooooooo—wooooooo - woooooo," he bleated with every thrust.

"Wooooooeeeeeooooo—wooooooeeeeeoooo," Teeelaaa bleated in unison to Maaawooo's thrusting hips.

Teeelaaa suddenly rolled to her side, almost twisting Maaawooo's love member off as she heard Olaaa's cries and gunshots.

Maaawooo clutched his thruster which had twisted like a corkscrew and screamed, "Eeeeeoooooeeee."

Olaaa's calls of danger echoed through the forest, followed by more rifle fire.

In a panic, Teeelaaa grabbed hold of Maaawooo's arm, "Eeeeeeee."

The Bigfoot lovers' hair puffed out with alarm. They ran off into the woods in the direction of familiar swirling smoke drifting from the tree tops.

THE HUNTERS HOLLERED and whooped with joy. Bob and Chuck tracked the obvious Bigfoot signs through the dense undergrowth. Bob lifted his fingers. Bigfoot blood!

Chuck was excited, "Jeez, Bob, we're gonna be so fucking rich."

Bob agreed, "Oh yeah. Come on, let's finish the job."

20

DUANE HEARD THE DREADFUL SOUND of gunshots. He was relaxing on the sofa, wearing his tartan long-johns and reading that week's TV guide, even though he didn't have a TV as his home had no electricity. He just liked to keep up on celebrity gossip.

He felt a sudden rush of panic and dread at the sound of the gunshots. He tossed the magazine onto the floor and got up off the sofa in one agile, fluid movement as he heard frantic Bigfoot panic cries.

"Eeeeeeeeee –eeeeeeeee—eeeeeeeee."

He rushed over to the side cabinet situated next to the cabin door. His rifle was beside the cabinet, propped against the wall. He checked the breach. It was loaded. His hands trembled as he held the hated thing. There was anguish in his eyes.

At the sound of another gunshot followed by more Bigfoot screams, Duane flung open the cabin door and stepped out onto the porch to determine from what direction the shots were coming.

OLAAA LOOKED UP to see the friendly swirls of smoke from Duane's cabin. Safety was so very close. *Bang!* Another bullet snapped a sapling less than an inch from her.

"Eeeeeeeee!" She crashed through the undergrowth towards the safety of Duane's cabin. She mewed as the hunters were getting closer.

Olaaa   let   out   a   loud   desperate   cry, "eeeeeaaaaoooooeeeeaaaooooooeeee."

A fearful Teeelaaa and Maaawooo joined her as they fled from the danger of the hunters. The three Bigfoot ran through the undergrowth, treading heavily, causing twigs and branches to break in their path, leaving an easy trail to follow.

THE HUNTERS' PACE had slowed. They were both winded and had lost sight of their Bigfoot. They faltered and looked at each other.

Bob scanned the woods around him looking for any sign of Bigfoot. He listened. He frowned.

"It looked real to me . . . but what if it was old Duane-o?"

Chuck nodded his head no, "Nah, couldn't be Duane-o. He don't make that sound when he's been shot."

Bob thought about that for a while. "True . . . when we shot the fucker last year he just screamed his balls off and shouted for us to stop shooting him."

Chuck chuckled, "Yeah, what a cry baby . . . we only nicked him some."

Bob grimaced with another thought. "Yeah, but if it was Duane-o then it sure as fuck wasn't a Bigfoot. We won't get nothing displaying that dumbass to anyone, even in his Bigfoot getup."

Chuck urged, "Come on Bob . . . better go see what we hit."

DUANE RAN IN THE direction of the Bigfoot's cries for help. He could clearly hear the crash of undergrowth heading towards him. He hoped the hunters weren't too close behind his friends.

Duane was knocked on his back as Olaaa crashed into him from a dense thicket. He gasped for air, making a gurgling sound. He saw Teeelaaa and Maaawooo emerge a few strides behind Olaaa. All were in a high state of panic with their hair ruffled and rippling. With eyes wide with terror, the Bigfoot desperately looked at Duane for help and protection.

They mewed pathetically, "Weeeeoooeee-aaaaeeeoooo-aaaaeee."

Duane's lungs returned to normal. He gulped down much-needed air.

Maaawooo hauled him to his feet and pointed to Olaaa's shoulder wound which was trickling blood.

Olaaa whimpered in pain, "Eeeeeeoooooeeeeeaaaa."

In between gasping for breath, Duane urged them all with a hand, and in a high-pitched kitten voice, "This way . . . come on."

Not wasting any time, he led the frightened Bigfoot in the direction of his cabin where he hoped they would be safe from whoever was shooting at them.

ONCE INSIDE THE CABIN, Duane opened the basement trapdoor in the living area, and ushered the three Bigfoot down. He rushed around the cabin, bolting all the doors and slamming shut all the shutters to the windows to prevent curious eyes from discovering his big secret.

Duane stepped down into the basement. Massive, rough cut logs propped up the basement ceiling. One would think that a little excessive, but he had his reasons.

"You safe now," he said in a soft tone, trying to calm the frantic Bigfoot by hugging them.

But all three Bigfoot were still in a high state of panic, looking around with desperate eyes and ears twitching for danger sign. Their hair was still bristled and fluffed up.

Olaaa pointed to the blood on her shoulder. "Eeeeaaaa," she whimpered with tears of pain.

Duane looked at the injured Bigfoot's shoulder and saw the tears in her eyes.

"Good girl, Olaaa," he said comfortingly patting her head. "There, there. Who's my brave girl?" He inspected the wound and smiled. It wasn't serious, just a minor scratch.

Duane was a sucker for Olaaa's pity-me look with those big blue eyes. He smiled sadly as she shrugged her shoulders and touched the wound. Her eyes rolled at the sight of blood on her fingers.

"Eeeeeeee!"

Duane had to make Olaaa understand the injury wasn't serious. He smiled and pointed at Olaaa's shoulder, doing a silly jig and laughing.

"Good girl, Olaaa."

Duane was relieved to see the look of understanding coming from Olaaa as she cocked her head to one side.

Olaaa gave a faint smile, bleating, "woooo-eeee-oooo."

Duane patted her head and kissed her snout. He looked at Teeelaaa and Maaawooo holding hands and smiled reassuringly to them. He walked over to a massive cupboard and opened the door. He disappeared inside the walk-in cupboard for a few moments then came back out with a bottle of antiseptic and a wad of cotton. He opened the bottle as he hurried over to Olaaa.

He dabbed antiseptic on the cotton and pressed it gently to Olaaa's shoulder.

Olaaa's eyes shot wide open. She winced in pain, "Eeeeeeee." She wrinkled her nose at the smell of the antiseptic. She exclaimed, nasally, "Ftftftftft!" She spat nasally with disgust. Her hair fluffed up.

Duane smiled comfortingly and patted Olaaa's head. "Good girl, Olaaa . . . good Olaaa."

Olaaa relaxed as her hair flattened and forced a brave smile, revealing her yellow teeth.

Teeelaaa and Maaawooo sensed Olaaa's relief. They too relaxed their hair.

Both Bigfoot mewed, "Oooooeeeeeoooo." They patted Olaaa's head.

After some moments, Duane stopped administering to Olaaa's wound. He smiled at all three Bigfoot.

"You stay here," he said pointing to the floor of the basement. "You safe here." Duane hugged himself to indicate safety.

The Bigfoot looked at each other then directly at Duane. They shook their heads no and looked fearful for they did not want to be left alone, nor did they want to be shot at by the hunters again. All three fluffed up their hair in fright.

Duane wasn't to be swayed. He knew what he had to do. This wasn't the first time a Bigfoot had been shot by a hunter. He had to do something drastic.

"I go," Duane insisted, pointing to the stairs.

Teeelaaa grabbed hold of his arm and shook her head, "Eeeeeeee."

"Please, Teeelaaa, I must go," Duane pleaded, trying to pull away from her firm hold, but she held him in her strong hands.

It dawned on Duane that the Bigfoot were afraid for his safety, too. So was he, come to think of it. He was reminded of one of MB's Old Indian legends—A man's gotta do what a man's gotta do. This was one of those times when he had to do what was necessary. He had to get mano-a-mano with those hunters. Get mean if necessary. Give them a taste of their own medicine.

That was when Duane froze.

A loud hammering came from the front door, followed by, "Anyone home?"

Duane put a finger to his mouth and shook his head no to the three Bigfoot. He scratched his butt as he tried to think who the voice belonged to. He tried to put a face to the voice, but his state of panic wouldn't let him. Then it dawned on him—the Feds! Willis! He had to see his best friend, but now was not the time, not with three frightened Bigfoot in his basement. Fuck it!

BOTH FBI AGENTS waited for a reply at Duane's front door. They split up. Willis walked around one side of the cabin and Merlot the other side. Each agent stopped and peered through cracks in the shutters with hands shielding the light. They met at the front door.

Merlot shrugged, "Guess he's out."

Willis grunted a reply and walked back to their car.

BOB AND CHUCK crouched in the undergrowth at the edge of the forest, watching the FBI agents.

Bob whispered to Chuck, "Shit, the Feds . . . let's get the fuck outta here."

Both hunters crept back into the forest.

DUANE HEARD THE CAR'S engine being turned over and driving off. He wondered when he would see Willis and give him a big hug and a kiss. He waited for a respectably long moment while comforting all three Bigfoot with strokes and pats to the head.

21

ON CLOSE INSPECTION, any idiot could see that the Bigfoot standing behind that Douglas fir with a rifle at the ready was someone dressed in a Bigfoot costume. But Duane, incurable lover of the forest, had fooled many such hunters hoping to bag the elusive creature by luring them away from the real thing. Problem was not getting bagged himself.

The sound of Chuck and Bob's hushed voices and of snapping twigs alerted Duane to the hunters' whereabouts. He remained motionless behind the tree and quietly waited with his rifle aimed straight down a well-worn path.

Duane's breathing was rapid, hurting his chest. Doing all this running was really taking it out of him. He wanted to wipe the rivers of sweat from his forehead, but dared not remove his Bigfoot head.

He was also aware that the sweat was running down his naked body causing the inner lining of his Bigfoot duds to stick to his skin. It tickled, infuriatingly so, especially as it trickled down his butt crack. Like a grizzly bear, Duane rubbed his butt up and down the bark of the tree he was leaning against to relieve the itch. It made little difference that his duds were made of light summer material with air vents under the armpits and crotch to let the body heat out in warm weather, for Duane was a real sweater.

And did he stink or what? Duane got a good whiff of his manly odor every time he shifted from one foot to the other. Fuck it! There was nothing for it, but to take off his Bigfoot head. He put it down on the ground between his feet, so it wouldn't roll away—something that had happened many times, giving away his position too early.

As he stood erect he spotted the asswipe hunters walking along the well-worn path in his direction. They were obviously unaware of his presence.

Duane didn't hesitate for a second. He raised his rifle and squeezed the trigger.

The bullet went over their heads and hit the side of a tree, exactly where it was meant to go. Duane smirked with pleasure at his accuracy. He still had what it took.

Bob and Chuck were startled—alarmed even.

"Shit," Chuck screeched like a girl.

They stopped in their stride and scanned their surroundings with their rifles aimed to shoot at whoever was shooting at them. They were unable to pinpoint the exact spot where the rifle shot had come from.

"It's only me, boys," Duane called out in an amiable tone of voice, though he was feeling anything but amiable towards the two men who had been trying to bag his hairy friends. But that said he had no intention of harming the two hunters.

"Lower your rifles and I'll do the same."

Bob called out, "For fuck's sake, Duane-o, what the hell are you doing?"

"This ain't no game . . . I said lower your rifles." Duane had an edge to his voice now. "'Cause I don't want you taking another pot shot at me today, if you don't mind."

The two hunters looked at one another and nodded their heads. They lowered their rifles and waited for Duane to come out from his hiding place, wherever that was.

Duane stepped out from the tree, but still kept his rifle aimed at the hunters.

"Shit, Duane . . . you're such a dumbass. Why the fuck do you insist on running about dressed up as Bigfoot? Jeez, we could've killed you back there," Bob said with genuine concern. "Sorry if I hit you though. My aim was off." He stifled a giggle.

Chuck sniggered, "Yeah, Bob, if you'd been on target, Duane would be dead now."

"Ha fucking ha! Haven't I told you boys not to go shooting at me?" Duane was real pissed now. "You damned well know it's me, so why bother thinking I'm the real thing?" He continued to aim his rifle at the hunters.

Chuck looked warily at Duane and raised a hand. "Come on now, Duane-o . . . we said we're sorry."

Duane tilted his head and looked at them. They didn't fool him. He could tell they weren't that sorry.

"Look, guys . . . if you see me in this get up, then it's me in this get up. Got that?" Duane shook his head with dismay. "Bigfoot don't exist . . . get it."

Bob and Chuck scuffed their feet like naughty boys, looking totally confused.

Bob asked, "Yeah, but how the fuck we gonna know the difference, Duane-o?"

Duane sighed with exasperation, "Come on guys, smarten up a little . . . it's just me dressed up as you can plainly see."

Bob looked a little less confused, "Sure thing, Duane. We got it."

"See you tonight at Abe's. Buy you a beer," Chuck offered as an apology. "No hard feelings, right?"

Duane shook his head. He was still upset with them for shooting at Olaaa. He thought it would take more than a free beer to smooth things over between him and Chuck and Bob.

"No, it isn't alright, Chuck. You can't go making things right with free beer. I'd rather buy my own. I'm real pissed with the pair of you . . . you've ruined my suit, see." Duane showed them a neat hole in the right shoulder where he had smeared some of Olaaa's blood.

"Shit, Duane you're bleeding," Bob said with genuine concern.

"Better take care of that." Chuck pleaded, "But don't say it was us. See . . . we're kinda already in deep shit probation from the last time we nicked you."

Bob nudged Chuck. They slung their rifles over their shoulders and sauntered off down the path in the direction towards Little Beaver picnic area.

Duane watched their backs until they had disappeared behind the trees. Yeah, they won't come back today. He picked up his Bigfoot head and sauntered off towards home.

AS DUANE GOT CLOSER to his cabin he heard Latin American music. He smiled knowing his Bigfoot friends were playing music on his battery operated CD player. He guessed Olaaa was feeling okay or they wouldn't be having fun.

Bigfoot love to dance—a salsa or a tango being their favorite. Olaaa especially loved to salsa. All the Bigfoot used the salsa in their wedding ritual now. Some might say Duane had contaminated the Bigfoot, but he knew better.

Duane stepped onto the porch and was relieved to see his hairy friends had kept the shutters closed. It wouldn't do for some unsuspecting local or inquisitive tourist getting the surprise of their life.

He opened the door to his cabin and stood in the doorway with a wide smile. He kept his rifle behind him. He watched all three Bigfoot dancing in the middle of the room. They'd pushed the armchairs and sofa back towards the walls to give them more space to dance. The whole cabin was rocking and creaking quite alarmingly. With each dance move, the furniture, tables and anything not nailed down hopped up and down in tune with Bigfoot stomp.

The Bigfoot continued to dance, bumping hips, rubbing groins together, shaking their shoulders and chest bumping.

Duane cringed as the floorboards groaned with displeasure at the thunderous abuse they were getting. Thank God for those supports in the basement.

Teeelaaa looked at him and beckoned with her hairy hand for him to join them.

Duane closed the door. He put his Bigfoot head on the side table by the door, and discretely propped his rifle next to the cabinet so his friends wouldn't see it and panic.

He noticed, with some annoyance, several empty tequila bottles scattered on the floor. Shit, they'd been at the booze again. Nothing changes. How many times had he told them that too much happy juice made them sick?

Duane sighed with exasperation. He stood, arms akimbo, and tried to look stern at his Bigfoot friends. He wagged his finger at them in a naughty way.

"Who's been drinking my happy juice? You know it makes you woozy," Duane said in his high-pitched kitten voice, mimicking stumbling around. He couldn't raise his voice against them, not after what they'd been through.

The Bigfoot continued to dance. Teeelaaa begged with an outstretched hand for Duane to join her. She wouldn't take no for an answer. She skipped over to him and grabbed hold of his hands, tugging on them. She shuffled her feet and swung her hips in tune with the salsa.

Duane didn't feel in the mood to dance. He was dog tired, hot, sweaty and stinky after all that running. All he wanted to do was to have a long hot soak and put his feet up for an hour or two before he ventured out that evening for some beers at Abe's.

Duane kept hold of Teeelaaa's huge hands and began to dance to the salsa, but he moved slowly to the rhythm. His dance movements were no more than a few shuffles of the feet and a slight sway of the hips. He tried to leave.

Teeelaaa thumped him with her hip, giggling, "Sfsfsfsfsfsfs." She grabbed Duane before he fell and pulled her to him. She kissed him on the cheek, "Woooo-woooo."

"Love you too, Teeelaaa," Duane replied. He stopped dancing and gave her a big hug. He got a face full of her massive suckle-bumps.

Maaawooo came to a sudden stop when he saw Teeelaaa deliberately rub Duane's face in her hairy boobs. He gave a loud growl directed at Duane.

"Graaaaaarrrrrrrraaaaaarrrr."

Olaaa seemed to be in a world of her own, oblivious to the discord between Duane and Maaawooo as she continued to salsa, her mind and heart somewhere else.

Duane saw the jealous glint in Maaawooo's eyes and noticed his greasy hair had spiked up. It wasn't Duane's fault that Teeelaaa still teased him—once a cock teaser always a cock teaser; and besides, he would never think of mating with a Bigfoot.

While Maaawooo did his jealous lover thing, Duane recalled that momentous day—the day he and Teeelaaa almost got hitched. At that time, he had no idea he was taking the lovely hand of Teeelaaa to be his wife. How could he have possibly known that by eating a bark full of the jooobaaa—wacky mushroom, offered to him by Teeelaaa all covered in flowers and dripping with red berries between her legs, was saying "I do" in Bigfoot.

Duane remembered how he had met Teeelaaa in the special meadow where most Bigfoot did their thing. After the jooobaaa had taken effect she shoved him to the ground and ripped his shorts off. Teeelaaa was most put out when he refused to go any further.

Duane shrugged his shoulders at Maaawooo. "Can I help it if Teeelaaa still woooo-woooos me?"

Although Maaawooo could understand some of the sounds spoken to him, he gave another growl when he heard 'woooo-woooo.'

"Gaaaaarrrrraaaaagggrrrraaaaa."

Teeelaaa stood with legs apart and arms akimbo, growling back at Maaawooo, "Eeeeaaaarrrrrreeeeaaaa."

Duane thought he might be witness to a Bigfoot brawl, something his cabin floor would never be able to withstand. In fact a Bigfoot brawl was nothing more than a lot of rough and tumble and the odd punch, with a few bites, hisses and spits. He'd never seen any Bigfoot get nasty with one another. Not even over a mate.

After years of studying Bigfoot, and being privy to their behavior, Duane knew that they were a very peaceful society as all the fight had been taken out of them. Unfortunately this meant they could not roam far enough to mate with males of other tribes as they were happy with their lot.

But the male gene was in short supply. Despite mating at the drop of a hat—which meant that females didn't have to be in heat, the females of the species didn't get pregnant so easily. There was also another reason for the shortage in active males—they sometimes migrated south to Florida when they got old and miserable, courtesy of the Bigfoot Mobile. Duane was always hysterical at seeing the looks on drivers' faces as his Bigfoot Mobile drove past with several elderly Bigfoot faces peering at them. Duane snapped out of it.

Duane caught a glance at the antique clock on the mantel— six p-fucking-m. Shit! It was time to get the ol' guitar out and rev up the hog and go. There was just enough time for a bath, but not to stick his feet up for an hour or two. He had an eager audience waiting for him and a thirst that needed quenching.

Teeelaaa continued to tug on his arm, though her woooo-woooo gaze was focused primarily on Maaawooo, who was still looking menacingly at Duane.

Duane looked nervously at Maaawooo, and wondered if he was going to be chased around the room like the last time Teeelaaa got too close. Maaawooo had marked his territory by spraying the armchair with his musk mixed with piss and semen. It was no wonder the cabin stunk.

Moments later, Duane's question was answered. He watched helplessly as Maaawooo aimed his chubby thruster at the armchair Lou had recently sat in, and started to spray it vigorously with his musk. There was nothing Duane could do, except hold his nostrils as the rotten eggs and garlic stink raped his olfactory system. He just stood and helplessly watched.

"Now, Maaawooo, what have I said about spraying the furniture. Ftftftftftf," Duane said, wagging his finger, although he couldn't get the Bigfoot word right. How to say ftftftftft through his nostrils was beyond him.

Maaawooo shrugged his shoulders and turned round to face Duane. He aimed his thruster at his love rival and growled.

Teeelaaa and Olaaa wriggled their hips to the music and giggled, "Sfsfsfsfsfsfsfssf."

Duane quickly stepped back a pace. He didn't want to be sprayed with Maaawooo's pungent love juice.

He wagged his finger again, "Bad Maaawooo."

Maaawooo started to chuckle, "Sfsfsfsfsfsfsfsf."

He lowered his hand from his thruster and started to dance with Teeelaaa and Olaaa, grinding his lower regions, revealing his growing hard on.

Duane saw the amorous glint Maaawooo gave Teeelaaa. It took little guesswork to know what Maaawooo was thinking and come to think of it, so did Duane.

22

THAT EVENING, around nine, Abe's Bar and Grill was practically bursting at the seams. The cacophony of chatter and laughter mixed with country and western music rivaled that of the joyful clinking of glassware.

MB sat alone at a table close to the stage, drinking a cool Little Beaver Light from a tall glass. He was wearing his usual jeans and a denim shirt. A bottle of the same beer and a tall glass awaited the arrival of his other singing half—Duane.

MB's attention was focused on a group of noisy male and female Japanese seated at several nearby tables. They looked as if they were enjoying the entertainment and having a good time.

On the stage was a middle-aged Japanese male, wearing a full country and western ensemble, playing a guitar and singing a country and western tune. The tune in question was a C and W rendition of "The Green, Green Grass of Home."

Not bad on the ol' geetar, but the singing was more than a tad off key, thought MB, with a disgusted look on his face. There's an Old Indian legend that tells us man who is tone deaf, can't sing.

MB took a sip of his beer and wondered where the hell Duane was. He would have to be here soon or they'd miss their spot.

Less than twenty seconds later, Duane stepped through the door of Abe's Bar and Grill. He was dressed in his Bigfoot duds, minus the head, which he had stuffed under his armpit. He waved and shook hands with everyone who said howdy—which was basically everyone.

MB caught sight of his friend and smiled. He stood up and waved to attract Duane's attention, indicating he was late with his non-existent watch. He was reminded of an Old Indian legend that told us man who depends on watch will be late for the rest of his life.

From across the crowded seating area of the bar and grill, Duane saw his friend. He cheerfully waved back. He sauntered through the crowded room saying his hellos to anyone that greeted him.

MB sat back down and waited with some amusement as Duane made his way toward him. *This is gonna take some time,* thought MB, as hands shook Duane's hand, and offers of free beer halted his progress.

MB was reminded of an Old Indian legend that tells us man who has a lot of friends is rich indeed.

A glass of beer was thrust into Duane's hand by a fellow male Beaverite. He accepted it and took a mouthful, then went on his merry way.

Another Beaverite, this time a familiar female clad in a cowboy get up, grabbed hold of Duane's arm and planted a kiss on his cheek, leaving a big red lip print on his skin.

Duane spilled half his beer over Collette.

Collette proudly looked down at her erect nipples showing through her wet blouse. She grabbed Duane by the hair and pulled his face into her breasts.

Everyone cheered.

It was obvious to all that a lot of people really liked Duane, MB mused. And why shouldn't they? Ol' Duane-o was one of the friendliest, if not *the* friendliest human being he'd come across.

Under MB's watchful gaze, Duane came across the only Beaverite not so enamored with Duane's cheerful personality. Duane faltered by Walt's table which was deliberately within earshot of MB, but due to the rowdy audience and performer on stage MB could only guess what was being said.

Walt sneered at the amiable Bigfoot and said something unpleasant.

Duane blew Walt a kiss.

Walt tried to get up, but was held down by his two close friends and hunting buddies. You guessed it—Chuck and Bob. All three were well and truly intoxicated on Bigfoot ESB.

MB's amused face transformed into a frown as Duane goaded Walt with an attempt at friendship by pretending to offer his hand, only to pull it away and display the bird. *Here we go,* thought MB. If Walt thought Duane was hiding Beau out at his place then things might get a little nasty. Many Beaverites were starting to come to the conclusion that Beau should have showed up by now—that his joke had gone too far.

23

BEFORE LEAVING HIS CABIN that night, Duane shooed his Bigfoot friends outside. He snatched up all his tequila and rushed into the kitchen.

Most kitchens are instantly recognizable as places to prepare food—not Duane's kitchen. Although it had a sink and an old-fashioned range, the rest of the available space was cluttered with boxes stacked to the ceiling. The boxes were labeled with various food stuffs—canned beans—canned sausage and beans—canned chili beans—canned curried beans and canned tuna. Duane never had the time to cook a meal, and why should he—he always ate out at Abe's, Annie's or at one of his nightly stop-offs for you-know-what.

In a brief moment of clarity, Duane decided to hide all his booze from Maaawooo, who had a strong liking for the stuff. He knew that while he was away, Maaawooo might search the cabin for more booze, something he had a habit of doing. So Duane opened the walk-in pantry. He walked in and pulled a lever. A trap door fell open from the ceiling.

Most of the available space was taken up by an array of bottles marked skunk, deer musk, grizzly piss and essence of Bigfoot. An empty plastic cleaner sprayer lay next to the bottles.

Duane slid the tequila into the tiny crawl space which was not big enough for a Bigfoot, not even for Duane. He was confident his Bigfoot friends would never think to look in the roof space.

But Duane's moment of clarity suddenly left him as it often did. In one of his frequent absent-minded episodes, he forgot to padlock the pantry door before he had left to go into town that night.

ॐ   ॐ   ॐ

THE COAST WAS CLEAR as all three Bigfoot stood facing the walk-in pantry. Maaawooo and Teeelaaa were impatient as Olaaa squeezed in. It was cramped inside the pantry. Every time she turned, she knocked something off a shelf. Flour, peanut butter and various contents of fruit jars covered the floor. Olaaa's footprints were clearly visible in the sticky mess that now resembled a cake mix.

From inside the pantry she looked out, shaking her head to indicate she couldn't find the happy juice.

Maaawooo gave a loud grunt of dissatisfaction and snorted, "Ftftftftftft!"

Teeelaaa gave Maaawooo a comforting pat on the shoulder, "Woooo-weeee."

Olaaa didn't like to see Maaawooo looking so miserable, but what could she do? She was about to step out of the pantry when she heard the clink of bottle striking bottle—happy juice! She looked up to see the trapdoor. She tried to reach it, but was not quite tall enough.

"Ftftftftftft!" Olaaa clambered up the shelves and was about to push her large hand through the trapdoor when the whole pantry collapsed. "Ftftftftftftftft!"

Olaaa slid across the kitchen floor leaving a thick trail of the flour mix, along with everything not stuck to the shelves by spilled honey.

Teeelaaa and Maaawooo sniggered, "Fsfsfsfsfsfsfs."

They sniggered some more as Olaaa attempted to stand up only to fall on her hairy behind which became matted with the sticky mixture.

Olaaa slid along the floor to rub her behind clean. This brought even more laughter from her friends. She finally got to her big messy feet and looked around at the disgusting mess.

Olaaa couldn't help but join in, "Fsfsfsfsfsfs."

Teeelaaa and Maaawooo sat down in the mess and rubbed their behinds along the floor, crashing into the wooden cabinet doors, splintering them into matchsticks.

Maaawooo staggered to his feet and proudly surveyed the wrecked kitchen. He trudged over to the ruined pantry and smashed a fist through the trapdoor. He deftly caught three bottles of happy juice.

Teeelaaa snorted, "Ftftftftft!"

Maaawooo grinned, showing his large yellow teeth.

Olaaa surveyed the kitchen and saw the look on Teeelaaa. She realized what a naughty girl she was, but it was such fun being naughty. She looked longingly at the bottles in Maaawooo's hands. She tried to grab one.

Teeelaaa knew what Olaaa wanted. She put both hands to her head and moaned as if in pain to imply what would happen if Olaaa drank the happy juice.

Maaawooo turned away from Olaaa.

Olaaa tried to grab the bottles.

Maaawooo held the bottles above his head and sniggered, "Sfsfsfsfsfsf."

Olaaa jumped as high as she could, but the bottles were out of reach. She gave up and slumped to the floor, exhausted after her antics. She kicked her feet in a hissy fit.

Maaawooo skidded to the watering hole and broke a bottle top into the sink. He up-ended the entire contents down his throat. His eyes rolled with delight. He tossed the empty bottle and belched loudly. He was about to start on the other bottles when a sudden thought occurred to him. He chuckled at the delicious idea he had.

Teeelaaa and Olaaa gave Maaawooo a suspicious look. They both knew that naughty face on Maaawooo meant more trouble.

24

DUANE BELCHED AT WALT and said to his hunting buddies, "Howdy guys."

Chuck and Bob gave wide drunken grins and replied together, "Howdy, Duane, ol' buddy."

But Walt continued to give Duane a nasty look.

Unperturbed by Walt's unfriendly attitude, Duane gave him a brotherly pat on the shoulder.

"Walt, ol' buddy."

"Don't you 'ol' buddy' me, asshole," Walt snarled.

Duane stepped back in feigned surprise and fear. He even managed to look a little offended by what Walt had just said. He guessed that Walt wasn't in a particularly good mood, due to the fact that his boy hadn't shown up yet and maybe he was also ticked off with him for taking a pot shot at his two asswipe buddies.

"Me, an asshole? I can't think why, ol' buddy." Duane gave that stupid grin, knowing how much it would infuriate Walt.

Walt didn't reply straight away. He took a swig of his strong beer, remarking, "You'd better wipe that stupid grin off your fucking face . . . and who gave you the right to go shooting at my friends, asshole." Burp!

Duane smiled amiably at Chuck and Bob, "No harm done was there, guys?"

Chuck pushed a Bigfoot ESB bottle across the table towards Duane. "Changed your mind about that free beer?"

Duane shook his head no, "No, I haven't." He winked, "Rain check?" He looked at Walt. "They don't seem too upset about it."

Chuck and Bob nodded their heads and grinned drunkenly, "No hard feelings."

Walt gave his buddies a nasty look for sucking up to Duane, "You stupid pair of fucking asswipes."

Bob and Chuck gave each other mock fearful looks then burst out laughing.

Walt certainly did seem miffed, mused Duane. Well, serves him right for thinking he had Beau up at his cabin.

Duane smiled his amiable smile at Walt and then glanced up at the Japanese male singer on stage, now giving everyone his rendition of "D-I-V-O-R-C-E." Duane listened, scratching his butt for a while, before he came to the conclusion that the performer couldn't sing, but he kept his thoughts to himself.

Duane would never jeer a performer no matter how bad they were. He was reminded of one of MB's Old Indian legends that told us man who sings bad on stage has nerves of steel.

"Fucking weirdo," Walt muttered under his breath, but loud enough for Duane to hear.

Duane realized Walt was referring to him and not the performer. Walt often called him weirdo for living in that cabin of his like some hermit. A lot of Beaverites thought Duane was weird. He didn't take offense, and why should he? It wasn't that Duane was thick skinned; he accepted that everyone was entitled to an opinion, and besides he agreed with them, he was weird.

"Yeah, I guess I am a little weird," Duane said. "Aren't we all, spaceman?"

Walt visibly jolted at that remark before he took a big sniff of Duane. He wrinkled his nose in disgust.

"You stink worse than a Bigfoot turd."

Duane sniffed under his free armpit. He couldn't disagree with that. He was getting a tad ripe, despite the hose down in the low down.

Duane shrugged amiably, "No need to tell me, ol' buddy."

Walt didn't reply. He just took another mouthful of beer and gave Duane a nasty look. Burp!

Duane left the asshole and two asswipes to their beers, but not before flashing them the bird one more time. He was gratified to see Chuck and Bob hold Walt down in his chair.

MB WATCHED HIS FRIEND approaching with a welcoming smile on his face. He noticed the red smudges of lipstick on Duane's cheeks and lips. That Duane was one lucky guy.

The door opened. MB was distracted in that direction. He saw both FBI agents entering the place. They failed to look inconspicuous at the far end of the bar, trying to attract Abe's attention as Duane arrived at his table.

Jesus! Something smells really bad around here, thought MB, as his nostrils got a sniff of something quite revolting. He looked up at his good friend and coughed. His keen olfactory senses were attuned to picking up forest smells—good or bad— before most people detected them, and this smell was by far the worst.

The air smelled musky like skunk, tainted with an earthy dampness mingled with manly odor and something else that he had occasionally got a whiff of in the woods and at Duane's cabin. But what that mysterious something was he could not say. It didn't smell exactly like grizzly or skunk, but the smell could be likened to grizzly piss and skunk spray. Most of all the smell reminded MB of the Phantom Bigfoot—rotten eggs.

"Howdy, Chief," Duane said with his trademark smile as he sat down opposite the chief, facing the stage. He placed his Bigfoot head on the table and took a mouthful of beer straight from the bottle offered to him. He savored it with a look of relief.

He burped.

"You're late, as usual," MB commented in an inoffensive, casual tone of voice.

An attractive barmaid with distinctive bright red hair was close by. She wore a short skirt and see-through t-shirt revealing ample breasts.

MB attracted the barmaid, "A pitcher of ESB and two whisky chasers, Tina."

Tina winked at MB, but started to cough. She rushed away as Duane's stink defiled her nostrils.

Duane took another sip of his light beer and sniffed his armpits.

MB took a whiff of the air just to be sure it was his ol' buddy stinking up the place with his pungent odor. *Phew— stinky*, he thought! He gave Duane a look of disgust and wrinkled his nose, but didn't say anything, as Duane often smelled bad.

DUANE LOOKED AWAY FROM the stage and noticed the look on MB's face. He recognized that look of disgust. He sniffed the air, then himself, paying particular attention to his armpits.

"I want you to be totally honest . . . do I stink that bad?" Duane chuckled as MB nodded yes. "Well it's mostly just manly odor." He gave himself another sniff, "I had a hose down, but I can't quite figure it. . . I still stink."

"When was the last time you washed them Bigfoot duds?"

Duane shrugged and took another mouthful of beer. He looked thoughtful as he mulled over what MB had just asked him, scratching his ass.

"Can't be sure . . ."

Tina dropped off the pitcher and chasers before rushing off without her usual tip. "That's so gross!"

Duane shrugged at Tina's cute ass now knowing why she had left so abruptly.

Duane filled both tall glasses with ESB. Clinked MB's before downing the ale in one go. Both friends followed with the chasers.

Duane let rip a loud burp. "That'll get the lower motor going for you-know-what."

"Better not waste any exhaust fumes before it's time." MB warned.

"Not to worry, I'll clench them in." Duane crossed his legs as if that would do the trick. "Did you know the human fart is pure methane gas?"

"Duh ... everyone on the planet knows that. But did you know there's a theory gaining momentum that the dinosaurs gassed themselves to death with their farts?"

"And did you know ... and this is a fact by the way ... when the warp engines on those Star Trek ships run low on anti-matter they have to resort to recycling their poop which gives off methane gas. The engineers convert it into anti-fart?"

MB gave Duane a look of pure awe in the presence of such stupidity. "I bet that's what Walt got up to when he was abducted ..." MB's words trailed off at the sight of the Feds approaching. He nudged Duane to look behind him.

Duane turned to see the Feds closing in on Walt's table and became misty-eyed at the sight of his old friend.

MB called out to Walt, "Hey, shit-for-brains, did you pump out those aliens' toilets for them?"

Walt jumped to his feet. Chuck and Bob grabbed him and forced him back to his chair.

"Hey, Willy!" Duane shouted, waving to Willis.

Walt grabbed Willis by the arm, causing both agents to stop in their tracks.

"This might be fun," MB sniggered.

"Huh . . . Bob and Chuck thought I was a Bigfoot again. It was close . . . real close. Those asswipes never learn."

"You've only got yourself to blame," MB chuckled. "Old Indian legend tells us man who dresses up in Bigfoot duds is likely to be displayed as a trophy on hunter's wall."

"I think, as my friend, you could show some concern for my safety," Duane said with a cheeky smile.

"Well, what do expect wandering about the woods dressed up as Bigfoot?"

Duane didn't reply as his attention was diverted to the Japanese performer as he bowed to his audience and left the stage. He applauded. The decibels were momentarily reduced to a level enabling him to hear what was going on at Walt's table. He agreed with MB, this could get interesting as Walt held onto Willis' arm.

"Can I buy you and the little woman a beer?" Walt asked in a slurred voice.

Bob and Chuck had a fit of the giggles as they noticed Merlot stiffening to the little woman remark.

"No thanks, Walt . . . we're on duty." Willis said curtly.

Walt glared at Willis. "No one refuses a free beer in this town, asshole—no fucking one."

Willis gave a disgruntled grunt. His cheeks took on a pinky hue.

"Let go of my arm, Walt."

"What're you goin' to do about it?"

Willis gave Walt a cold smile. "It has occurred to me that you put your son up to this disappearing act."

Walt heard childish giggling. He glanced over at Duane and MB who were looking in his direction.

"If anyone has my put my boy up to this, it's that asshole over there." Walt pointed to Duane.

Duane waved at Walt then gave him the bird. He was gratified to see the look of anger on Walt's face.

"Let go of my arm," Willis said with menace.

Instead, Walt tightened his hold.

In response, Willis grabbed Walt's little finger and snapped it back, but not enough to break it.

Walt released Willis' arm and fell backwards off his chair.

Bob, Chuck, Duane, MB and Merlot had a sudden bout of giggles at Walt's expense.

Walt spat on the floor, just missing Willis' regulation, shiny, black leather shoes. He rubbed his painful pinky as he got to his feet and picked up his chair.

"I knew you'd sink so low the FBI would take you in." Walt laughed at his own comment. He took a hefty swig of beer. He belched loudly at Willis as he sat back down.

Walt gave his hunting buddies a nasty look for laughing at him.

They ignored the asshole and laughed some more.

Merlot tugged on Willis' arm and directed him away from Walt.

But Walt jumped up from his chair and poked Willis in the shoulder.

"Fuck you, Willis Johnson," Walt raged.

Willis clenched his fists but kept them at his sides. He fixed Walt with his ice-blue eyes. He felt another firm tug on his arm and finally relented to Merlot.

"Meeeow - meeeeow," Walt teased.

The smile on Duane's face widened as both agents loomed over his table.

"If it isn't my old buddy, Willis," he said in a voice choked with emotion.

"Hello, Duane," Willis said rather coolly.

To any observer it would seem that Willis no longer thought of Duane as his old buddy.

Duane wiped the tears from his eyes. He got up from his chair and grabbed hold of a surprised Willis in a bear hug.

Willis gagged and struggled to be free. "Get away from me!"

Duane realized his awful stink was too much for his old friend to stomach. But Duane kept a firm hold on him. And without giving a damn what other people said or thought he planted a big kiss on Willis' cheek.

"Love you, man."

"About that let ..." Willis started to choke on the pungent odor. He was rendered speechless.

After some moments of manly hugging, Duane let go of Willis.

"Knew you'd come back," Duane said with tears running down his face. He noticed the ravishing beauty next to Willis and went to hug her.

Merlot looked aghast and stepped back from the stench that was Duane. She offered her hand rather reluctantly.

Duane shook Merlot's hand then cheekily kissed it.

Merlot snatched her hand back with revulsion.

"You must be Duane Dexter . . . stinky, but cute for driftwood," Merlot said out loud.

Duane frowned at MB. "Driftwood?"

MB shrugged.

Willis gave his partner a sharp look, "Keep your thoughts to yourself, Agent Merlot."

"Yes, massah," Merlot teased. She gave MB a come-on wink as she sat down next to him. She took a mouthful of beer from his glass. "This is good stuff."

Merlot ignored the disparaging look Willis gave her and sipped more of MB's beer.

Duane sat back down in his chair and wiped more tears from his eyes. He took a mouthful of beer and looked lovingly at his old friend over the rim of his beer bottle.

MB gave Duane a reassuring pat on the back of his hand and commented, "Old Indian legend tells us that man whose friend comes back home after many years away should give friend a big hug and a kiss."

"Willy!" Duane tearfully exclaimed. "Take a load off." Duane kicked a chair from the table.

Willis remained serious and on his feet. "If you insist on calling me by my first name . . . then it's Willis."

"Oops," Duane apologized. "Still touchy about being called Willy, I see. How could I forget, ol' buddy? Sorry." Duane gave a wide smile. "We've got a lot of catching up to do, Willis." He emphasized Willis.

Willis sat down rather stiffly. He avoided looking Duane in the eyes.

It seemed obvious to Duane that Willis was feeling guilty and owed him an apology for the way he'd left Big Beaver. And not once in all the years Willis had been away had he tried to contact Duane by letter or phone. Duane had every right to be hurt, but couldn't help being overjoyed at seeing Willis again.

A thought crossed Duane's mind . . . what did Lou think about her old love coming back to town? She might want to inflict injury on Willis for ditching her the way he did. Well, he's got it coming if she does.

There was something else, something at the back of his mind, but his brain fog wouldn't allow that something to surface. He had a feeling he'd forgotten something very important concerning Willis. He scratched his butt to get his brain in gear, but nothing would come to mind.

"Duane . . . we'd like to ask you a few questions," Willis stated in his regulation, matter-of-fact tone of voice.

Willis continued to sit stiff-backed with a serious look on his face while Merlot was a little too relaxed, helping herself to a handful of salted peanuts from a bowl while ogling MB.

After several moments of studying his old friend over the rim of his glass, Duane remarked, "So you're on Beau's case."

Willis nodded his head slightly to indicate yes.

Duane glanced over at Walt and saw him still glaring in their direction with a hostile look on his face.

"You know Walt will never forgive you, Willis," Duane mused.

Willis shrugged, "Fuck him."

Merlot looked askance at Duane and frowned, "Forgive Willis for what?"

Duane opened his mouth to reply.

Willis quickly cut him off, "Nothing you need to know about. It's not relevant to the case."

Merlot didn't push the matter, giving her partner a questioning look then glancing over at Walt.

Walt was still looking in their direction and pointing an unfriendly finger at them.

Duane glanced back at Walt and gave him the bird. Duane was gratified to see Walt visibly jolt.

"No, he certainly hasn't forgiven you, Willis, old friend. You'd think after all these years your family and his would let bygones be bygones."

The puzzled look on Merlot's face deepened. "After all these years?" She looked for an answer from MB, "Do tell."

MB opened his mouth to enlighten the bewildered FBI agent.

Willis quickly cut him off, too. "Shut it, if you know what's good for you, Mocking Bird."

MB folded his arms across his chest. "Old Indian legend tells us man who doesn't keep his mouth shut sticks his big foot in it."

Merlot looked even more perplexed.

Duane sensed there was tension at his table, and all of it was emanating from Willy. As he recalled, Willy could always be a little uptight and a little too quick to lose his cool. Now that he was older, those undesirable traits had gone up a few notches.

"Walt's family founded the town at the same time Willis' family did. The feud started over its name." Duane saw the angry glare on Willis and continued. "Even the Johnsons knew their name was inappropriate so the river's name was used."

"But welcome to Flucker has a nice ring to it, don't you think?" Merlot said, suppressing giggles.

Duane scratched his butt as he thought for a moment. He looked mischievously at Willis, "Oh yeah."

"Enough with the Flucking history lesson!" Willis glared at Duane. "Just for the record . . . have you seen anyone in the woods who you thought was acting out of the ordinary?"

"I keep a close look out for undesirables and such like . . . none of which I have seen recently." Duane smiled proudly to himself. "Gotta take care of my woods, you know. So many people these days got no respect for nature."

MB remained with his arms folded over his chest, and exclaimed in a serious tone, "Old Indian legend tells us that man who disrespects nature will only have fools for friends."

That was a good one, agreed Duane. That should keep the agents' thoughts rattling around in confusion. He had to admire MB for his moralistic depth—real fucking deep, man.

Willis gave MB a nasty glance then abruptly asked, "Duane . . . do we need a warrant to search your place?"

Duane was hurt. Why would his old friend need a warrant? As long his Bigfoot friends were nowhere in sight, Willy could drop in any time.

"Be my guest, Willis. My home is your home. But why do you want to search my place?"

"Because we and certain people in town . . ." He gave Walt a glance. ". . . Suspect you might be hiding the boy up at your cabin." Willis wasn't smiling. "After all, you've got a reputation for pulling pranks."

So what if he did have a reputation for pulling pranks; but to think he might be foolish enough to hide Beau at his cabin was ludicrous indeed. Duane contemplated the notion for a moment with his brow furrowed and an irresistible urge to scratch his butt, but he'd done so much thinking of late with his butt finger that he was getting tired of thinking. He needed to rest his brain whichever end that was at. He sighed heavily as he could see why the FBI agents thought he might be hiding the boy.

"Feel free to drop in anytime you like," he smiled. "But if I'm not in, then you can't see me . . . and sometimes when I am in you can't see me . . . but when I'm out, you can call on me." Duane chuckled at the puzzled look on Willis' face. "Lighten up, Willis. Lou doesn't seem to think I've got anything to do with Beau going missing."

With those prophetic words, Duane glanced over at the empty stage. "That's it . . . time for more live entertainment."

BOTH AGENTS REMAINED SEATED as they watched Duane take his Bigfoot head onto the stage where his guitar waited.

Duane tested the microphone by blowing a raspberry into it. A spotlight shone down on him like a silvery moon.

MB stood a few paces behind Duane, looking casual with his hands in his pockets. He also had a microphone in front of him.

The audience continued to chatter. The sound of clinking glasses continued. But most of the audience's attention was focused on the stage while they waited for Duane to break into his signature Bigfoot song.

"Can the idiot sing?" Merlot asked.

"He seems to think so," Willis replied.

Duane tapped the microphone, "Hi folks. It's us again—Duane-o the Bigfoot and the Chief."

Duane began to strum his guitar.

MB drew close to his microphone in readiness.

Duane burst into song:

"Nobody loves a Bigfoot, like a Bigfoot Babe,
Nobody likes a Bigfoot, until he's been laid,
Big and hairy,
He's a Sasquatch."
MB joined in, "he's a Sasquatch."
Duane continued to sing, "Big and hairy,
He loves his snatch,
They roam the land of woods and trees,
Plagued by bugs and pesky fleas."
MB joined in, "bugs and pesky fleas."
Duane continued to sing, "but all he wants is the birds and
bees."
MB burst into chorus with Duane.
"I'm a Bigfoot, I'm a Bigfoot,
Nobody loves a Bigfoot,
Like a Bigfoot babe."

The audience applauded and stamped their feet to the rhythm.

MERLOT CLAPPED HER HANDS and smiled. She glanced over at her partner and saw the slightest smile on his face. Agent Tightass was starting to melt.

Duane broke into a further rendition of his theme song.

"Nobody loves a Bigfoot, like a Bigfoot babe."

A sudden clatter of chairs and loud male voices caused Merlot to look over her shoulder. She watched with rising apprehension as a fight broke out between two men in the audience. The fight spilled over onto another table. In moments, several more of the audience began to throw random punches at the nearest person. Even a few of the women got involved in a tussle, tugging their hair and screaming and kicking.

Merlot looked back to the stage.

Unperturbed by the fray, the song continued—

"I'm a Bigfoot,

I'm a Bigfoot,

Nobody loves a Bigfoot,

Like a Bigfoot Babe."

Several empty beer bottles flew across the stage. Duane and MB expertly dodged the projectiles aimed at them.

The Japanese tourists excitedly watched the fracas and clicked away with their cameras, shouting, "Banzai-Banzai-Banzai!"

With an alarmed look on her face, Merlot surveyed the barroom brawl. She looked to her partner.

"Um . . . shouldn't we do something?"

"No need. Leave it to the law." Willis looked at his watch. "They'll be here any second now," he said somewhat confidently.

What the fuck was going on, thought Merlot, raising a quizzical eyebrow on hearing this reply.

Suddenly, a chair flew past Merlot's head and shattered against the wall behind her. Things were getting a bit too rough. She looked at Willis and saw that his attention was focused on Walt and the broken leg of a chair in Walt's hand. Merlot placed a hand to her gun, concealed within her jacket.

Like some caveman, Walt was waving the chair leg in a hostile manner directed at Willis.

Walt's beer-guzzling companions tried to hold him back.

Instinctively, Merlot unsnapped the harness from the butt of her gun. She didn't plan on using it on Walt. Just let him see she meant business. She looked all around the barroom and focused on the stage.

While the barroom brawl went on unabated, Duane and MB continued to sing though they were off key and a tad distracted by the fracas and flying beer bottles.

Hardly anyone seemed to be listening to them now.

Duane shrugged his shoulders, stopped singing and slung his guitar off. He glanced at MB. Wordless communication passed between them.

MB nodded his head in agreement and announced to all, "Okay folks, you asked for it."

Duane spoke into the microphone, "Time for the Awesome Asshole to strike again."

With an amused look, Merlot watched Duane turn his back to the audience and drop his Bigfoot duds to his knees. The glare of the spotlight reflected off his white ass making it hard for anyone not to get a glimpse of his perfect moon.

Heads turned in his direction, though not too many. There were a few wolf whistles from randy females.

The Japanese clicked away at Duane's perky buttocks, amid gasps of, "Banzai!"

But the fracas continued despite the sight of Duane's white ass up on stage.

For a brief moment, the sight of Duane's dumb ass had the desired effect of distracting Walt and Willis.

Walt sneered at the hideous sight. He relaxed his fighting stance and lowered the chair leg. "Not again . . . what an asshole."

This is just too much, Merlot mused. She burst into childish giggling at the sight of Duane's hairy butt. She closed her jacket and relaxed a little. She quickly and furtively snapped Duane's ass with her cell phone.

MB prompted Duane over the microphone, "It's time for the Blazing Butthole to reveal his true colors." MB offered his firelighter.

Duane grabbed the lighter and squeezed out an almighty fart. The flame from the lighter exploded Duane's methane cloud. A three foot flame singed all the hair from his ass and caused several Beaverites to duck out of the way.

One Beaverite wasn't quick enough. His eyebrows were seared off.

Merlot took a snap of that, too.

Duane looked duly satisfied. He pulled up his Bigfoot duds and turned around to look at the barroom brawl that was still in progress. The Blazing Butthole and his accomplice exchanged glances and shrugged their shoulders. They grinned mischievously at each other.

MB looked at his invisible wrist and nodded his head. "5-4-3-2-1," he counted and then pointed at the door.

Merlot also noticed Willis check his watch and count down the seconds. Her confused look said - *What the hell is going on here?*

25

THE IDEA RATTLING AROUND in Maaawooo's head was quite simple—he intended preparing his harem of blond Bigfoot babes for some serious wooing with the happy juice. It was easier than going through the whole mating ritual. He was in the mood for some passionate three-way woooo-woooo.

But, as Maaawooo tried to leave the kitchen with arms raised, Olaaa hopped up and tickled his armpit. A bottle of happy juice clonked her on the head.

"Ftftft!" she spat, rubbing her sore head and scowling at Maaawooo.

Maaawooo grinned as he caught the bottle and frantically looked around for something suitable to carry it in so his hands would be free. He growled. He beamed with large yellow teeth. He saw Duane's old moth-eaten rucksack lying on the floor. Maaawooo grabbed the rucksack and took a peek inside. He tossed a set of Duane's dirty Bigfoot duds on the floor and stuffed both bottles into it. He heard a loud clink. Maaawooo gave Teeelaaa a worried look. He picked the rucksack up and could see it was dry. That was a close call.

Maaawooo slung the woooo-woooo sack over a massive shoulder and in his excitement at the thought of some wild mating he forgot to open Duane's rear door from the kitchen. He smashed straight through the flimsy door which shattered like kindling.

Teeelaaa and Olaaa looked at the mess they had made. Olaaa giggled. Teeelaaa grabbed her hand and followed Maaawooo, skipping and jigging to the salsa music still playing loudly from Duane's living room.

The three Bigfoot headed back to their secret home, deep in the forest where no pale one, except Duane of course, had seen.

But Maaawooo's thruster got all a-twitching and frisky. He diverted the babes into a well-known Bigfoot clearing used for woooo-woooo purposes.

A NEAR-FULL MOON illuminated Olaaa as she sat on a large boulder amid the trees, looking up at the twinkling stars in the clear night sky. She sighed heavily. Tears filled her eyes as she listened to the loud grunts and howls coming from behind a thicket. She longed to mate with her plaything. A shooting star trailed across the night sky. Olaaa made a wish—that her pale plaything and she would get hitched on the jooobaaa and woooo-woooo their brains out.

"Wooooeeeeeooooo," she bleated. "Weeeeeooooeeeee-ooooo."

Olaaa stared at the tiny white flowers in her palm and sniffed them. She sighed deeply, looking up to the heavens.

"Wooooo-aaaaaa-woooo-eee-oooo," she howled plaintively to the moon.

Her heart ached for a love she knew deep down she could never have. She was so much in love it hurt. She was overwhelmed with sadness. She saw another shooting star and wished she could be like her plaything and not be a Bigfoot anymore.

She sighed heavily and cried unaware that Teeelaaa and Maaawooo had stopped their noisy lovemaking and now stood behind her. She felt Teeelaaa's comforting large hand on her shoulder.

Olaaa looked up into Teeelaaa and Maaawooo's big round, concerned eyes. Olaaa had not told any of her Bigfoot tribe that she had taken her plaything. She feared if they knew they would force her to let him go and chastise her.

Teeelaaa patted Olaaa's head, mewling pathetically.

Olaaa forced a sad smile and nodded her head, mewling in unison.

Maaawooo suddenly looked as though a thunderbolt had struck his ass. He gave a wide grin and went over to the stash of tequila.

Olaaa watched him rummage inside the rucksack and pull out a bottle. He looked around for something to open it with. He tapped the bottle top on a rock, wiped any glass with a calloused hand and gave it to Olaaa.

Olaaa snatched the bottled and sniffed its contents. Her twitching snout sensed something was very wrong. She took a sip. She gulped it nearly all down.

Maaawooo tried to snatch his woooo-woooo prize away from her.

Olaaa turned from Maaawooo's grasping hand. She knew that Maaawooo was trying to cheer her up by offering her his precious gift. She thought Maaawooo might be right. It would have cheered her up except it tasted just like their local drinking hole.

Olaaa pouted and spat, "Ftftftftft!" She tossed the almost empty bottle in the air.

Maaawooo caught the gift and sniffed it. "Ftftftftft!" He gave a low dissatisfied growl on inspection. He ripped open the rucksack and snatched the other bottle. He smashed the top off and drank, spitting out the contents. "Ftftftftft!" He howled to the moon. Duane had out-foxed him. Maaawooo was displeased to say the least.

Olaaa and Teeelaaa giggled. Olaaa didn't mind the deception, but she knew that Maaawooo would be more than a little miffed with Duane.

26

BACK AT ABE'S, WILLIS looked up from his watch and pointed to the entrance, knowing what was about to happen. He smirked at Merlot's look of astonishment as the door to Abe's rowdy establishment opened on Willis' count of "one."

Sheriff Lou and her four deputies entered meaning business with their guns at the ready. They had a job to do and they were looking tough. The fight continued.

Willis wanted to laugh, but maintained his serious pose, as Deputy Dwight was shoved to the floor by two brawling females. The deputy slithered on his back as both women rolled across his wobbling girth.

Lou saw the singing duo on the stage. They had stopped their performance and were looking in her direction. She smiled as she aimed her pistol up at the ceiling and fired.

The fracas suddenly stopped. All attention focused on the sheriff and her deputies and most of all on the massive Magnum .44 still smoking in Lou's hand.

The excited Japanese continued to click-click away with their cameras.

Lou scanned the room with her gun still at the ready. "Okay boys . . . round 'em up."

Abe walked up to her and checked his watch, "On the nose, as usual, Lou."

"I aim to serve," she said, swaggering up to the bar. She was engulfed in flashing lights from the Japanese cameras.

One of the brawlers staggered over to Sheriff Lou. Brad was in his mid-thirties, a good-looking dude—except his eyebrows had been burnt off. Brad held out his hands to be cuffed. He swayed from side to side as he tried to give the sheriff a peck on the cheek. He suddenly grabbed her and planted a passionate one smack on her lips.

"Marry me, Lou," Brad loudly declared just as the whole place went silent.

Willis heard Brad's declaration and scowled. So that's it, he thought. It was Brad who wanted to marry Lou. Whoever had written the letter, and that must've been Duane, was right about Brad. Fuck, it would have to be the old sawmill owner's son and second richest guy in town who had taken Lou's heart. At that moment he felt just about as miserable as he could get.

LOU REARED HER HEAD away from Brad's drunken advances, but not before she got a whiff of his intoxicated breath and strong aftershave.

"Hey Lou, you can cuff me any time you like now," he slurred.

Lou smiled and replaced her gun into her holster. With a nod of her head she signaled Deputy Heidi to put the cuffs on the amorous fool.

Lou didn't wait for Deputy Heidi to cuff Brad. With her hand on the butt of her gun and looking tough she sauntered into the carnage left by the brawling patrons of Abe's Bar and Grill.

Upturned chairs and tables littered the floor amid broken drinking glasses and bottles of alcohol.

She soon caught sight of the FBI agents seated at a table. They were looking in her direction. In particular, she focused her attention on Willis. She could well imagine what he'd put in his regulation report to his regulation superiors, and didn't give a regulation fuck.

As she made her way over to their table, she had to step over several bruised and bloody, drunken Beaverites floundering in her path. It was good to let off steam, she mused. Besides, the tourists, especially the Japanese, loved a good knock-down-drag-out barroom brawl. It was good for business.

A few paces away from the FBI agents' table, she called out, "Hope you enjoyed our little show."

A bemused Merlot looked more than a bit incredulous as she blurted out, "The show! You mean all that wasn't for real?" She pointed to the devastation.

Lou stopped at their table and put her hands on her hips. She grinned. "Sure, some of the punches were genuine, that can't be helped, but the tourists love to see a good, old-fashioned knock-down-drag-out." She pulled out her pistol and waved it about. "Just blanks." She glanced at Willis and gave a faint smile. "Don't need real ammo here."

"Thought as much," Willis said with a hint of a smirk.

Lou put her pistol back in her holster and sat down on a chair next to Merlot. Her attention focused on her old flame.

He was looking directly at her. His expression was thoughtful, even on the soft side. Could he be thinking of her? She hoped so.

Merlot glanced all around her with a look of disbelief. She turned to the sheriff. "I'm in the Twilight Zone."

Lou smiled at the Japanese cameras aimed at Deputy Heidi man-handling a horny Brad trying to plant a wet kiss on her lips. "This is more like The Outer Limits."

"You going to lock anyone up?" Merlot asked.

Lou laughed, "I'll keep the drunkards in jail overnight to sober up, but the rest can go free."

Merlot continued to look confused. She looked at her partner for further explanation, "Please explain."

"I remember your father doing exactly the same thing. Nothing much has changed around here," Willis commented.

Lou didn't reply straight away. Her eyes wandered over his chiseled, handsome face. Her heart skipped a beat. Shit! It hit her like a bullet, right there and then that she still loved the heartless bastard. Really loved him!

Their eyes met. Lou could feel how warm her cheeks had become. She sensed he was still attracted to her. Was there more to his gaze than just mere attraction? Did he still love her too? Her heart skipped another beat.

Lou gave a gentle little cough and glanced over to the stage to see Duane and MB being cuffed by Deputy Dwight. She looked back at Willis. Their eyes locked. She quickly avoided eye contact with him and inwardly cursed herself—*you idiot— he was the one that left, not you.*

"I like our town just the way it is. We don't get much crime. I know some people might say Big Beaver's a bit backward compared to life in a place like Sacramento . . . but that's the way we Beaverites like it."

"Not all Beaverites," Willis said dryly.

"Is that why you left, because nothing much happened in Big Beaver?" Lou gave him a hard look. "Or was there another reason?"

Willis' gaze lingered on Lou's face, "Maybe."

Merlot was uncharacteristically silent as she eavesdropped on the sheriff and her partner's conversation.

Lou sensed Merlot's watchful gaze and directed her attention towards the female agent. "You don't have to be FBI to guess we were once an item, Agent Merlot."

"Before we arrived I thought it was Annie tugging at Willis' heartstrings," Merlot admitted.

Willis gave Merlot a deranged glare, "Annie!"

Merlot giggled, "Okay, I was off track a little." She looked at her partner and smiled. "So what went wrong? Why didn't you two settle down?"

Willis stiffened in his chair. He gave his partner a withering look, "None of your business."

As Willis spoke, Deputy Dwight approached with the infamous singing duo cuffed together and looking very pleased about it.

Lou turned her attention to her deputy and his charges.

"What should I do with these two?" Dwight asked.

Duane chuckled, "Nice timing, Lou."

It was a shame she couldn't arrest them, but the jail was going to be full tonight. She shrugged.

"How much have you two had to drink?" Lou cringed at Duane's pungent aroma.

"You know . . . the usual," MB said with a boyish grin. "Old Indian legend tells us that a man who drinks too much falls flat on his face."

Merlot chuckled at MB's remark, "You know what, Mocking Bird . . . you're full of it."

MB smiled and nodded his head in agreement.

"Okay, Dwight . . . let 'em go," Lou said with a sigh.

Deputy Dwight hesitated. "A little bird told me Duane-o mooned the audience again." The deputy looked pleased with himself. "You gotta arrest him for that."

Lou tilted her head and looked disparagingly at the lame brain. "Is that true?"

With a certain amount of pride in his voice, Duane replied, "Sure is, Sheriff. I confess."

"Damn it to hell, you know I should charge you with indecent exposure."

The no-brainer solemnly nodded his head and smiled apologetically with that disarming smile of his.

Yet another warning would have to do, Lou mused. She sighed. "This is absolutely the last time I let you off. Got that?" Knowing full well he'll do it again.

Duane leaned forward and slapped a big, wet kiss on her full red lips.

Lou was a sucker for that sweet smile of Duane's. She allowed him to kiss her as she knew it would make Willis mad. She was gratified to see the jealous glare from her first love. It worked! Unfortunately for Lou, the powerful Duane odor hit her full on. She wanted to gag right there. She reared away from Duane's lips.

Dwight pouted. "But, Sheriff, you said the next time Duane pulled down his duds . . ."

Lou raised her hand to silence her deputy's objections. "Un-cuff 'em, Dwight." As she spoke her gaze was drawn back towards Willis. They looked into each other's eyes.

All present could see that the sheriff and Willis had certain feelings for one another.

MB commented, "Old Indian legend tells us that man who never gets tired of his woman's face, even when she's old and wrinkled, is really in love."

Duane sighed heavily. "That's so romantic . . . it gets you right here." He put a hand to his heart.

Dwight sniffed back a tear. "That's a beautiful thing to say. It makes me want to cry."

MB consoled a teary-eyed Dwight with an arm around his shoulder.

Merlot focused her attention on the sheriff and Willis.

MB nudged Dwight and indicated Lou and Willis were in love with a pucker of his lips and fluttering eyelids. He smirked as Dwight wobbled all over as he cried.

Lou was unaware that all attention was focused on her and Willis. She was all a-tingle with emotion: a hot kind of tingle that meant only one thing—she wanted Willis to do her.

27

SHERIFF LOU ENTERED Grace Hotel a little after one in the morning. She was wearing a very sexy black number, slutty, bright red lip gloss and gelled spiky hair. She swayed with intoxication as she walked across the pine-walled lobby covered with stuffed animals. She nodded to the desk clerk and sauntered to the stairs.

Earlier that day, after returning from Little Beaver, the FBI agents had returned to their booked rooms at the Grace Hotel. They had been given single rooms with an adjoining bathroom. Like the hotel, the rooms were clean, neat and rustic. And as befitting a town with such a strong hunting tradition, stuffed animal heads hung on the walls of all the rooms and stuffed fish in the bathrooms.

Lou stood outside Agent Willis Johnson's bedroom, staring nervously at the closed door. She hesitated to give the door a knock, knowing that when she did she would be at his mercy, and that she would no longer be in control of the situation.

He would either tell her to go away or invite her in. If he invited her in, one of two things would happen—they would talk and nothing sexual would happen between them or they would end up tearing each other's clothes off and go at it all night. Whether sex provided the basis for a more lasting relationship, Lou didn't know. She only knew that she wanted some real sex, and Willis was it.

She glanced down at her boobs poking out from the low cut dress. She thought perhaps she was looking a tad too slutty. Was she wearing too much make-up?

She was unsure if Willis liked his women to dress up sexy and wear make-up. She was unsure about so many things concerning Willis. For one thing—and it was a niggling question, was there someone else in his life? If so, then all this would be a complete waste of her time. Lou prided herself on being the type of woman who would never split up couples.

She took in a deep breath to calm her nerves. She clenched her hands into fists. For one brief moment, Lou hesitated before she knocked at his door, thus perhaps sealing her fate with one gentle tap.

Was she doing the right thing by throwing herself at him? The voice inside her told her yes. *Yes! You still love him.* But did Willis love her? Something, women's intuition or even Lou's trusty gut feeling, told her that he did love her. She hoped she was right.

But first things first, she wanted him between her legs, and it didn't have to be meaningful. She told herself, first sex with Willis then if things went well she could pledge her undying love for the heartless bastard who had left her without even saying goodbye.

The hurt was still there. Would it ever go away? There was only one way to find out. But could she forgive him?

MERLOT WAS IN THE bathroom when she heard the gentle tap on the door of the neighboring room. She was almost ready for bed, wearing a skimpy, black baby doll and shimmering gold panties. She gave her reflection a big smile in the bathroom mirror. She tilted her ear and wondered who was calling on Willis at this time of night?

She skipped over to the interconnecting door of the bathroom and put her ear to the door. And listened...

THERE WAS ANOTHER GENTLE TAP on the door. Willis was tucked up in bed reading a crime novel. He gave the door an irritated look.

"Who the fuck is that?" he muttered under his breath.

He guessed it had to be Duane. If that dumbass tried to give him another kiss he knew he'd have no choice but to punch his lights out.

With a scowl on his face, Willis got out of bed. He was wearing regulation white boxer shorts and a regulation white t-shirt that showed off his lean physique. He picked his dressing gown up off a nearby armchair and put it on. He wrapped the belt of the dressing gown tightly around his waist as he walked towards the door.

On opening the door, Willis was met by the sheriff standing in the hallway looking like she wanted to get laid. He looked surprised at seeing Lou looking horny as hell. Willis ran an appreciative eye over Lou's revealing dress.

As Lou brushed past him into the room without saying a word, he got a strong whiff of her heady, intoxicating perfume, an overdose of pheromones and alcohol.

He couldn't help but notice how unsteady she was on her feet. He surmised her perfume wasn't the only thing that was intoxicating. Willis hesitated for a few moments before he quietly closed the door, not wanting to wake that nosy partner of his.

Lou surveyed the bedclothes tossed back and swung around to give Willis a wanton look. She swayed slightly.

Willis stared at her, poker-faced and without saying a word. Though beneath the regulation serious façade, he was getting more turned on by the minute. He ached for her, but couldn't let her see that.

"Oops . . . naughty me, I've been drinking," she hiccupped.

Yeah, I can see that, thought Willis.

She looked from Willis' stern face back at the bed and sashayed over to it. She fell backwards with sexual abandonment, stretching out fully, resting her head on the pillow. She licked her full lips seductively as she looked up at him.

"I want you, right now."

Willis could feel his pulse rate go up several more notches. His light blue eyes looked at her with wanton desire. But he didn't make a move in her direction. He stood as motionless as a rock. His expression was serious. He wondered if his boner was showing. He slowly approached the bed.

Lou smiled seductively at him as she fondled her breasts and writhed with wanton abandon.

A voice inside him told Willis not to go any further. For one thing, it would complicate the investigation—those damned pesky regulations again. And there was also the fact that Lou had had too much to drink. He didn't want to take advantage of her, for that too would complicate things. He felt sure that if they had sex right now, when she'd sobered up in the morning, she'd really regret what she'd done. And hate him even more for taking advantage of her while she was drunk, even though she was the instigator. What a dilemma!

Willis sighed heavily and reached out for her hand. "Come on Lou, enough's enough."

But as he reached out to her, Lou completely caught him off-guard. She grabbed his hand and gave a forceful tug, pulling him onto the bed next to her. She ran her fingertips through his hair.

He tried to get off the bed but she wrapped her arms tightly around his waist. He could feel her slender body rubbing against his. He sighed as she quickly found his erection.

Lou giggled, "That's my Willis . . . hard as a rock." She pulled him to her and kissed him hard on the lips.

The rush was just like that first kiss, all those years ago. Willis couldn't help it as her tongue found his, but then those regulations kicked in. He desperately tried to pull away.

Lou loosened her hold of him, by removing one hand which slipped down his body into Willis' boxer shorts. She hiccupped.

Willis didn't want to make a break for it but knew it was for the best. He yanked himself free of her embrace and got up quickly from the bed.

"Damn it, Willis," she pouted. "Now I really hate you." Lou lunged at him.

Willis jumped back as Lou slumped to the floor. He picked her up and dropped her back on the bed. He wondered if she behaved like this with Brad or that dumbass, Duane.

Lou's eyes widened at the sight of his twitching erection inside his boxer shorts.

Willis tugged on his robe to cover his rampant manhood. "I think you'd better leave."

Lou sat up on the bed and looked petulantly at him.

She begged in a girlish voice with a finger to her lips, "Please don't send me away, Mister FBI man." She licked her fingers provocatively.

Willis so wanted to make mad, passionate love to her. But the timing just didn't seem right. He was on a case, and having sex with the sheriff would surely complicate the investigation, not to mention that Merlot would pick up on the situation and blab her big mouth off.

Willis took Lou by the arm and heaved her off the bed. He started to lead her towards the door but Lou dug her heels in and refused to move further.

She swung around to face him and pressed her body against his. Lou tried once more to kiss Willis on the lips but he avoided her by rearing his head slightly backwards.

Don't succumb whatever you do, and no matter how tempted, he urged himself. His eyes wandered over the beautiful contours of her face. Did he still love her? He didn't have to ask that question.

"Come on, Lou, it's been a long day," he urged in a tender voice.

"You really want me to go?" she asked with a pout on her lips and a hurt look in her eyes.

Willis hesitated as he looked at her inviting, full red lips. "Yes. Now go!"

The hurt look in Lou's eyes deepened. Her lower lip trembled as if she was about cry.

"You miserable, heartless bastard," she said with all her raging emotions in full view. She let go of Willis and swayed over to the door with sagging shoulders.

Willis followed her and with every step he took he regretted sending her away. His heart yearned for her lips again, but those damned regulations kept getting in the way.

Lou swung the bedroom door open and turned round to face the heartless bastard. She couldn't hide the hurt and anger in her condemning eyes.

"So that's it then?"

Willis opened his mouth to speak—to say stay—but no words came out. He watched her hesitating to leave as if waiting for him to say that all-important something. He drew his lips together and sealed them tight.

A few lovelorn moments passed before Lou finally stepped out into the hallway. She staggered as if on the deck of a boat in a storm.

Willis poked his head out into the hallway and looked left and right. He was grateful to be alone with Lou. He knew that in a town like Big Beaver people loved to gossip.

Lou glanced back over her shoulder to look at him. Tears filled her eyes.

"You bastard . . . you know you want me." She wiped tears from her eyes. "I don't do this for just anyone, you know."

Willis remained silent. *Do you do this for Brad*, he wondered? His expression was serious, but inwardly his emotions were in turmoil over his desire for Lou.

"That's it then." Lou shrugged her shoulders and began to walk down the hallway, leaning against the wall for support.

Willis wanted to call out to her to come back, but his rock-hard inner-self forced him to remain silent. With a miserable sigh, he stepped back into his room and quietly closed the door.

Had he made the right choice sending the woman he loved away? Willis heaved a woeful sigh of regret. She loves you, you stupid jerk, and you still love her. That's another round to Doctor Fernandez.

LOU STIFLED HER TEARS as she walked away from Willis' bedroom. She didn't want anyone seeing her in a slinky black dress balling her eyes out. She knew what some people would say—they mostly being men—that a woman had no place being a sheriff if she allowed her emotions to get out of hand and to go about the place in such a drunken state.

And so, with this in mind, Lou pushed back the tears, knowing she would save them for later when she was home and where no one would see her crying—for no one ever came to see Lou at her home.

She consoled herself with the thought that he still wanted her. That much was evident with his erection, but did he still love her? His hard on was not proof of that, just a man wanting sex. So, why did Willis throw her out and why was she walking away from his room without so much as having a quickie? She didn't know what to think anymore.

Lou slipped out of the hotel lobby and into the cool night air. The thought that Willis didn't hold the same feelings for her made Lou's eyes fill up with tears once more. Don't cry, don't you dare. *Don't give up yet*, she told herself. *He might be playing hard to get, something you should be doing, you slut.* Then the full force of the alcohol hit Lou. She rushed into an alley and threw up.

A GRINNING MERLOT stepped away from the interconnecting door. *Well, what do you know*, she mused.

Won't Doctor Ramón love to hear this? This trip was certainly turning out to be a revealing one at that. She wondered what more did Big Beaver have to offer. She giggled at the thought of defiling the town welcome sign.

28

HIROSHI, ONE OF THE twenty-something Japanese tourists who had used several memory sticks of his camera at Abe's, awoke with a strong urge to relieve his bladder. He was not surprised, as he had drunk copious amounts of beer the previous night, and his head throbbed and his tongue felt like a Bigfoot had slept on it.

He shared the room with his older brother, Akira. They slept in single beds. He glanced over at his brother and could make out the shadowy shape tucked up in the neighboring bed.

Akira snored loudly indicating to his brother that he was asleep and equally as intoxicated on Abe's beer, for Akira only snored when he was drunk.

Hiroshi looked at the travel clock on his bedside table. It was two-thirty in the morning. The only light in the room came from the hall light that filtered through the gap under the door.

Hiroshi threw back the bedclothes. Wearing only boxer shorts with the rising sun emblazoned on the ass end, he swung his legs over the side of the bed and sprung to his feet with the agility of a cat. He moaned quietly as this action caused his head to ache even more. He quickly glanced over at his brother. He hadn't woken him. *Good*, thought Hiroshi, for it had taken several interminable hours of listening to Akira bleat on and on about the rumpus at the bar, and if he had awoken, he would continue all through the night.

Hiroshi picked up his black, silk kimono off a nearby chair. As he tied the kimono, Hiroshi quietly opened the door and peered into the hallway. He stepped out of his room and carefully closed the door without making a sound.

Unlike the FBI agents and several of his Japanese companions, Hiroshi and his brother were not fortunate enough to have a room with a private bathroom. They had to share a communal bathroom—of which there were two—on the second floor.

Hiroshi yawned and rubbed the sleep from his eyes. Quietly, and with the light tread of someone trained in martial arts, he walked on bare feet down the hall towards the bathroom at the far end of the hallway. He had to pass the stairs to get to the bathroom. Something hit him like an express train of stink. He coughed.

And what he saw going down the stairs caused Hiroshi's sleepy eyes to widen with surprise. There before him was a stinky Bigfoot descending the stairs.

As if sensing someone was watching, the Bigfoot came to a sudden stop and looked over its shoulder. It stared at Hiroshi for a brief, wondrous moment.

Hiroshi blinked at the sight before his eyes. Was it a real Bigfoot or just someone dressed up as the creature? It looked real to Hiroshi, but since when did Bigfoot stay at hotels? His heart pounded with excitement, and with just a hint of fear, for supposing it was a real Bigfoot and was in a bad mood. It could attack. Hiroshi was a black belt in karate. He thought if the creature attacked he could defend himself, for this Bigfoot wasn't exactly as tall as everyone was made to believe.

"Bigfoot san . . . Hiroshi friend," he said pointing a finger at himself and bowing.

The Bigfoot looked away from Hiroshi with a growl and continued on its way down the stairs two steps at a time.

"Hey, Bigfoot, wait for me," Hiroshi called out excitedly in a raised voice. He pointed his finger at Bigfoot.

At that moment lights were turned on in virtually every room in the hotel. Frantic Japanese clambered with sleepy eyes for their cameras as the alert to the presence of a Bigfoot could be heard.

The Bigfoot became frantic also, and in its eagerness to flee, missed the lower step, tumbling onto the floor at the bottom of the stairs and rolling across the lobby.

Hiroshi charged down the stairs after the clumsy Bigfoot.

The Bigfoot got quickly to its feet, swaying slightly, as if it had had a little too much to drink.

Hiroshi reached the lower step and dived across the lobby. He grabbed a hold of the Bigfoot's furry ankle.

The furry creature wriggled itself free of Hiroshi's hold and gave the Japanese a hefty kick, causing him to roll backwards across the floor. The Bigfoot then made haste to leave and headed for the main door to the hotel.

A stunned Hiroshi could only watch as the Bigfoot ran across the hotel lobby. He noticed the stunned look on the female desk clerk as she watched the incredible sight.

THE BIGFOOT HIROSHI had seen that night was none other than MB. His plan was to create a stir. The plan apparently succeeded. Why he did such a thing and allowed himself to become one with the Phantom Bigfoot was quite simple—he'd had too many at Abe's that night. And once Duane had told him he was the Phantom Bigfoot, MB jumped in with both big feet. Old Indian legend tells us that man who drinks too much gets up to all kinds of mischief.

BOTH FBI AGENTS—like the majority of those present in the hotel that summer's night—had been awoken by Hiroshi's cry of Bigfoot. And like the majority of those present in the hotel that night, they opened their bedroom doors and stepped into the hallway to see what the commotion was all about.

Guests spilled out into the hallway. Excited Japanese with cameras and camcorders at the ready were eager to finally catch a glimpse of Bigfoot. Who would have thought it would be at the hotel?

MERLOT, DRESSED IN HER skimpy baby-doll, looked at a tousled-haired and sleepy-eyed Willis, dressed in his regulation white boxer shorts, as he stepped out into the hallway.

"Someone called out Bigfoot," Merlot commented with a yawn. She glanced down the hallway at the Japanese en masse making their way towards the stairs.

"Yeah, I heard," Willis replied with an irritated edge to his voice. "I was sound asleep."

Merlot glanced back at her partner and could see he wasn't in the best of moods by the scowl on his face. She knew her partner was always in a better frame of mind if he'd had a good night's sleep. If he didn't he could be real touchy, not that anyone could tell the difference these days.

"Go back to bed. I'll see what's going on," Merlot offered.

"What's the point . . . I'm awake now. Huh, won't get back off to sleep now, anyway. Better get dressed and see what's going on."

Merlot nodded her head in agreement as she attempted to go back into her room, but was swept away by the throng of guests heading for the stairs.

Willis was also swept away by the tide of fervent, camera-happy guests, most of which were Japanese.

MERLOT AND WILLIS LISTENED TO an excited Hiroshi pointing at the hotel exit and exclaiming in a confused mixture of Japanese and English what he had seen. Neither agent could speak Japanese, but Merlot quickly deduced that Hiroshi had seen someone dressed up in a Bigfoot costume leaving the hotel through the lobby door. Probably that piece of driftwood, Duane!

Merlot was all smiles, for unlike her cranky partner, she didn't mind being woken up, especially for something as stupid as this. "Must have been someone dressed up in a Bigfoot costume . . ." She chuckled, ". . . Unless Bigfoot likes room service. Wouldn't surprise me in this town."

A petite Japanese woman, dressed in a red kimono, ran down the stairs holding something in her hand and waving it excitedly in the air.

"Bigfoot photo. Bigfoot photo," she gasped in a voice breathless with excitement.

The FBI agents gave her questioning looks as she made her way over to them.

The woman bowed. "Please, I found photo slid under door of bedroom."

She handed the photograph to Merlot.

Merlot and Willis looked with total surprise at the photograph of a Bigfoot seated upon a toilet eating a doughnut. Both agents grimaced with disgust at the image totally lacking in couth.

"Yuck!" Willis said.

"Double yuck. How can anyone eat on the toilet?" Merlot exclaimed.

"Exactly," Willis agreed with a shudder.

Several Japanese who were standing nearby spied the photograph with excited gasps.

Akira exclaimed, "It's the sewial bather." He stared at Merlot's body.

Willis turned from the lurid photograph. He glanced at his partner and saw the grin on her face. "This keeps getting worse."

Keep it coming, mused Merlot. She was flattered by Akira's drooling ogle. She smiled coyly at him. She was having the time of her life.

29

IT TOOK SHERIFF LOU forty minutes to show up at the hotel and by then Dwight had already taken Hiroshi's and the Japanese woman's statements. She was in a very low mood, having to scramble into her cop's outfit and sober up with a couple of cups of strong black coffee.

All of the sheriff's deputies were on the scene and asking questions when Lou walked in through the lobby door, a little wobbly on her feet. She saw Willis resplendent in his boxer shorts talking to a Japanese woman and Dwight. She saw the elderly hotel owner, Grace, handing out cups of tea and coffee with biscuits to her excited guests.

Merlot looked in Lou's direction and attracted her over with a wave of her hand.

Lou approached the agent slowly, careful not to make it obvious that she was a little unsteady on her feet. She knew if any of her deputies asked her to walk in a straight line, she would fail. Thankfully, it was impossible to do that in the crowded room. Her weaving this way and that to dodge excited guests helped hide her drunken state.

"Agent Merlot," she said in a matter-of-fact tone of voice. On noticing Merlot's see-through attire, Lou removed her jacket and handed it to her. She saw the disappointed looks on the men and heard their sighs.

Merlot gave Lou the photograph to look at, suppressing a fit of the giggles while putting on Lou's jacket. "Thank you, Lou."

"Don't mention it." Lou grimaced as she studied the image of the Bigfoot eating the doughnut. She shook her head and frowned. *Hold on—the MO was different.* The Phantom Bigfoot entered people's homes and bathed or whatever he did—he never left a photo of said crime. She looked up from the photograph and noticed Willis staring at her. She made eye contact with him but was distracted by the sound of Merlot's giggles.

Lou gave Merlot a cool look then looked back at the photograph, for something didn't gel.

"The toilet doesn't match any of the toilets in the hotel," she commented. "They're all white low flush jobs to save our precious water." Lou paused and looked thoughtful, "Though I'm not that much of an expert on Big Beaver's facilities . . . but I know this beige toilet from somewhere. Guess we'd have to do a house to house search." She paused again and gave another thoughtful look. "Well, this is certainly something new."

Dwight said, "Hey, Lou, we could put up posters around town and pictures on milk cartons? You know—has anyone seen this toilet?"

Merlot erupted into laughter at such a stupid suggestion.

Dwight looked upset at the effect his brilliant idea was having.

"Give your brain a rest, Dwight," Lou insisted with eyebrows raised.

"Could be a copycat . . . or it could be the perp has changed his MO by taking photographs of the . . ." Merlot faltered and bit down on her lower lip in an attempt to hold back a fit of the giggles.

Lou gave Merlot another cool look. She could see that the agent was about to break into a fresh bout of giggles.

"The crime scene," Lou said, finishing off Merlot's sentence.

Lou directed her attention towards Willis and couldn't believe how much of a complete fool she had been last night—no, make that *this* night. What an idiot she'd been to think they could get back together. It was over. Her chin began to wobble.

He'd changed so much. Just look at him. Look at that block of ice. To think she ever had a chance to thaw that iceberg? How could she still want him? Problem was—she did still want him—more than ever. Damn him!

"This sounds like Duane's doing," Dwight remarked, trying to restore what little dignity he ever had.

"Yeah, well duh . . . it goes without saying." Lou frowned. "Guess we'd better go ask him." As she spoke she and Willis tried to avoid eye contact and failed.

Willis had a pensive look on his face. He didn't say a word. He appeared deep in thought.

Lou's trusty gut told her that Willis had something other than the Phantom Bigfoot on his mind. She took a guess and thought he was thinking about what had happened between them earlier that night. She didn't know if that was a good thing or not.

Deputy Heidi overheard their conversation and pulled Sheriff Lou aside.

She whispered into Lou's ear, "Uh, it couldn't have been Duane."

"It couldn't?" Lou asked with a questioning frown on her face.

Heidi continued to whisper, "No way sheriff! He's been with me and Annie. We've sort of had him cuffed to the bed all night . . . well . . . almost all night. He stunk up the place so bad we gave him a sponge bath, and well, you know . . . one thing led to another."

It was no secret that Duane was doing the Bumsen Sisters. They sure had a thing for him, thought Lou. She'd heard talk that Duane was quite a vigorous lover when he put his mind to it. And he'd have to be damned vigorous to satisfy the Bumsen Sisters.

"You don't say," Lou said.

The FBI agents and Deputy Dwight watched and listened as Lou and Deputy Heidi talked about Duane's love life.

Lou knew she should be annoyed with Deputy Heidi for using sheriff's department issue handcuffs to facilitate a sexual act. She smiled. She could only imagine what the two sisters were capable of doing with Duane cuffed to the bed. She suppressed her desire to chuckle and remained serious-faced. This she had to see.

"Come on, Heidi."

෧   ෧   ෧

LESS THAN TEN MINUTES later—the time it took for both agents to get dressed, Sheriff Lou, Willis, Merlot and Deputy Heidi stood in the alley outside a door marked private. Familiar muted music could be heard.

Lou and the agents followed Deputy Heidi through an alleyway entrance and up a flight of narrow stairs to the apartment above Annie's Diner. Lou recognized James Brown's timeless classic "Sex Machine" blasting through the building.

They reached the upper hallway and stood on the landing listening to the words—"*Get on up like a sex machine.*"

"This way," Deputy Heidi said as she led the way down the hallway.

The sheriff and the FBI agents followed.

Outside a closed door to one of the rooms, Deputy Heidi halted. The sheriff and the FBI agents did the same.

They listened to the loud music coming from within the room.

Just as Lou put her hand on the doorknob, Annie came down the hall carrying a tray with food. She was wearing a sexy, female Native-American outfit and Bigfoot slippers.

Annie froze in surprise at the sight of the unexpected visitors. She gave her sister a questioning look.

"Oh . . . hi, Annie, we need to speak to Duane," her sister explained.

"Sure thing," Annie replied, a little unsure of the situation.

"Someone dressed in a Bigfoot outfit caused quite a ruckus at the hotel just over an hour ago," Lou explained.

Annie shrugged her shoulders. "Ooh, you don't say."

"Can you confirm that Duane has been with you for the past two hours?" Willis asked in his regulation voice.

Annie's eyes rounded and she gave a naughty grin. "Oh yeah, I can confirm Duane's been with me for the past few hours."

As Annie spoke, Lou turned the doorknob and opened the door. She looked inside the candlelit room with its mirrored ceiling.

And there, cuffed by his ankles and wrists to a big four-poster bed with police issue restraints, was Duane. He was almost naked, apart from a leather loincloth that barely covered his goods.

James Brown went silent. A muted pause filled the air.

Lou gave a wry smile. She knew she should look away from the sight of Duane spread-eagled on the bed, but couldn't. She was thankful he didn't have a hard on, that would have been too much.

The FBI agents and Deputy Heidi looked into the room and saw Duane, apparently asleep. The music started up with Robert Palmer's "Addicted to Love."

Robert Palmer sang, *"The lights are on, but no one's home."*

Lou looked at Duane and smirked. That line sure summed him up.

Willis grimaced with disgust.

Merlot sniggered then giggled, "What's gonna happen next?" She had to shout above the music. She immortalized Duane on her cell phone, blurting out, "Nicely hung for a piece of driftwood."

Willis gave a sharp look to Merlot.

Merlot shrugged it off with a poke of her tongue.

Duane opened his eyes and looked at his audience with a wide sloppy grin on his face.

"Hi, guys."

Lou had to bite down on her lower lip to stop herself from laughing. It wouldn't do to have a fit of the giggles in front of Willis and Merlot. She needed to be professional about all of this and laughing like a schoolgirl was not the way to go about the place if she wanted to maintain appearances. She was the sheriff, not like Merlot, a giggling twinkie. She gave Merlot a quick look to stop giggling.

Merlot couldn't stop.

"Duane, I don't know what to say," Lou smirked, walking a few paces into the room.

The FBI agents followed the sheriff into the room, followed by Annie with the tray in her hands.

Showing no sign of embarrassment at being caught with his pants off, Duane continued to smile. "Real nice to see you all," he said, waving rather limply. "Come on in and take a load off."

Merlot suddenly burst out into paroxysms of laughter. "This is too much."

Willis gave his partner a scathing look, but didn't say anything. He had to bite his lip from joining Merlot in laughter.

Merlot's infectious laughter was all Lou needed to hear. She began to laugh, though it was no more than a titter and chuckle.

"Duane! You sure look a sight to behold."

"Why, thank you, Lou," he agreed with a boyish grin.

Willis' disgusted look began to falter and the corners of his lips turned upwards into a smile. And if anyone looked close enough they would have seen the humor in his eyes.

"Duane, you horny, dumbass bastard," Willis said with a smirk.

Both sisters joined in on the merriment and started laughing.

Duane nodded his head in agreement, "That I am, Willis. That I am."

"How long have you been . . . uh . . . here like this, Duane?" Lou asked, thoroughly amused.

Duane tried to look at his wristwatch, only to see he wasn't wearing one, "Can't honestly say, Lou." He looked to Annie for an answer.

Annie, still holding the tray, filled in the timeslot, "It's gotta be at least . . . four times ago . . . oh, I'd say three hours. That's about right, Heidi?"

Deputy Heidi nodded in agreement with absolutely no hint of embarrassment.

Lou looked impressed with Duane's sexual endurance. She was about to leave when something dawned on her. "Oh by the way, where's your Bigfoot costume?"

"It's being aired," Annie chipped in.

Lou seemed satisfied with Annie's reply and left.

30

WHILE THE SHERIFF and both FBI agents stared dumbfounded at Duane's private parts, Olaaa stared with lovesick eyes at her pale plaything.

The lights were on as the cave was illuminated by one of Duane's battery-operated storm lamps that she had sort of borrowed.

Olaaa sat on her haunches looking wantonly at Boo with her large, round eyes. She had good eyesight in the dark, as did all Bigfoot. The storm light was for her plaything's benefit so he could see his surroundings and would not be afraid.

She lovingly watched Boo slowly awaken. She sighed with a faraway smile on her face, sniffing a dog rose in her hand. The entire floor of the cave was festooned with various forest flowers of every color.

She sniffed the sweet scented air and gave a bleat, "Woooooooo."

Boo was still tied up but he was no longer gagged. He suddenly sat upright and looked afraid and confused at Olaaa. He tried to back away from her, but she had used vines to bind his hands to a large boulder. He quickly gave up and slumped on his side.

Olaaa smiled sweetly at him, "woooooo-woooooo-wooooo."

On the floor at Boo's feet was a chunk of bark piled with various berries and nuts that Olaaa had collected just for him.

She indicated hunger by rubbing her belly and shoving fingers to her mouth.

He eased himself up to a sitting position, moistening his dry lips with his tongue.

"Look . . . I know you're not a real Bigfoot. This is some kind of joke . . . right, Duane?"

Olaaa didn't fully understand what he'd just said, but the word "Duane" struck a chord. She tilted her head and looked questioningly at him for several moments.

"Please untie me," Boo begged, showing his bound wrists.

Olaaa stared at her plaything for several seconds without responding then shook her head, no, as she understood his meaning.

"Is that a no?" Boo asked with a frown.

Olaaa smiled a sweet smile.

"I know you're not for real. If you ain't Duane, you must be MB. So stop fooling around and let me go."

Olaaa cocked her head at his strange words then leaned forward and picked up several berries from the plate. She held them in front of Boo's mouth.

Boo looked at the delicious berries with obvious hunger. He opened his mouth and allowed himself to be baby fed by Olaaa.

After he'd eaten everything from the bark, Olaaa removed a bright white dog rose from her hair and tried to place it behind Boo's ear.

The teenager looked warily into Olaaa's beautiful, big eyes and reared away.

She gave a hurt look and bleated.

Boo relaxed with a timid smile and offered his ear for the rose.

"No funny stuff, Duane, or whoever the fuck you are."

Olaaa mewled pathetically as she slipped the flower behind his ear. If only she could make him understand that she wouldn't hurt him—that she loved him.

"Woooo-woooo-woooo."

"Okay, I've had enough of this kinky shit," Boo exclaimed. "It's time to let me go."

Olaaa picked up on his fear. She gave a shrug of her shoulders and mewled, "Woooo-woooo-woooo."

Suddenly, a loud growl filled the cave, "Raaaaarrrrrraaaaarrrrraaaaaaarrrrrr."

Boo's expression turned to abject terror. He squealed and tried to hide behind the boulder.

Olaaa turned her attention away from Boo to look at a massive, shimmering blond Bigfoot with perky suckle-bumps standing in the entrance to the cave. She knew Ooonaaa couldn't keep a secret. Ooonaaa would tell the other Bigfoot she had taken a pale plaything.

"Weeeeeeaaaaaaeeeeeeoooooeeeeee," Olaaa screamed hysterically, which basically meant—get outta my cave, bitch.

Tears filled Olaaa's eyes as Ooonaaa threatened her with the stamping-of-feet ritual. Olaaa knew it was time to let Boo go home. Olaaa slumped to the floor and began to weep.

"Hey guys, is that real fur or what?" Boo asked. With increasing confusion and awe his eyes took in the excessively large muscles rippling beneath the fur on the larger, blond Bigfoot. He stared at her pert breasts clearly visible through her blond chest fur.

"You ain't Duane ... I know that's gotta be you, Annie 'cause Bigfoot can't be stacked like that. Come on, let me go. I've had enough, okay?" He looked into the large blue eyes glaring at him, "Annie?"

Ooonaaa stomped up to the pale one and raised a massive big foot above his head.

Boo closed his eyes, "Oh, fuck no!"

The big foot crashed down on the lamp, plunging the cave into darkness. By the light of the silvery moon, Boo fainted to the floor.

Olaaa realized Ooonaaa had actually facilitated Boo's escape by removing the light so she could sneak out with him. She untied the vines binding Boo to the boulder with clumsy fingers, weeping for her plaything.

31

THE DINING ROOM of the Grace Hotel was bursting with guests eating a hearty breakfast after the previous night's fun at Abe's. Almost a full, three-quarters of the guests were the Japanese tourists still happily chatting and wildly gesticulating about the Bigfoot sighting.

Merlot entered the pine-clad restaurant with its quota of animal heads stuck here and there, along with local American Indian paraphernalia—arrows, spears and leather shields. She casually walked over to her designated table.

As Merlot perused the breakfast menu, a good looking young waiter arrived at her table to take her order. He was just her type on her woodometer—good fresh mahogany sapling full of sap. Merlot eyed him up and down with an amorous glint in her eye.

The tall, muscular waiter with shiny black hair appreciated the look the FBI agent gave him and smiled.

"Hello there, gorgeous, my name's Agent Merlot, Candice Merlot, but my friends call me Merlot, because I go down in a velvety, smooth way."

The waiter smiled and tried to look coy. He obviously understood the sexual metaphor by the expression on his face.

"You're something I could drink any day, Merlot."

Merlot gave a confident smile. She knew it wasn't FBI policy to chat up the locals, but in a town like Big Beaver such rules seemed trivial and nonsensical. And yet surprisingly there was no major crime, she thought.

"And what's your name, sweet thing?"

"Mario," he replied with a blush, pointing to his name label on his chest.

"Well, Mario, if you would be so kind to fetch me one egg over easy, a couple of rashers of bacon, not too crispy, four waffles, orange juice and plenty of black coffee." She noticed Mario's eyebrows raised, "Breakfast is the most important meal of the day . . . oh, and a big glass of prune juice for my partner, Agent Tightass. He sure needs it."

Mario chuckled at Merlot's reference to her bunged-up partner as he scribbled down the order in his notebook.

"Will there be anything else, Merlot?" Mario looked at the sexy FBI agent and moistened his lips with his tongue.

Yes, there was, Merlot thought, but there wasn't any time to nibble on Mario's board-au-fare. She sighed with regret at his firm butt as he walked away.

Merlot looked up to see Willis enter the room. She quickly surmised that her partner was not in the best of moods, as was the case every damned morning these days. Her thoughts of Mario dissipated at the sight of her partner.

Willis looked disgruntled at the boisterous Japanese who had started to re-enact the previous night's barroom brawl and Hiroshi's encounter with Bigfoot. He shook his head with dismay as he approached Merlot.

Mario soon returned with Merlot's orange juice, coffee and a glass of prune juice.

"Breakfast will be another few more minutes."

Merlot didn't mind the wait as she watched him saunter to another table. She picked up the glass of orange juice and sipped. *Hmm, freshly squeezed! Perfect!* Over the rim of her glass she watched Willis approaching their table.

Willis sat down opposite Merlot without saying a word. He glanced up as Mario arrived with notebook and pencil at the ready.

The waiter stood at the table in an impatient manner waiting to take his order.

"Coffee, black, a large bowl of oatmeal and two bran muffins," Willis ordered in his matter-of-fact tone of voice.

Mario scribbled the order down, glanced at Merlot and gave her a smile before saying, "Oh yeah, he sure needs it." With that he hurried off to the kitchens.

Willis glanced at the waiter and frowned, "What do you suppose he meant by that?"

Merlot watched her partner take a sip of his prune juice. "You really need to lighten up." She took a sip of her freshly ground coffee. Even more perfect! She looked at Willis' prune juice. "You ever tried mixing some rum with that stuff?" She chuckled. "Guaranteed to reach the parts that others cannot, real fast."

Willis didn't reply at his partner's crude remark.

"That was quite a night, wouldn't you say? And that Duane . . . he sure is one of a kind," Merlot commented.

Willis didn't reply, he just quietly sipped his prune juice and nodded his head in agreement.

Merlot eyed her partner with a mixture of mischief and curiosity. "You know, I could have sworn I heard you talking to someone last night."

Willis narrowed his eyes and looked coolly at his partner.

"Someone of the female persuasion . . . about an hour or so before Bigfoot paid a visit." Merlot studied her partner's unsmiling face wondering if there'd be a reaction.

Willis stiffened in his chair and gave his partner a withering look. He didn't speak. He sighed heavily.

Merlot continued, "What a night . . . first a barroom brawl, then the sheriff pays you a visit begging you to do her brains out . . . and last, but not least, Bigfoot shows up at our hotel. Oh, let's not forget Duane caught with his pants down." Merlot sniggered, "I'll never forget that sight as long as I live."

Willis' annoyance was beginning to boil over and yet he didn't reply. He scowled at Merlot's grinning face over the rim of his glass of prune juice.

Merlot thought about dropping the subject, but she had a devilish streak in her that forced her to push Willis until something gave. When it came to teasing her partner, Merlot knew no bounds. Up until the last couple of months, Willis didn't seem to mind the teasing, but that was then, in the good old days. Merlot knew from her partner's nasty look that she was pissing him off. It was so much fun!

"Sheriff Lou could do with a hunk of real wood," she said with a devious smirk. "Something maybe you can't offer."

Willis' eyes narrowed as he slowly put down his glass of prune juice. "Don't push it, Candice."

Merlot hesitated for a moment. She knew she was treading a thin line when Willis called her by that name.

"Take this anyway you like, Willis, but if you don't do her then I'm sure Duane will." She gave her partner a cheeky grin and showed her cell phone.

Willis didn't reply straight away. His cheeks turned a bright pink, a clear indication that he was getting riled. "If you were a man, I'd deck you."

Merlot feigned fear, putting her hands up in defense. "Please don't whip me, massah . . . I'll be a good slave, massah," she said in her "*Roots*" voice.

The entire room went ominously quiet. All the guests stopped what they were doing to look at the feuding FBI agents. Startled murmurings emanated from the wide-eyed audience. Hushed words were spoken in Japanese, because most of the guests were Japanese.

Willis glared at Merlot, whispering harshly, "Keep it down, Candice." He picked up his glass of prune juice and took another sip. He licked his lips savoring his drink as if nothing had just happened.

"Looks like it's gonna be another shi . . . uh, fine day," Willis commented.

Despite the verbal fracas, Merlot couldn't stop herself from saying, "It's gotta be love, Willis."

Willis didn't reply. He just quietly sipped his prune juice and looked coolly at Merlot over the rim of his glass.

32

AN EXHAUSTED DUANE returned home that morning. He hoped his Bigfoot friends had left the place in a decent state as he was not in the mood for a cleanup. He propped up his Harley and removed his Bigfoot helmet.

Wearing his freshly laundered Bigfoot duds, minus the head which was strapped to the back of his bike, he entered his cabin by the front door and stopped in his tracks.

He shook his head and muttered, "How many times have I told them not to do that?"

Duane looked all around at the Bigfoot handprints, made from flour, on the walls and ceiling of the living area. Bigfoot footprints completely covered the floor, leading from the kitchen then back into it. The pantry!

Of course, Teeelaaa might still be home and sound asleep and had forgotten to clean up after their party.

"Teeelaaa, I'm home." He gave the come-hither whistle.

No reply. All was silent.

It occurred to him that they could still be inside sleeping. Bigfoot liked to sleep a lot, more so in the winter when the temperature dropped and there was snow on the ground and less food to forage. Though they didn't hibernate as long as bears, they did sleep, huddled together for warmth for very long periods. The longest Duane had measured was one week.

He wondered if they'd found his stash of water in the crawl space above the pantry. He didn't mind them getting loaded but they had a habit of throwing up and totally trashing the place—like now. Maybe Maaawooo had thrown a hissy fit when he had discovered Duane had tricked him.

Oh what the hell! He gave a big yawn as he trudged into the kitchen. Shit! He stared aghast at the remains of his kitchen, the missing rear door and the space where the pantry used to be. He could clearly see where his friends had scraped their butts along the wooden floor leaving a trail of thick goo. And yet he couldn't feel angry. It was just play to Bigfoot, and they loved to play.

Duane was feeling hungover and exhausted from spending the night pleasing the Bumsen Sisters. They'd drained him of his manly juices. He realized that just like his Bigfoot friends, the Bumsen Sisters took advantage of his good nature. They just won't take no for an answer, even when he told them he couldn't get it up for the fourth time in one night. Maybe if the sisters weren't such vigorous lovers he wouldn't feel so exhausted, but they liked to do a lot of active stuff.

Duane gave another big yawn. He was looking forward to some quality sack time, and if Duane had been wide awake and not thinking about getting some Zs he might have sensed danger when he had entered his cabin, but he didn't sense danger because it would never occur to him to expect danger here.

Duane sauntered back into the living room looking around at the empty bottles of tequila on the floor.

He called out, "Teeelaaa, Maaawooo, Olaaa—anyone here?"

No reply. All was silent.

Duane listened to the silence. A perplexed look came over his face. The hairs on the back of his neck started to prickle and his stomach started to gurgle. But Duane was tired and hungover. He wasn't paying too much attention to the prickles on the back of his neck and his gurgling stomach that was telling him something was wrong. His bleary eyes didn't see the heavy boot prints mixed with Bigfoot prints.

From somewhere in the cabin he heard floorboards creaking. He gave another frown. It crossed his mind that Teeelaaa was playing hide and seek. She loved that game. All Bigfoot loved to play hide and seek. It helped to hone their skills at evading capture.

Duane heard another creak.

Suddenly the door to the bedroom swung open, and there standing in the doorway was that big bully of a bear, Walt Flucker, brandishing a rifle at a startled and alarmed Duane.

"Shit, Walt, I almost crapped my pants." Duane blew out air and breathed deeply. "What the fuck're you doing here?"

Walt sauntered into the room looking mean and tough. He wasn't alone.

Chuck and Bob emerged from behind him with rifles at the ready.

Duane suddenly felt a bit queasy at the sight of his unwelcome visitors. Not that he thought they had plans to take pot shots at him, but more than likely they planned on roughing him up. It had happened before. And no doubt Chuck and Bob were looking to even the score for what he'd done to them the previous day in the woods.

Duane smiled amiably, in the vain hope that if he gave them one of his amiable smiles they'd change their minds about roughing him up. It sometimes worked.

Walt narrowed his eyes. "Where's my boy, Beau?" He snarled like a grizzly.

"How the fuck should I know?" Duane shrugged.

Walt took a few menacing steps closer to Duane. "Don't believe you, asshole." He looked around the living room and wrinkled his nose with disgust. "Something weird's going on here . . . and what's that God awful smell?" Walt sniffed the pungent air. "It ain't skunk and it ain't grizzly shit." Walt glared at Duane, "That stink's gotta be you . . . and anything that smells that bad's gotta be guilty of something."

Duane decided to play the innocent—something he was good at doing, and took a big sniff. He got a faint waft of air freshener, but even he had to admit the place smelt bad with Bigfoot body odor.

Duane chuckled and sniffed his armpits, "Maybe it's you."

Walt's face darkened. "You asshole!" he shouted. He aimed his rifle at Duane's head. "You're gonna get it for sure if you don't tell me where you've stashed Beau."

All of a sudden there was a loud growl as Maaawooo stood in the doorway behind Duane.

"Raaaaarrrraaaarrrrraaaaarrrr."

Duane looked over his shoulder and saw his Bigfoot buddy.

He muttered under his breath, "Just fucking great."

What was Maaawooo doing here? How was he going to explain him to Walt and the other two idiots?

Walt narrowed his eyes and looked at the menacing Bigfoot, standing at least seven feet tall. He walked towards the Bigfoot without showing any fear.

"Is that you Beau?" Walt asked without much conviction. Beau wasn't that tall.

Maaawooo growled a big ferocious growl at Walt and the two hunters. He showed his yellowed teeth.

"Rrrrraaaaaarrrrrraaaaarrrrrraaaaa."

Walt must be fucking blind drunk if he can't see that Maaawooo is a real Bigfoot, thought Duane.

"Uh, Walt . . . I wouldn't get too close if I were you," he warned, knowing that Maaawooo had a strong dislike of men with guns and had a justifiable grudge towards them.

Not that Maaawooo or any Bigfoot that he knew went about the place pouncing on people and having them for dinner, like some grizzlies he knew. Bigfoot were generally peaceful creatures, and didn't like to get into fights, but Maaawooo always had a bit of temper and like all Bigfoot—a long memory.

Undeterred, and no doubt still thinking the big creature in front of him was a mock-up, Walt continued to advance on Maaawooo. He came to a stop in front of the big creature.

Maaawooo scowled at the rifle in Walt's hand and growled a low menacing growl, "Rrrraaaarrrr."

With one swift yank, Maaawooo tore the rifle from a surprised Walt's grasp. With his massive hands, Maaawooo bent the rifle in two and tossed it onto the floor.

It must be obvious to Walt by now that the big creature could not be a mock-up, mused Duane.

Walt looked at the bent rifle on the floor and stepped back a pace.

He shook his head in fear and disbelief, spluttering, "No fucking way, man . . . I-i-i-it can't be." He began to whimper.

This could get ugly, thought Duane as he saw Chuck and Bob take aim at Maaawooo. Teeelaaa got up from behind the sofa and quietly crept behind Chuck and Bob.

Chuck and Bob dropped their guns and squealed as Teeelaaa picked them up by the scruff of the neck.

Teeelaaa let out a ferocious growl, "Rrrraaaarrrrraaaarrrr."

Duane shook his head, "You'll never learn, Walt."

"L-l-l-earn w-w-what?" Walt stammered in terror for his life.

Duane casually raised the trapdoor to the basement. He whistled to Maaawooo and Teeelaaa to bring the three assholes down into the basement.

SOME TWENTY MINUTES LATER Walt and his buddies were back to back on the basement floor, trussed up like turkeys. All three whimpered, struggling to get free.

The overhead light was dim and cast dark shadows into the corners of the room, but Walt could see the two Bigfoot looming over him with snarling faces.

Duane sat on a chair facing them. He thought the situation called for him to act mean. But he knew that Walt and his buddies wouldn't think him capable of doing anything unpleasant to them. So Duane scratched his butt—it worked—he had a brainwave—he would act the good guy. His two Bigfoot friends would play the bad guys.

Maaawooo and Teeelaaa stood behind him, looking menacing. They were already in bad guy character, and didn't need any directions on his part.

In fact, Duane sensed that Maaawooo was in a very bad mood and not just because of Walt and his buddies. Maaawooo was sorely displeased with him—Duane-o.

Duane guessed that after he'd left to go into town last night his Bigfoot friends must have gone looking for more booze. Duane pondered the matter for some moments and came to the conclusion that he must have forgotten to lock the pantry door. After finishing scratching his butt, he realized that Maaawooo would want some real tequila to get his harem of Bigfoot babes in the mood for some serious three-way woooo-woooo.

Duane made a promise to himself that after he'd sorted things out with Walt and his buddies, he'd give Maaawooo three bottles of the real thing.

"First things first . . . let me introduce you to Maaawooo and Teeelaaa . . . hmm, friends of mine."

Walt looked fearfully at the Bigfoot.

But Chuck and Bob didn't look fearful at all as they craned their necks to get a better look. They had amused looks on their faces.

"Nice tits," Chuck chuckled.

Teeelaaa growled at Chuck.

"Are they . . . you know . . . for real?" Walt asked with a tremor of fear in his voice.

Duane shrugged, "Come on Walt . . . we all know Bigfoot doesn't exist . . . and yet, if they don't exist, then who are these two cuddly critters in the basement with us right now?"

Maaawooo growled a big growl at Walt and his buddies and took a few menacing steps towards them. He stomped his foot down in a suggestive way.

Bob shook his head. He gave the Bigfoot a skeptical look.

"You ain't for real. No such fucking thing as Bigfoot."

"Yeah, if they was real, we would have shot one by now," Chuck said.

"Yeah, you could both be right," Duane agreed.

"I say they are fucking real," Walt insisted with eyes wide in terror. "Shit . . . haven't I always said Bigfoot exists?"

Chuck laughed at his gullible friend. "Yeah, well, I say they ain't for real. It's typical of you, Walt, to think this furry piece of shit is genuine." He gave Maaawooo a mocking look then looked at Walt. "Tell me again, Walt, what did those sexy Swedish-looking female aliens do to you?"

Walt gave his companion a nasty look. He struggled to be free of his restraints. "Shut your stupid fucking mouth," he sneered.

Duane smiled as he listened to Walt's and Chuck's discord, "Now, now boys." He pointed to Maaawooo. "You don't want to upset these guys more than you already have."

"You can let us fucking go any time you want," Walt snarled. "If you don't, I'm gonna rip you a new one."

Of course, Duane knew he'd have to let them go. There was no choice. He gave Walt and his companions a keen look.

"You can't go to the sheriff . . . she'll lock you up for trespass with intent."

Walt thought for a moment, "That's true, but there's no reason we can't tell the press about your Bigfoot friends."

It occurred to Duane that no one would believe Walt, no matter how true his story might be, not after his alien abduction tales.

"Who's gonna believe you?" Duane asked. "I'll tell you who—no one."

Walt nodded his head yes in agreement, "Huh, that's also true, damn it."

Maaawooo gave another growl. He took a step forward with a thunderous stomp. His immense size cast a shadow over Walt and his buddies.

Walt looked fearfully up at Maaawooo, "please, don't hurt me."

"Please, don't hurt me," Chuck mimicked in a teasing voice with a snigger.

Then Maaawooo did something strange, something that not even Duane would have figured. Maaawooo leaned real close, face-to-face with Walt and sniffed him. He sniffed Walt all over then as a final insult, kissed Walt on the cheek. Maaawooo waved Teeelaaa to have a go. She did the same. Both Bigfoot stepped back and mewed.

Duane frowned at his Bigfoot friends and wondered what they were up to.

"They must love you, Walt," Bob chuckled.

"Okay, I'll let you three go," Duane said with a smile. "But be warned, if you ever go after Maaawooo or his Bigfoot friends, I'll let Maaawooo do what he wants to you." Duane laughed as he started for the stairs.

"What the fuck, Duane? You said you'd let us go," Walt pleaded desperately.

Duane waved to the three butt holes tied up in his basement and exited with a chuckle, "Be seeing you."

"You fucking asshole," Walt shouted just as Maaawooo gripped his thruster and pissed all over them.

33

A LITTLE OVER AN HOUR LATER, a thoroughly hungover MB was crouched behind some thickly tangled brambles with his listening gear attached to his ears. The sound of heavy feet had piqued his interest.

MB used his hands to spread a hole in the thicket and peered into the forest. His eyes bulged almost from their sockets. He told himself what he was looking at wasn't real.

Trees and undergrowth partly obscured his view of the tall Bigfoot as it strode across the small meadow.

It had to be Duane-o, he thought.

MB was quick to notice the wild flowers behind the Bigfoot's ears and a string of dog rose around its neck. Who else could it be, but Duane-o?

But something was different about Duane's Bigfoot costume. It was a different color—it was a reddish foxy color and streaked with golden flashes with a golden flash down its snout. The hair appeared to look like real hair, not the lifeless fur on Duane's costume, and quite fluffy and rippled with muscular movements. There was also very little hair on the creature's face which, to MB, seemed very feminine, almost attractive. He frowned as he seemed to recognize the face. He concluded that his friend had bought fancy new duds and had given them to a female friend of his. Most of all, MB noticed the large breasts swinging free.

MB started to film the creature with his camcorder, but as he aimed his directional microphone at the Bigfoot, a perplexed look came over his face.

It wasn't just the color of the costume that was different—the Bigfoot had a different stride. It was a smooth, fluid stride, but a heavy stride, as if the creature was heavier in weight—much heavier than a human. And something else bothered him—the strides seemed further apart and the Bigfoot didn't lean forward as if it couldn't lock its knees in an upright position, as was the consensus of opinion. These Bigfoot walked like humans. And something else bothered MB—Duane just wasn't that tall.

The Bigfoot stopped walking to pick some flowers.

MB wondered if someone else was masquerading as Bigfoot, apart from himself and Duane, but no one came to mind. MB excitedly concluded that the hairy creature was a real Bigfoot, or miserably concluded some newcomers had trespassed into the woods for reasons unknown.

Another Bigfoot suddenly stepped out from behind some trees at the edge of the meadow and walked over to the female Bigfoot, carrying a rucksack.

MB immediately recognized the rucksack as belonging to his friend and thought the Bigfoot he was looking at had to be Duane-o. But again, the color of the Bigfoot's hair was different, almost raven black and slick as if wet or greasy, and the way it walked was exactly like the first Bigfoot. And if it was Duane, he had suddenly put on a lot of muscle.

The big-breasted Bigfoot stopped picking flowers and watched what MB assumed was her mate as he approached her.

She bleated plaintively, "woooeeeooo—wooooeeeeeooooo."

Her mate replied, "woooooo-woooooo-wooooooo."

The two Bigfoot nudged noses. There was a lot of mewls, snorts, hoots, glugs, yowls and weeee-woooos.

MB watched the amazing spectacle and recorded the animal sounds that he had heard so many times before. Yeah, it had to be old Duane-o. The no-brainer must have leg extensions on or something similar. They nudged noses again and the big male Bigfoot licked the snout of the tall female Bigfoot. It could even look like they were getting frisky. This might get interesting, thought MB.

Something big crashed through the nearby undergrowth, causing MB to give a start. A mean-looking grizzly came charging out of the woods towards the Bigfoot. It jammed its claws down and came to a stop. It gave a menacing roar and pawed the air.

MB watched the scene with eyes wide in amazement and disbelief. He didn't feel so afraid now because what he was witnessing couldn't be for real. It just couldn't. Could it?

At the sight of the grizzly, the sexy reddish Bigfoot yelped in fear and quickly hid for protection behind the bigger, muscular Bigfoot.

The grizzly charged menacingly towards them.

The male Bigfoot carefully placed the rucksack on the ground and stood erect. He gave a ferocious growl at the grizzly, revealing his yellowed teeth, beating his chest and stomping the ground.

Duane sure was getting into character, MB thought-if it was Duane?

The grizzly stopped and reared up on its hind legs and growled back.

The stacked Bigfoot stepped out from behind her mate and growled at the grizzly.

The three creatures faced each other in a Bigfoot-bear standoff.

To MB's well-attuned ears, the growls emanating from the three critters sounded like genuine animal sounds—not that he'd ever heard a genuine Bigfoot growl, except those strange noises in the woods he had heard from time to time and couldn't identify, but assumed it was Duane. The grizzly sure sounded and looked real, though. But how could it be, unless the other two creatures were also real? Nah, that's impossible.

The giant Bigfoot thumped his chest with both fists and growled ferociously. To MB's utter amazement, the Bigfoot did a clumsy roundhouse kick, clipping the grizzly's head with his massive big foot, thus confirming these were not real Bigfoot. He felt deflated, thinking Duane had fooled him yet again. Or had he?

A few moments later, the grizzly landed back down on all fours and trudged off into the woods, looking totally miserable and mewling pathetically.

MB continued to film the scene. As he watched, he thought, *nah, someone was fooling around and that someone was probably the Phantom Bigfoot.* The three creatures couldn't be real, or his name wasn't Chief Mocking Bird.

He thought the matter over for several moments before he concluded that he had just witnessed one of those kinky dress-up-as-animal sex things he'd heard about and the three creatures were performing some animal mating ritual before they did what nature intended. That meant one of the Bigfoot was Duane-o—the rucksack Bigfoot.

Yeah, it was some kinky, sex thing, thought MB, as he watched the two fluffy creatures walk hand-in-hand across the meadow. What else could it be?

And sure enough, the bigger of the two Bigfoot mounted the smaller one, and rammed the biggest bright pink cock MB had ever seen between the other's hairy hindquarters.

The rutting was over in seconds. The two Bigfoot nudged noses then skipped off across the meadow.

Duane must have had his dick surgically altered—not that MB had ever seen Duane's goods in that agitated state, or maybe Duane was wearing a massive strap-on. *You kinky bastard,* MB thought.

MB watched until the two Bigfoot disappeared into the woods and then quickly followed after the creatures. But in no time they were no longer in his sight as the trees and undergrowth became thicker. All he could do was follow his instincts and the distant sounds of crunching undergrowth.

OLAAA WALKED THROUGH the same woods with her pale plaything slung over her shoulder, fireman style. The undergrowth crackled and snapped beneath her heavy feet. The journey from her lair to Duane's cabin had taken longer than usual because her pale one had walked some of the way. She realized that he wasn't like her. He was slow on his feet and took smaller strides. He wasn't capable of walking for endless miles and he tired easily. And he also moaned and groaned a lot. Overall, Olaaa decided her precious plaything was a bit of a baby boy.

Olaaa was disappointed when Boo had collapsed in a state of exhaustion some hours ago. At first, Olaaa had carried him in her arms then she was forced to sling him over her back when her arms got tired.

Olaaa stopped and sniffed the familiar meadow air. She knew Maaawooo and Teeelaaa had been there not so long ago. The unmistakable smell of grizzly wafted through her keen, twitching snout.

Another scent caused danger signals to attack her brain—a pale one was close by. She looked all around with her keen eyesight, but saw nothing with a fire stick.

She did look up however to see the familiar swirling trails of smoke from Duane's cabin. Smoke that Duane always ensured would direct his hairy friends to safety. Olaaa surmised the cabin was no more than three thousand strides away. All Bigfoot measured distance and time by their stride.

Olaaa sighed. She felt sad at having to leave her woooo-woooo plaything. She also felt sad at how much of a baby he was and knew he wasn't meant for her. He needed to be with his own kind. So Olaaa paced off the three thousand strides towards Duane's cabin with Boo slung over her shoulder. Her puppy love moment had gone. She had grown up.

MB WAS HIDING WITHIN A thicket at the edge of Little Beaver picnic area staring at another scene that was so extraordinary that he had to film it. Before MB's astonished eyes were Walt, Bob and Chuck, tied butt naked to that damned leaky tree with the yellow crime scene tape. *Gives a new meaning to tie a yellow ribbon,* MB mused. All three were gagged with their own torn clothing which lay in tatters at their feet. MB suppressed the urge to giggle as all three assholes struggled to be free. *So that's what you three get up to in the woods,* mused MB. He wondered if they were involved in the kinky, animal sex thing. Probably not.

Maybe this is how the Swedish-looking aliens leave Walt? Cool! He suppressed chuckles and silently left the three assholes tied to their tree to do whatever three assholes tied to a tree could possibly do.

But MB was distracted by excited Japanese voices approaching from the west. He crouched back down and filmed Hiroshi and Akira busting their guts at the sight of three naked men tied to the tree. Hiroshi pointed at a large hairy spider crawling up Walt's leg. Both brothers became hysterical as they watched Walt squirm. *Don't untie them you idiots. Shit!* Too late, as Hiroshi and his brother released the three assholes. Time to move on.

34

FOR THE SECOND TIME in twenty-four hours, Agent Merlot looked at Duane's rustic home as if it should be in the film *Deliverance*.

The dried, brown grass grew in scattered clumps. The path leading up to the porch was just a dust trail. The remnants of a tattered picket fence stubbornly resisted nature's desire to return its wood to the forest.

She and Willis noticed Duane's Harley and shiny new Winnebago motor home.

Both agents opened the door to the Winnebago and entered. The stink of rotten eggs was quite overpowering.

Merlot looked into the tiny toilet. Beau wasn't hiding there. She failed to notice the color of the toilet – beige!

Moments later they exited the Winnebago.

Willis carefully touched the bike's engine. It was still ticking as it cooled off. He nodded to Merlot.

Willis was the first to step onto the creaky boards and waited for his partner at the front door.

Merlot gingerly stepped onto the porch and tapped each board with her foot placing any weight on it.

As Willis was about to hammer on the door, it opened, revealing a bleary-eyed, tousle-haired Duane, wearing Bigfoot pajamas and massive slippers that looked like Bigfoot feet.

Duane rubbed the sleep from his eyes and smiled his usual friendly smile, "Glad to see you've taken me up on my invite . . . so soon." He yawned widely. "Please, come in."

He stepped aside for his guests, still yawning profusely. "I guess you think I'm hiding Beau?"

"Maybe . . . maybe not," Willis replied in his regulation, stern voice.

Once inside the living room, the FBI agents surveyed their surroundings with even more disgusted looks on their faces.

Merlot sniffed the air. Her nostrils detected floral air freshener, a damp grassy smell, and something stinky like body odor mixed with something musky and unpleasant similar to the leaky tree.

"What do you think of the old place?" Duane asked his old friend in a congenial tone of voice, gesticulating proudly. "Hasn't changed much from when you used to come up here. We had some good times, back then, old buddy."

WILLIS AGREED WITH A CURT nod of his head. It looked as though the place hadn't been cleaned in—well, never. He stared with nostalgia at the stuffed steelhead on the wall above the stone fireplace. His eyes filled with tears at the sight of the faded photo above the fireplace. He clearly remembered Duane reeling in that ten-pounder. It was a day he could never forget. Willis fought back tears of regret and guilt. Doctor Fernandez was right, yet again.

Duane continued to smile and pointed to the furniture.

"Take a load off. Stick your feet up. Make yourselves at home while I make us some coffee." He continued to point to the threadbare sofa with the clumps of stuffing hanging out.

Both FBI agents exchanged glances of disgust at the prospect of sitting on such a filthy object. They hesitated for a respectable moment before using hankies to wipe it before sitting down. They tossed their hankies to the floor.

Duane smiled with amusement at the agents' unease and once they had seated themselves, he wandered off towards the kitchen.

Willis fidgeted uncomfortably. He pulled out a clump of stuffing that dug into his butt. The big problem was—the stuffing was hiding a busted spring which jabbed his tight ass. He slid over a ways.

Willis called out, "You've really tied the flow to the motif, Duane."

Duane poked his head around the door frame to the kitchen, "Nice of you to notice."

Willis said under his breath, "That's not what I meant, dumbass." He saw large Bigfoot prints made of flour and frowned, what the fuck went on here?

SEVERAL MINUTES PASSED before Duane returned from the kitchen carrying a tray with three mugs of coffee and a plate of doughnuts.

To look at Duane, no one would suspect that just over two hours ago he'd been held at gunpoint by Walt and his buddies. Not to mention the raging hangover pounding in his head and the frantic cleaning he endured—not that he had done much cleaning as the need to sleep took over his weary body.

But it wasn't every day his old friend Willis dropped in on him. He was overjoyed to see his best friend, despite feeling a tad under the weather. He wanted to hug Willis, but realized, after last night at Abe's, his dear friend wasn't into hugging and tearful reunions.

Duane placed the tray on the tree trunk section that served as a table in front of his welcome guests and sat down in his favorite, shabby armchair, the one he kept hidden from Maaawooo.

"Help yourselves," Duane offered. He picked up a mug of coffee, a doughnut and eased back into the armchair. He waited for his guests to help themselves before he took a sip of his coffee.

"Doughnuts!" Merlot wrinkled her nose. "I don't seem to have much appetite for doughnuts these days." She picked up a mug of coffee.

"Me neither," Willis said. He picked up the remaining mug of coffee.

Duane smiled as he took a mouthful of doughnut. He chewed happily on the confection, smiling at his guests' unease.

"Oh, by the way . . . did either of you see the Bigfoot at Grace Hotel?"

"No," Willis replied in a curt voice.

"If you didn't see it, it must be the Phantom Bigfoot. Heard the Bigfoot left a photograph . . . and wasn't there something about a half-eaten doughnut left at the crime scene?" Duane's expression remained casual as he bit into his doughnut. He shook his head and feigned a look of disgust. "DNA might get something from it . . . but not mine . . . wonder who it could be?"

Willis didn't reply.

"Do you have any idea?" Duane asked. He warned himself to be on his guard. He was in the presence of professionals trained in the art of detecting subterfuge and tricking individuals they suspected of committing or being a party to a crime into confessing.

"I don't really care." Willis hesitated. "But Lou is convinced it wasn't the Phantom Bigfoot . . . the MO is all wrong."

"Must be a copycat then," Duane said with a thoughtful look. He took a mouthful of doughnut and watched both agents keenly. "The things people do these days . . . makes me wonder what this world is coming to."

"Yes, most likely a copycat," Willis replied, giving Duane a curious glance.

Duane casually scratched his butt and allowed his thoughts to wander from this interrogation to MB and how eager he had been to follow in his big feet. Duane hadn't told him the whole truth as it might spread around town, but he knew one day the truth would come out about his tribe of Bigfoot and their ancestry.

Of course, Duane had no intention of hanging up the Bigfoot duds any day soon, but who could say what the future held. He had an urge—not dissimilar to geese migrating in the winter, to take a trip and see the sea. He'd like to visit his property in Florida. Say hello to a few old friends he hadn't seen for a while, and possibly reunite them with some relatives.

"So you agree it wasn't the Phantom Bigfoot?" Merlot probed, suppressing a fit of the giggles.

With a sigh, Duane drew himself out of his pleasant contemplations. "No . . . uh yeah, it must be a copycat."

Merlot fidgeted as a spring forced its way through the rotting material and poked her in the ass. "Really nice sofa you have, Duane." She chuckled, "must have set you back some?"

The sofa wasn't at all comfortable, thought Duane. Merlot was being a tad sarcastic. Duane took another bite of doughnut.

"You sure you won't have a doughnut . . . you could do with a few extra pounds?" Duane added, "No offense."

"None taken," Merlot replied with a bat of her eyelids.

Willis gave his partner a quick glare and kicked her foot.

"Beau's gotta show up soon, don't you think?" Duane asked, maintaining the serious façade.

"We hope so," Willis replied.

Duane looked keenly at his old friend and changed the subject again. He was reminded of a little ditty he and Willis used to sing. He gave a smile.

"You remember that tune we used to sing about Walt? It would sure piss him off."

Willis gave his old friend a wary look. "A shame . . . but I remember."

"We were younger then," Duane said, watching his friend stir uncomfortably on the sofa.

"Enough of this reminiscing . . . we're here to ask you about Beau," Willis demanded in his matter-of-fact tone of voice.

Duane didn't hear his old friend's grouchy request. He was lost in a world of his own where he and Willis would hide in the forest and tease Walt the hunter as he was about to bag his prey. Walt's anger would never fail to cause him to miss his target.

Duane started to hum to himself then a moment later he broke into song—

"Walt Flucker thinks he's so tough,
Acts so mean but it ain't enough.

Likes to run naked round a big ol' tree,
Chased by a big, randy grizzilly.
Coz he's a bear mother fucker,
That's Walt Flucker—a bear mother fucker."

Willis bit down on his lower lip suppressing a smile. "Give it a rest, Duane."

Merlot sniggered. "I love it . . . don't stop."

"For fuck's sake, don't encourage him." Willis gave Merlot a kick.

"Walt Flucker likes to...." Duane was interrupted in mid verse by the sound of several rapid knocks on the door.

All three looked curiously at the front door.

"Wonder who that is? Excuse me," Duane said, rather too politely. He placed the remainder of the doughnut back onto the plate with the uneaten doughnuts and got up.

He sauntered over to the door with the mug of coffee in his hand.

A SWEATY MB STOOD on the porch of Duane's cabin. He was more than a little excited at what he had witnessed, but told himself the creatures he had seen couldn't have been for real. But supposing they were for real? There was one way to find out for sure.

He glanced over his shoulder back at the FBI car. He cautioned himself to be careful and not say too much in front of the nosy FBI agents, for Old Indian legend tells us that man who isn't careful is likely to get scalped.

Duane opened the door and smiled. "Mocking Bird, guess who's here?" He whispered, "The FBI."

"You don't say," MB replied in an obvious way. "Uh . . . what time did you get back from town?"

Duane shrugged his shoulders and replied, "Dunno for sure . . . hmm . . . about eight this morning, I guess." He winked at MB, "Needed some quality sack time after spending the night with the Bumsen Sisters."

MB looked speculative, "Who wouldn't? You go out afterwards in your Bigfoot duds?"

Duane looked thoughtful as he scratched his butt and looked rather vague. "Nope . . . not that I can recall."

What sort of reply was that? MB thought. Either the Phantom Bigfoot had been out today or he hadn't. Sometimes it was impossible to get a straightforward answer from his friend.

"You want some coffee and doughnuts . . . ring doughnuts?" Duane gave MB a cheeky smile.

MB frowned at Duane to be careful, peeking into the living room to check on the FBI agents who were obviously trying to listen in on their chat. What the fuck! He smiled at them as he entered Duane's humble abode.

"Sure thing, Duane-o. I could really do with a cup of your coffee, but hold the doughnuts."

MB mimicked disgust at the lurid image of the Bigfoot eating a doughnut on the toilet. He watched for any reaction from Duane's guests, but got nothing. MB smiled timidly to both agents as Duane handed him his own half cup of coffee.

MB frowned at his friend, thinking, Old Indian legends told us beggars can't be choosers. He stood by the sofa drinking coffee. There was no way he was going to sit in the stinky armchair. That would have been the final insult.

Willis broke the silence, "What did you see in the woods, MB?"

MB was as cautious as an elk on a frozen lake. "Not quite sure . . . just a blur of movement . . . probably a grizzly?"

He looked away from Willis' intense gaze and stared at the frightful mess all over the floor. Bigfoot footprints were everywhere. His keen eye detected three different sets of Bigfoot prints and several boot prints in the flour. He gave Duane a curious look. *Old friend, you've been holding out on me.*

Willis put his empty coffee mug on the log table and asked, "What's in the basement, Duane?"

Duane colored slightly and shrugged, "Nothing that could be of interest . . . but be my guest if you don't trust me."

Willis nodded to Duane, "Thanks for the coffee."   He indicated to Merlot it was time to leave.

Merlot dropped her cup on the table and sprang from the sofa with all the eagerness of someone who was desperate to leave. She brushed her suit with her hands.

Duane was curious, "Was there something else you wanted to ask me, Willis?"

Willis hesitated by the door as if he were about to ask something. But he shook his head. "It can keep."

35

AS SOON AS THE AGENTS DROVE OFF, MB turned to Duane. "Guess what I saw in the woods today?"

Duane shrugged, "No, I can't guess."

MB narrowed his eyes and looked questioningly at his friend. "I didn't want to say anything in front of the Feds. Didn't want to tell them I saw Bigfoot, not just one Bigfoot, but two and a mean old grizzly in the woods not far from here."

"Someone else must be dressing up as Bigfoot," Duane replied with a casual shrug.

MB studied his friend to see if he would give himself away. But no, there was nothing to indicate that Duane wasn't telling the truth. MB realized a long time back that his friend could tell a lie as easy as he could down a glass of beer. But sometimes Duane would get a twinkle in his eye that would give him away.

"I could have sworn it was you," MB probed. "One of them had your old rucksack."

Duane shrugged his shoulders and smiled, "I lost it a while back."

MB looked keenly at his friend. He saw the tell-tale twinkle in Duane-o's eyes and knew that he was holding back. "If you ask me you're involved in one of those kinky, dress-up-as-animals sex things you hear about."

Duane looked aghast at MB for suggesting such a lewd thing. "Not me!" He looked lecherous, "Got enough on my plate as it is."

MB studied Duane's smirk for that give-away twinkle of humor in his friend's eye. He got nothing. He felt a little hurt that the Phantom Bigfoot wouldn't confide in his apprentice on such a matter. Even more hurt that his friend hadn't asked him if he'd like to join in on the kinky, animal sex thing.   That would be fun.

MB thought what else he saw in the woods, "Guess who I saw trussed like a turkey?"

As he spoke he was distracted at what he thought to be movement in the bushes at the edge of the clearing to Duane's property. He stared for a moment with his keen eyesight, but got nothing. *Just a raccoon.*

Duane yawned with exhaustion, "Can it wait, MB, I'm real bushed."

MB shrugged, "Sure thing, buddy." He only wanted to know who could have tied Walt and his buddies to a tree, as butt naked as they were born. It couldn't have been Duane as it would've taken several strong guys to man-handle those three. The thought of man-handling three naked men made MB a little squeamish.

࿇ ࿇ ࿇

OLAAA SKIRTED THE EDGE of the clearing, staying hidden by the surrounding bushes and trees. There she waited until the pale one had left. After counting off one thousand strides in her head she decided to approach the cabin as quiet as a field mouse just in case Duane had other pale ones inside.

She walked up to the cabin careful not to make a sound and peered in through a dirty windowpane. She saw Duane asleep on the sofa in his Bigfoot pajamas. There was no one else in the room. She sniffed the air and could clearly discern the strong scent of a pale one leaving the cabin and the foul stench of their four-legged thing. She was sure he was alone.

Olaaa gently tapped the window with one of her pudgy fingers knowing that if she used her hand she might break the window, as she and her Bigfoot friends had done on several occasions previously.

Duane didn't stir. He was sound asleep.

She could tell he was asleep by the sound he was making. Olaaa walked around to the front of the cabin and tried to open the door. It was locked. Olaaa frowned. She scratched her butt and thought a while. Duane had never locked his door before. She gave the door a loud knock being careful not to put her hand through the rotting wood.

DUANE WOKE TO the loud knock on the door. He licked his dry lips for he still had a hangover. Another loud knock caused him to wince. He glanced at the door and remembered that he'd locked it in case Walt and his buddies managed to free themselves.

Duane slowly got up from the sofa and walked over to the door. He picked up his rifle.

"Who's there?"

There was another loud knock in response to his question.

Duane thought it had to be one of his Bigfoot friends. He put his rifle down then unlocked the door and opened it.

"Olaaa," he said with a smile. He beckoned her into the living room with a wave of his hand. "Come on in."

But Olaaa stood on the porch and hesitated to enter.

Duane wondered why she was reluctant to come into his home.   Was everything alright? He studied her face. She looked upset.

"Olaaa sick?" he asked, wiping his brow as if sick.

Olaaa shook her head no and wiped a tear from her eye.

Duane could feel his concern growing, "Olaaa sad?" He mimicked wiping tears from his eyes.

Olaaa nodded her head yes. She grabbed hold of Duane's arm and pulled him out onto the porch.

Duane realized she wanted him to come with her. "Alright I'm coming."

He fell to the floor as Olaaa dragged him. He didn't have time to put anything on his feet.

Olaaa dragged Duane from his cabin across the small clearing and into the edge of the woods.

Suddenly, Duane stopped as Olaaa let him go. He stared wide-eyed at Beau tied to a tree with vines and a gag over his mouth. At first he thought Olaaa must have found Beau and had brought him here. But why tie him up? Had Olaaa taken Beau in the first place?

The teenager looked desperately at Duane as he struggled to be free of the vines. He muttered and wriggled.

Duane looked curiously at Olaaa. She had a sheepish look on her face that told him she had been a naughty girl.

"Olaaa, naughty girl!" he said in a not-too-angry tone of voice, wagging a finger at her. It then occurred to him to help Beau.

Duane rushed up to Beau and removed the gag from his mouth. "Are you hurt?"

Beau spat bits of cloth from his mouth. "I'm okay . . . I guess." He glanced curiously at Olaaa.

Duane started to undo Beau's restraints. He looked at Olaaa, "Did Olaaa take you?" He knew he needed to be real careful what he said to the teenager.

"Yeah," Beau replied, tugging himself free of the loose vines.

"Olaaa bad," Duane said a little more sharply.

Olaaa bleated miserably, "Weeee-woooo-weeee."

Duane never got annoyed with his Bigfoot friends, but today was different. She had done a very naughty thing.

"Olaaa bad." He slapped his behind.

Olaaa looked at Duane with tears in her eyes, and mewed pathetically, "Weeeeeooooo—weeeeeooooo."

Duane was immediately sorry for telling her off. He turned his attention back to Beau. He wondered if the teenager was aware that Olaaa was a real Bigfoot.

"She's not a real one, you know."

Beau looked keenly at Olaaa. "If she ain't real . . . then why are you talking like that? Uh-uh, I think she is for real. That's no costume." He looked back at Duane. "She carried me through the forest for miles and miles. No human, male or female, would have the strength to do that."

Yeah, well, the kid was right about Olaaa being strong, thought Duane with a scratch of his butt. He blew out his cheeks and gave a long sigh. What now? Continue with the façade or should he tell Beau the truth? And if he told him, could the kid keep a secret?

Duane contemplated the matter with a scratch of his butt. Even if the kid talked and said there were real Bigfoot in the woods, not many people would take him seriously—not with a father like Walt.

"Okay, she's real," he admitted. "So the big question is . . . can you keep it a secret?"

"I guess," Beau said sounding a little put out. "What a bummer ... I've been abducted by a real Bigfoot and can't blab about it." He shook his head. "That sucks big time."

"Best you tell people you got lost in the woods or aliens abducted you. Don't mention Olaaa." Duane scratched his butt. "Damn . . . this is real fucked-up. The FBI are involved and if they think you've wasted their time you might be in a whole lot of trouble."

"Shit . . . that *is* fucked-up." Beau looked concerned at Olaaa. "I think you've upset her."

"Good! She's been a very bad girl," Duane said.

Olaaa began to sob.

Duane was by nature a forgiving person, but his head was throbbing due to his hangover and he was tired and wanted some Zs.

"Olaaa bad . . . go!" he shouted, pointing to the forest. "Go!" he insisted.

Olaaa looked sadly at her pale friend and burst into tears. She hunched her shoulders and turned away from him.

"You didn't have to speak to her like that, Duane-o."

Beau sounded quite concerned, thought Duane. Probably the Stockholm Syndrome. What a real no-brainer.

Duane watched Olaaa skulk away but didn't try to stop her. She'd been a bad girl for taking Beau. And now his big secret would be all over town if Beau decided to blab. That was surely fucked-up! A tear ran down Duane's face at the thought of his Bigfoot friends being carted away by government scientists.

36

AGENT WILLIS LOOMED OVER BEAU, who was seated in a chair with a blanket wrapped around him, drinking hot coffee from a large mug with shaking hands.

Sheriff Lou sat behind her desk looking real pissed.

Opposite Beau was Duane in scruffy jeans and a t-shirt, leaning against a wall looking nonchalant.

And sitting on the edge of Lou's desk, giving Beau a hard time with her tough guy act was Agent Merlot with arms crossed.

As yet, Beau's parents hadn't arrived to claim their son, but Lou had given instructions to Deputy Dwight to give them the good news that their son was back safe and sound in Big Beaver.

Willis looked dubiously at the teenager, pointing an angry finger. "So . . . that's the story you're sticking to . . . that you simply got lost in the woods?" His tone of voice was his regular matter-of-fact, and somewhat stern with an obvious hint of disbelief thrown in.

Beau gave Willis a worried glance then turned to Duane who gave him a reassuring smile to continue.

Willis noticed the faint smile Duane gave Beau. His keen instincts told him that the kid and Duane weren't being truthful as to the facts of Beau's disappearance.

Beau looked back at Agent Willis. He shrugged his shoulders.

"How many times do you want me say this?" Beau looked exasperated. "Like I said, I got lost in the woods after eating these weird mushrooms. I went all weird as if weightless and the next thing I remember is coming out of the woods. It was real weird."

Willis looked at him disbelievingly.

"You must have eaten more than just mushrooms." Willis demanded.

Beau nodded his head, "Sure . . . the forest is full of berries and such."

"And you just found your way to Duane's cabin?" Merlot exclaimed with disbelief.

Beau looked from one agent to the other. "Like I said before . . . I saw this smoke above the trees and made for it, thinking I'd be safe."

Duane chipped in, "Yeah, like I said . . . there was this knock on the door and there was Beau, as large as life and looking none-the-worse for his ordeal."

Sheriff Lou gave Beau and Duane a dubious look and sighed heavily, "That don't cut it guys. I don't believe either of you." She concentrated on Beau, "Are you aware the sheriff's department and the FBI have spent a great deal of time and effort looking for you?"

Beau smiled apologetically. "So what . . . I mean sorry, but I couldn't help getting lost. I know I must've wandered off, but I can't remember . . . it's all fuzzy."

The two FBI agents exchanged irritated glances, but didn't speak.

Sheriff Lou shrugged her shoulders. "Well, you didn't come to any harm. Let's be grateful for that."

Beau gave Duane a furtive look.

Duane smiled reassuringly at him.

Willis saw the smile on Duane's face and looked dubiously at the two idiots, but there wasn't a damned thing could be done about it.

"Well, I guess that just about wraps things up here in Big Beaver," Merlot said as she hopped off the table. "We should be leaving, right?"

Willis didn't hear his partner. His full attention was focused on the only woman he had ever loved. A big part of him didn't want to leave, not yet anyway. There was unfinished business between himself, Lou and Duane. But if he stayed, even for an extra day, what good would that do? Sure they'd end up settling their differences, but then what?

LOU SENSED WILLIS was looking directly at her. She glanced in his direction. Their eyes met. They held each other's gaze for several moments, unaware that all attention was focused on her and Willis.

She could feel tears starting to well up in her eyes. She didn't want him to leave—ever.

Duane gave a gentle cough, "Lou, you feeling okay?"

No, she was not feeling okay. Lou felt quite heady and overcome with her strong feelings towards Willis Johnson, the heartless bastard. And now he was going to walk out of her life, maybe for good. When would she see him again? Maybe when they were old and gray? She wanted to bawl her eyes out, but instead, she bit down on her lower lip to stifle her tears.

The arrival of Walt and Rose Flucker drew Lou out of her miserable contemplations.

Rose rushed over to her son to give him a big smothering hug. "There's my boy."

Walt stood in the background glaring straight at Duane with sheer malice. He pointed a finger at Duane and then mimicked cutting his throat. He looked sorely pissed.

Duane sniggered.

"Hey, Mom," Beau said in a cheerful tone of voice.

"Oh, my baby," Rose blurted amid lots of hugs and tears. She felt her son all over, "Are you hurt?"

Walt didn't say a word. His gaze remained fixed on Duane.

"He's okay, Rose. Apparently he got lost," Lou said in a sarcastic tone of voice.

Walt nodded his head but kept his gaze on Duane. "Yeah, Dwight told us he'd been found after getting lost." He looked at the sheriff and hesitated before he spoke. "I was at Duane's this morning, with Chuck and Bob . . . and guess what I saw?"

Lou had a hunch what he was about to say, "Bigfoot?"

"Damned straight they was . . . not one, but two of 'em." Walt glared at Duane. "And they were too big to be human."

Duane chuckled. "Come on . . . I told you they weren't for real, shit-for-brains."

"I say they was real, asshole," Walt insisted with a snarl.

Lou continued, "And do Chuck and Bob think they were real Bigfoot?"

Walt was slow to reply. He gave a barely audible dissatisfied grunt.

"Well . . . No, damn it . . . they think a couple of Duane's friends got dressed up in Bigfoot costumes. What do they know? But I know what I saw and I say they was real."

Willis gave Walt a scathing look and muttered under his breath, "What an asshole."

Walt's sharp ears picked up what Willis had just said. He looked nastily at him. "You watch your mouth, Agent Asshole."

"Takes one to know one," Duane chipped in.

Lou raised a hand for them to be quiet before the name-calling got out of hand. She looked questioningly at Duane.

"These friends of yours—give me their names."

Duane looked thoughtful for a moment as he scratched his butt. "No can do, Lou . . . they'd like to remain . . . uh, kinda anonymous."

Lou had a hunch as to the identity of at least one of Duane's two friends that Walt was referring to—MB.

37

LATER THAT DAY, Agent Willis Johnson sat in the passenger seat, looking as miserable as hell, as Merlot drove them back to Sacramento. They passed the Big Beaver welcome sign and saw that someone had scribbled on it—"Welcome to Big juicy Beaver."

Willis gave a wry smile.

Merlot observed her partner's demeanor.

The endless row of fir trees that lined the two-lane blacktop were reflected in Willis' eyes. He inwardly sighed with remorse. He'd said a friendly goodbye to Lou and Duane with more than a hint of regret. Was he doing the right thing in leaving Big Beaver and the woman he loved and the friend who thought so much of him? He could have stayed an extra couple of days.

Willis should have asked Duane about that damned letter. Then why didn't he? He reluctantly admitted it was because he was afraid. Afraid of Lou and letting his emotions get the better of him. He would have been at her mercy. He didn't want that to happen. He couldn't lose control.

He told himself he didn't need to love someone or for someone to love him, and besides, if Lou wanted to marry Brad, he had no right to stop her.

The Bigfoot Bend sign approached. Duane's hog was parked next to the sign and Duane was standing in the middle of the road looking somewhat frantic, waving his arms, dressed as Bigfoot.

Willis sat up with surprise as he recognized Duane in his Bigfoot costume, minus the head.

Merlot commented, "Not again!"

"What now?" Willis replied with a weary sigh.

Some moments later they were close enough to see what Duane was up to.

"No way," exclaimed Merlot. She slammed on the brakes and scrambled for her cell phone. She hurriedly flicked it open and pointed the camera at the trees opposite. "I don't believe my eyes."

Willis turned in that direction and sat up even more straight-backed. A look of total shock was frozen on his face. At least ten Bigfoot stood at the edge of the forest. They seemed to be waiting for Duane to allow them to cross the road safely.

Merlot looked from the Bigfoot to Duane to Willis with her mouth wide open. She concentrated on the Bigfoot with her cell phone camera. Her hands shook with excitement.

"Is this for real, Willis?"

"How the hell should I know?"

Duane remained in the middle of the road. He didn't make any attempt to walk towards the FBI car. He just grinned at the agents with that dumb smile of his and waved the Bigfoot tribe across the road.

The Bigfoot tribe casually crossed the road with a lumbering stride, keeping a close eye on the car. In moments they had all vanished into the forest on the other side.

Willis thought about ordering Merlot to drive around Duane, but he didn't want to hurt Duane's feelings. He got out of the car and walked over to his friend.

"Okay, dumbass, what the fuck's going on?" Willis' stern voice had finally melted. "Were they . . . you know . . . for real?"

"As real as it gets," Duane said with a wide grin.

"No wonder this town's so fucked-up." Willis laughed. He saw the look on Duane's face. "Is there something else?"

"I . . . " Duane faltered as his lip began to tremble with emotion. His eyes moistened with tears as he held out his arms. "I need a big hug."

Willis backed a few paces from his teary-eyed friend. "No hugging."

Duane sniffed back his tears. He continued to hold out his arms, "Big hug . . . now."

The wall of emotion that Willis had been holding back began to crumble. He looked over his shoulder back at his partner and saw her staring at them with a big grin on her face. He knew if he allowed Duane to give him a hug, Merlot would tell everyone back in the office that she'd seen him hugging a male friend, the second such occasion in less than twenty-four hours. Willis realized that people would start saying he was on the same team. So what if they did?

Willis looked back at Duane, "Okay, but make it a quickie."

That was all Duane needed to hear. He grabbed hold of his friend and hugged him tightly for several moments.

Willis instinctively flinched from Duane's stink, but to his surprise he smelled sweet and fresh.

To Willis' horror, Duane got down on one knee and looked as if he was about to propose.

"I love you . . . in a manly sort of way, Willis."

Willis was taken aback. He looked down at Duane then at Merlot's smiling face. He saw the cell phone in his partner's hand and panicked.

"For fuck's sake, get up, you dumbass," he frantically urged.

Duane remained on one knee. "Not until you say you love me in a manly sort of way."

Willis was frantic, "Get up now."

Without warning, Duane grabbed hold of Willis by the leg. "I won't let go . . . not until you say you love me in a manly sort of way." He looked into Willis' eyes, "And I don't care how bad this looks."

What should Willis do? What could he do? There was only one thing he could do if he wanted to get away from his overly emotional friend.

"Okay, I love you . . . in a manly sort of way." And Willis meant what he said. He did love Duane in a manly sort of way, but never thought he would have to say it—not like this.

Duane was all smiles as he released his friend's leg and stood up. "Promise me you'll come back."

"I promise." *But would he keep his promise and return one day?* This was it. It might be the last chance he had to ask, "About that fucking letter . . . ?"

Duane scratched his butt in confusion. "Uh . . . what letter might that be?"

"The letter you sent me two months ago." Willis said, thoroughly exasperated.

Duane laughed out loud, "Now you come to mention it, I do remember sending you a letter." He looked puzzled as he continued to scratch his butt. "What did I say?"

Willis blew out his cheeks. "You said Lou's gonna marry this rich guy in town. There are two rich guys in town . . . and there's no way she'll marry you . . . so it has to be Brad."

Duane was finally home and all the lights were on—well almost all. He suddenly remembered.

He looked a little sheepish as he explained, "Well, you see, it's kinda like this, Willis . . . Lou isn't gonna marry anyone this fall." He shrugged his shoulders, "Had to think of something to get you two idiots back together."

Willis knocked Duane to the asphalt with a right hook.

Duane lay sprawled on his back laughing his brains out while feeling his jaw. "Guess I deserved that?"

Willis suddenly burst into laughter. "You dumb son-of-a-bitch!" He pulled his friend to his Bigfoot feet and hugged him. "Love you . . . you dumb asshole."

ߠ   ߠ   ߠ

THE AGENTS WERE ONCE MORE en route back to Big Beaver but at breakneck speed.

Agent Merlot saw the sheriff's car being driven at an equal speed towards them. She glanced at Willis and saw him looking at the approaching patrol car with a look of excitement.

Lou was some distance away but gaining on them fast. Her headlights were flashing and the horn blaring.

"Looks like the sheriff's in hot pursuit of someone," Merlot commented.

"Yeah, sure looks like."

It was obvious to Merlot's mind that they were the ones the sheriff was in hot pursuit of. If so, there could only be one reason why—Willis Johnson. Merlot took her foot off the gas and came to a stop right next to the town welcome sign. *How appropriate*, she thought. She wasn't at all surprised when

Sheriff Lou took her foot off the gas and came to a stop in front of them.

LOU GOT OUT and walked over to the passenger side of the FBI car.

Willis sat looking up at her as she approached.

"Would you mind getting out of the car, Agent Johnson," she said in a matter-of-fact tone of voice.

Willis nodded his head and obediently got out. He gave her a faint smile.

Lou didn't say anything. She just walked back to her patrol car and waited for Willis to join her.

She put her hands on her hips and looked at him with narrowed eyes. She knew it was either now or never to make her move.

"Agent Merlot tells me you've got some vacation time stacked up."

"Oh, she did, did she?" Willis turned to see a grinning Merlot. "As a matter of fact I do," he replied in his matter-of-fact tone of voice.

She thought over those wondrous words "I do." Were those the words she wanted him to say one day? She swallowed nervously. It was now or never. She took a big, deep breath to steady her nerves. Her gaze wandered questioningly over his face. A face she knew she could love for the rest of her life.

"You want to spend it here in Big Beaver, or what?"

Willis hesitated. His expression was serious.

Lou was sure he was going to say no. She held her breath as she saw his face relaxing into a smile. Lou knew beyond all doubt what his answer would be. She smiled lovingly back at him.

"Nothing would please me more . . . ," he replied in a soft tone of voice, ". . . with the woman I love."

All the uncertainty she had been feeling washed away in a heartbeat. Her eyes moistened. She knew she was about to cry with joy and relief.

She took a step towards Willis. He moved a step towards her. Lou put her arms around his neck. Tears ran down her beautiful face.

Lou allowed Willis to kiss away her tears and use the tip of his tongue to lick her earlobe before travelling down the nape of her neck.

Lou arched her back in total ecstasy. Her tongue found Willis' and became entwined with the heat of passion. She was lost in his urgent desire as she tightened her grip on his back. She remembered their first kiss all those years ago. More tears flowed.

They kissed and kissed and kissed.

Lou's legs turned to jelly. She fell across the hood of her car as Willis pinned her. Lou suddenly pushed Willis away. She panted for breath, almost forgetting how to draw precious air into her bursting lungs. Her ample breasts heaved within the tight confines of her light blue sheriff's shirt.

Lou groaned out loud, "Not here, Willis . . . come on."

Merlot punched the air with joy and took a snapshot of them with her cell phone, "You're gonna love this, Ramón."

LOU SCRAMBLED BACK into her driver's seat with Willis sitting next to her. They kissed again, but Lou pulled away and revved the engine. She spun the car around and drove back to her lonely home. The car had barely stopped before Lou and

Willis sprang from it and rushed up the stone steps to the front door.

Willis grabbed Lou and kissed her intensely. They fell against the door which swung open. They stumbled into the hall ripping at each other's clothing. With strong, muscular arms, Willis pinned Lou against a wall in the hallway. He ripped Lou's shirt into tatters, revealing her soft, pale breasts trembling within their satin embrace.

Willis kissed Lou all the way up to her gasping lips as he gently thrust his member to the hilt. He wrapped his body around Lou in an exquisite embrace and cried tears of relief and joy.

38

BENEATH A BRIGHT FULL MOON, a whimpering Olaaa crouched amongst a thicket of brambles and honeysuckle, watching two honey-blond females—Ooonaaa and Meeelaaa play with Teeelaaa in Little Beaver Creek.

Olaaa smelled her strong odor and concluded she also needed to get a wash. She watched with almost childish fascination as each female Bigfoot playfully splashed water over one another, screaming and giggling.

Maaawooo sat on a nearby rock stroking his erect thruster, closely guarding the three bottles of happy juice Duane had given him. With his free hand he counted the time with his fingers—one stride—two strides—three strides. After two hundred strides, Maaawooo estimated that enough time had elapsed for his harem of Bigfoot babes to be ready and willing for some serious woooo-woooo.

"Raaaarrrr," he growled. Oops! Maaawooo let rip with a thunderous fart. He wrinkled his snout at the stink. He walked away from the methane cloud. Several midges flew into the cloud and crashed to the ground.

The three Bigfoot females stopped their ablutions and giggled at Maaawooo. They waited for the amorous Maaawooo to join them. Each female Bigfoot allowed Maaawooo to pour the entire contents of a bottle down their eager throats. Once all three Bigfoot had been thoroughly prepared they began to splash water over themselves and Maaawooo.

With a lustful glint in his eyes, the horny Maaawooo licked his lips and pushed out with his rampant thruster.

The two honey-blond Bigfoot females and Teeelaaa giggled and squeaked as they beckoned him to woooo-woooo their brains out.

Maaawooo pummeled his chest enthusiastically and gave a low growl, "rrrraaaarrrrrraaaa." Followed by, "woooooo—wooooo—woooooo."

In unison, the three female Bigfoot replied, "wooooeeeeoooo—wooooeeeeeoooo—wooooeeeeeoooo."

Olaaa's eyes widened as Maaawooo mounted Teeelaaa first. She thought about her plaything and yearned for him. She gave a deep, guttural growl of discontent. She was envious of the Bigfoot females, but knew she was too young for woooo-woooo.

Olaaa sighed and thought of Boo. She bleated plaintively so as not to disturb the others. She wiped away tears. She watched Meeelaaa and Ooonaaa dance a salsa to an imaginary tune. She wanted to join in so much it hurt. But most of all, Olaaa was upset for being told off so sharply by Duane.

SOME CONSIDERABLE DISTANCE away, yet deep in the forest, MB recorded the now familiar sounds of Bigfoot, mating their brains out.

The somewhat bewildered crypto-zoologist decided the calls were Duane and his two sex-freak companions, but nevertheless he recorded the animal sounds.

The directional microphone told him the rampant calls were due north-west of his position and too far to trek to in the night.

So he set up camp where the Little Beaver Creek joined the larger confluence of the Big Beaver River.

After a light snack washed down with coffee from his thermos, MB retired for the night in his one-man tent. He didn't dare set up a campfire, not this deep in the forest, for he didn't want to give away his position to anything worth recording.

೨ ೨ ೨

CHEERFUL BIRDSONG WOKE MB at the crack of dawn. He unzipped his tent and peered out into the misty, early morning. He breathed in the rich scent of pine and his own stench of sweat, but it was honest sweat.

MB suddenly heard the unmistakable sound of heavy feet carelessly snapping twigs.

He leapt out fully clothed in his army-style fatigues. He slipped on his earphones and listened intently. North, north-west was the direction the sound was coming from, but diminishing in volume. Without further delay, MB hurried in the same direction.

Behind mist-covered undergrowth, MB watched and waited, careful not to make a sound or movement. He heard branches and undergrowth being broken and trodden on by heavy feet. Something big was nearby. Could it be Duane and his freaky companions? If so, MB hoped they'd let him have some fun with them.

A moment later, MB saw Duane dressed up in his Bigfoot duds crunching through the forest. MB had no doubt it was Duane, as he had his Bigfoot head tucked under his arm.

With him was another Bigfoot, but this Bigfoot didn't have a furry fake head tucked under its arm. It looked familiar, like the Bigfoot he'd seen the other day.

MB recognized the gold flash on the lightly-haired snout, and the massive breasts swinging freely due to its vigorous stride.

MB watched with mounting curiosity. He was tempted to call out and say hello, but something told him to remain silent. He wanted to see where Duane and his friend were going and what they got up to. But MB, the eternal voyeur, knew that if Duane started to get amorous, he'd make his presence known. The last thing he wanted to see was Duane getting some booty call.

MB's instincts told him to follow them, for Old Indian legend tells us a wise man always follows his instincts. He watched until Duane and his furry friend were almost out of sight then followed them, careful not to make a sound.

For many hours, MB followed behind Duane and the Bigfoot, keeping a discreet distance, until he came upon a remote, flat area ringed with caves.

He crouched behind a large rock, and watched Duane and the Bigfoot entering one of the caves. He looked up. The sun was directly above. Where had the time gone?

THE INTERIOR OF THE CAVE was festooned with flowers of every color and the floor covered with clean, fresh straw. The walls were covered with drawings of mating Bigfoot, large thrusters entering enormous nether regions and tall spacemen with pale hair patting the heads of Bigfoot. In the furthest corners of the cave were several straw beds.

Duane and Teeelaaa greeted the two honey-blond female Bigfoot—Meeelaaa and Ooonaaa by nudging noses.

The Bigfoot babes were glad to see them, especially Duane. They pawed at him excitedly, and rubbed their groins against his hips. They were getting a bit frisky.

Duane checked each blond Bigfoot babe for skin lesions. As he did this the Bigfoot babes became very aroused indeed, pawing Duane and licking his hair. Duane was satisfied of no side effects to the hair colorant. He smelled alcohol. He sniffed each babe's breath and laughed. That Maaawooo had wasted no time in giving them the tequila. Old habits die hard.

"You girls look so pretty," he said mimicking beauty.

They continued to paw him excitedly, trying to remove his Bigfoot duds.

Ooonaaa grabbed hold of Duane's arm, almost yanking it out of his socket, and tried to pull him towards the cave entrance.

Duane figured she wanted him to go somewhere with her.

"Okay I'm coming," he sighed, without putting up any resistance. And so Duane was dragged towards the cave entrance by Ooonaaa.

MB WATCHED with a strange fascination as Duane emerged from the cave with a dappled, honey-blond Bigfoot tugging on his arm. He was extremely surprised to see that the Bigfoot's hair was honey-blond. He recorded the Bigfoot with his camcorder.

MB was tempted to call out, but something told him to stay quiet and do nothing, except watch and learn. Suddenly a wild and wonderful thought occurred to him. It was such a wild and wonderful thought that he dismissed it a moment later as sheer crap. But the wild and wonderful thought kept nagging at him—they were real Bigfoot.

MB shook his head to clear it of this wild and wonderful thought. Reason told him that the Bigfoot with Duane could not possibly be a real Bigfoot, not with honey-blond hair. Nah impossible! They were just girlfriends of Duane's who liked to dress up in animal duds and have kinky sex. That had to be it. Could they be Annie and Heidi? He hoped so.

He watched the Bigfoot tug on Duane's furry arm so hard, he fell face first into the dust.

The blond Bigfoot chuckled in a peculiar snorting way. Several moments later, the stacked reddish Bigfoot and another honey-blond Bigfoot with equally large breasts emerged from the cave.

Wow! How many kinky girlfriends does Duane have in there, MB thought, with a surprised look on his face. His buddy had a lot of explaining to do, keeping all this free sex from him. He watched and listened.

Duane rubbed his arm. "That hurts, Ooonaaa. Naughty Ooonaaa."

Ooonaaa snorted, "Ftftftftft!"

The other honey-blond Bigfoot helped Duane to his feet and nudged his nose with her snout.

"Woooo you too, Meeelaaa." Duane patted her hairy ass.

Ooonaaa grabbed Duane's arm and whisked him away into the forest.

Once Duane was out of sight, MB decided to make his presence known. He got up slowly, careful not to startle them. Even though he didn't think they were genuine Bigfoot, his presence might spook them, all the same.

Both Bigfoot babes were indeed surprised to see MB. They immediately started to back away towards the cave entrance mewling and spitting with their hair bristled.

MB remained standing behind the rock, as motionless as a rock. He was sure if he moved towards them, they'd run back inside the cave or into the woods. He didn't want that. Not that he thought the Bigfoot were real Bigfoot, but he didn't want to scare them.

MB smiled disarmingly and gave a gentle wave, "Hey there Meeelaaa."

The two Bigfoot babes were frightened of MB, and ran back inside the cave.

MB's shoulders slumped. He called out to them, "It's okay. . . I'm a friend of Duane's. I'm your friend, too."

A few interminable moments went by. MB suddenly perked up as both Bigfoot babes emerged from the cave. They stood looking curiously at him, sniffing the air with twitching, cute snouts.

Both Bigfoot babes nudged noses and mewled, pointing at MB.

MB pointed to himself and said, "Duane-o's friend— Doooane." He pointed to where Duane had vanished into the woods.

The Bigfoot babes tilted their heads, and with wary, watchful eyes looked curiously at him, mewing and sniffing.

MB slowly approached, still under the misguided notion that the two Bigfoot babes were humans in animal duds.

Meeelaaa and the foxy red Bigfoot looked at each other, nodding their heads in an affirmative fashion and smiled. They looked back at MB, snorting and squeaking then they beckoned him to come towards them.

Should he go with them? MB hesitated for only a brief moment. He was reminded of an Old Indian legend that tells us man who refuses sex with two gorgeous babes is a fool to behold.

Yet despite the Old Indian Legend, MB followed them into the cave with trepidation and unease, thinking they could not be real Bigfoot, but what if they were?

❧   ❧   ❧

DUANE WINCED IN PAIN. His arm was beginning to feel sore with Ooonaaa continually tugging on it as she led him through the woods. They arrived at another cave, the last one on the left.

Ooonaaa stopped and pointed to the cave entrance, covered with ferns and saplings.

Duane pointed at the cave. "You want me to go into Olaaa's cave?" He knew that Olaaa didn't like anyone going into her cave, unannounced.

Ooonaaa gave Duane a hefty shove for him to move.

Duane stumbled forward. He gave Ooonaaa a concerned look thinking that Olaaa wasn't well. He hoped it wasn't anything serious.

Ooonaaa shoved Duane into the cave.

Duane entered the cave in a rush and saw Olaaa curled on the floor. She had her back to the entrance and mewed sadly. There were several pieces of bark containing berries and wild mushrooms, obviously untouched. It looked to Duane as if Olaaa was off her food. Did Olaaa have an upset tummy?

Olaaa sensed his presence and rolled over on her side to look at him. She didn't try to sit up. Her large round eyes looked at him full of hurt and tears.

Duane could see the hurt in her eyes. It suddenly dawned on him. Olaaa was upset because he had been annoyed with her. He had hurt her feelings. He knew how sensitive some Bigfoot females could be. He smiled apologetically.

Olaaa sat up and began to sob.

Duane walked over to her and knelt down on the ground by her side. He put his arm around her shoulder and wiped the tears from her eyes. He kissed her snout.

Olaaa pushed his arm off her shoulder and shook her head in a spoilt fashion.

Duane persisted by tenderly stroking the bridge of her snout, making cooing noises.

Olaaa slowly turned to look at him and pouted, "Woooo-woooo-woooo."

Duane gave Olaaa a wide smile and nodded yes. He nudged her snout.

Olaaa's face brightened up. She smiled back at Duane. The tears stopped. She jumped to her feet and started to dance around Duane.

Duane shrugged what the hell and danced with Olaaa, but was soon knocked to the floor with a bump from her hips.

Olaaa giggled, "Sfsfsfsfsfsfsfsf."

Duane gave Olaaa a playful angry look and then laughed with pure joy.

આ   આ   આ

AT THE SAME TIME that Duane was dancing with Olaaa, MB was stretched out on a carpet made of flowers with both Bigfoot babes as they lovingly pawed him. He was in bliss land. He heaved a relaxed sigh. He was reminded of an Old Indian legend that tells us man who finds himself the sex object of two beautiful Bigfoot babes should thank his lucky stars.

At this point, MB still believed the Bigfoot babes cuddling up to him were human females all dressed up as Bigfoot and acting the part.

The foxy red Bigfoot stopped pawing MB and offered him a drink from a hollow branch.

MB sniffed the heady aroma coming from the branch. What the fuck, he took a sip. It tasted okay-ish, a little too sweet for his liking. His lips went numb. He shrugged. The second mouthful tasted better, and the third even better again.

MB paused and looked at the Bigfoot babe with a frown. He was feeling a little light-headed. He allowed her to pour all the liquid down his throat. By the sixth mouthful he realized he was feeling as if he'd had one too many beers. Only then did he think that what he'd been given was drugged in some way.

MB could feel himself drifting off to sleep. He looked at the Bigfoot babes and thought they were really into character with their creature-like behavior and sounds. He hoped they wouldn't be too rough with him.

"Be gentle," he begged.

39

WHEN MB CAME AROUND some time later, he found himself well outside the cave lying on a bed of sweet-smelling flower petals in a beautiful glade surrounded by Bigfoot of all shapes and sizes, sitting on their haunches in a circle. He saw Meeelaaa with them.

Some Bigfoot looked old with graying hair, and long, sagging breasts.

Each Bigfoot held the hand of the Bigfoot next to them. All of them had a profusion of flowers in their hair, especially behind their pert, short, tufted ears, and necklaces of petals around their necks.

MB looked quizzically at them and thought he must be tripping out. He watched two little Bigfoot, both heavily spotted in reddish-brown over light fawn hair, pointing at him and chuckling in a nasal snorting way. If he didn't know any better he would have assumed they were Bigfoot offspring. But then he did know better and immediately assumed that was so fucked-up because they weren't Bigfoot. Nothing made any sense. What the fuck!

MB jumped as the foxy babe gave him a hefty shove to notice her standing behind him.

All the Bigfoot giggled with quick-fire snorting.

MB's favorite Bigfoot babe squatted down next to him and pointed to a piece of bark containing chunks of bright yellow fungus, similar to a mushroom. She pointed and indicated with her hand to eat.

"I don't even know your name?" Not knowing her name wouldn't stop him having sex with her, but it seemed polite to ask.

He waited for a reply and got nothing. MB still felt more than a little light-headed from whatever he had drunk before. He wondered if he'd had sex. He couldn't remember. He felt down below. His love machine didn't feel as though he had done it, but his eyes widened as he realized he was as naked as a jay bird.

All the Bigfoot pointed to MB's groin and chuckled, "Sfsfsfsfsfsfsfsf."

It wouldn't be the first time, thought MB, that he'd consumed one too many alcoholic beverages and had sex without any recollection. He remembered the Bigfoot babes giving him something to drink that made him feel intoxicated and quite sleepy.

MB frowned as he contemplated what might have happened. He shook his head in an attempt to clear the fog. Instead, the act of moving his head, made him feel a little more light-headed, and everything left trails of colors in his mind's vision. Cool!

MB slowly sat up and waved, "Hi there, everyone."

As he spoke he realized how dehydrated he was. Whatever they'd given him to drink had not only knocked him out, but had given him a big thirst.

Foxy babe picked up the bark containing the jooobaaa fungus and offered it to him. She indicated with her fingers to eat.

As MB took a piece of jooobaaa, she nudged his nose with her wet snout. He could smell tequila on her breath, thus confirming they were not real Bigfoot. He had a nagging feeling that he had seen her before or even knew her, but from where?

He took a tentative mouthful, thinking it might be the stuff he'd drunk earlier that had knocked him out. To his relief, it tasted like raw mushroom. He ate most of the jooobaaa, and quenched his thirst from the same hollow branch containing the whacky liquid.

MB smacked his lips and rubbed his tummy, "Mmm, that was good."

Foxy babe smiled, revealing sharp, crooked yellow teeth. She snatched the branch out of his hand and threw it away, under MB's curious and watchful gaze. She picked up the empty bark and threw that away.

MB was in another world where all the colors took on new and exciting hues. His anxiety over the existence of Bigfoot had vanished. He looked at the gathering of Bigfoot watching him and smiled at them.

Foxy babe spoke in a deep, husky voice, "Woooo-woooo-woooo-woooo." She picked up a handful of red berries and rubbed them over her rear end.

MB looked perplexed, for he did not know what she had just said to him or why she was rubbing berries between her legs. He just smiled amiably in his confused state, shrugging his shoulders and thought what the hell. So he played along hoping this would end with sex.

Suddenly, all the Bigfoot screamed loudly, "Wooooooeeeeeeooooooooeeeeeeooooooo." They raised their arms to the heavens.

MB looked startled at his audience.

The Bigfoot started to happily chant, "Woooo-woooo–woooo-woooo."

Latin American music started up—a salsa.

A thoroughly bemused MB looked around at the Bigfoot and saw Duane's portable CD player on the ground. As yet, he had no idea he was the only human present.

Moments later, all the Bigfoot started to salsa and did a ring around the roses around MB and Foxy babe, throwing all the flowers from their bodies at the soon-to-be newlyweds.

In that sun-drenched clearing full of bright flowers, the Bigfoot continued to dance in a circle. Butterflies flitted over the flowers. Rabbits hopped closer, twitching their snouts. A pair of wolves sat at the clearing edge, howling in unison. Raccoons, elks, grizzlies, deer, weasels and birds of every species filled the clearing as spectators to the Bigfoot wedding.

It was at this point that Duane finally showed up with Olaaa.

As the Bigfoot continued to dance around MB and his Foxy babe, Duane broke through the circle.

MB was glad to see his friend, "Hey Duane-o, guess what?"

"Shit, MB, what have you gone and done, now?" Duane declared, looking quite troubled.

MB smiled innocently and shrugged. He hadn't done anything untoward, not that he could remember. And even now, he still didn't think the Bigfoot were real.

"Did you eat a mushroom . . . a big yellow mushroom?" Duane asked with a worried look.

"Oh yeah . . . yellow's my favorite color," MB replied, looking puzzled.

Why did his friend seem so troubled? It was a beautiful day. The birds were tweeting. The Bigfoot were real friendly. Even the animals seemed to be tame. He was having a really good time.

"You idiot," Duane exclaimed. "Do you know what you've done?" Duane looked real pissed. "Have you done the deed yet?"

MB shrugged. He didn't have a clue what he'd done. He nodded no with a shrug.

Duane slapped MB across the head, "Wake up, you dufus. You've gotten engaged to a Bigfoot babe."

MB rubbed his head, "I'd know if I'd done anything like that . . . and within the realms of reason and logic, I'm certain I didn't." He shook his head in confusion.

Duane gave MB an exasperated look. "These aren't sexy playthings, MB . . . don't you get it . . . these are real Bigfoot." Duane pointed to his hairy friends.

"No such thing as Bigfoot," MB blurted with a chuckle.

Duane's face grew serious. "Yes there are," he insisted. "And you just got engaged to one of them—Teeelaaa." He pointed to Teeelaaa.

MB gave his friend a speculative look then beamed, "Uh . . . hi, Teeelaaa."

Teeelaaa mewed and chuckled, looking very fetching, twirling her hips around to the music.

MB could see that Duane didn't look as if he was kidding. He shook his head, still reluctant to believe that these Bigfoot were real. A moment of clarity kicked in as MB upchucked the jooobaaa. He shuddered as he wondered if this was still a dream.

"Well, who'd have thought . . . I've got engaged to a Bigfoot babe!" MB smiled lecherously at Teeelaaa, thinking, *no way she's a Bigfoot.*

"Oh yeah, you sure did," Duane said adamantly. "I almost married Teeelaaa, too. She's a real cock-teaser and it's Maaawooo's cock being teased." He pointed to the massive dangerous-looking Bigfoot, entering the circle.

Teeelaaa squealed with delight as Maaawooo picked up a piece of jooobaaa and munched it. She threw petals all over herself and Maaawooo.

"She's been trying to get hitched to Maaawooo for the last twelve moons without much success."

"Really? What happens now, old buddy?" MB chuckled, still not believing a word Duane had told him. He watched Maaawooo mount Teeelaaa just inches from his face.

But something in Duane's serious manner troubled MB. He looked at Teeelaaa as she groaned with each thrust from Maaawooo. Her hair really looked too good. Her gorgeous tits looked too good! Maaawooo's humungous cock looked too real and impossibly big for a human as he dismounted.

MB reached out and grabbed Teeelaaa's arm. His eyes opened wide in shock. He felt the hair and rippling muscles.

"Fuck . . . they're real Bigfoot!" MB looked with awe into Teeelaaa's big, round blue eyes. He jumped to his feet in shock.

"That's what I've been trying to tell you . . . and my advice to you, my friend, is to get on good terms with Maaawooo."

Maaawooo growled with menace.

MB swallowed nervously and looked wide-eyed with disbelief and excitement at Teeelaaa. No one would ever believe him, that he, Chief Mocking Bird had been engaged to a real Bigfoot babe. He pinched himself, thinking he was still asleep and having a wet dream.

"I must be dreaming," MB insisted. He couldn't feel the pinch with all the whacky shit he'd taken.

Duane gave MB another smack across the head, "Feel that, dufus?" Duane smirked as MB rubbed his head. "It's for real."

Duane shook some sense into his naked and completely confused friend. "Now there are two ways you can get out of this. One is the old fashioned way." Duane grinned mischievously. "And that is to allow your ex-mate—Teeelaaa in this case, to tie you up naked and cover you all over in berry juice . . ." He faltered to allow this to sink into MB's befuddled brain.

MB liked the sound of where this was going so far. He was eager for Duane to continue.

Duane continued with a twinkle in his eyes, ".... After that you would be left outside a raccoons' nest to let them—the raccoons, lick off the berry juice." Duane pointed to several voracious-looking raccoons. "Sometimes they get quite ravenous."

The raccoons stood on their hind legs and chuckled with delight, showing sharp teeth.

MB looked horrified at the raccoons and swallowed hard.

Duane finished off with, "if you're lucky, the raccoons will leave you intact, so to speak, but without any body hair whatsoever, and if you're not so lucky . . . well, do I need to go down there?"

MB was ready to puke at the thought of his beloved beef bayonet being bitten off. He looked fearfully at Teeelaaa. The thought of a pack of rabid raccoons slurping berries off his naked body was so unpleasant that he started to shake with sheer dread.

"Not recommended! And the second way . . ." Duane paused and grinned. His eyes twinkled with delight and mischief. "Well, it's more of a dare really. In my case, Teeelaaa, my soon-to-be ex-mate, drew a picture of what she wanted me to do. Bigfoot are really good artists, by the way. I bet not many people know that. You know most of those ancient Indian drawings on rocks and in caves?" Duane waited for MB to nod yes. ".... Well, Bigfoot drew them."

MB had a look of total shock on his face, "No way, man. That's our heritage you're messing with."

"It's me you're talking to now, MB . . . you're no more an Indian than that grandfather of yours—the one always falling off his horse in *The High Chaparral*."

MB sobered up some. "It's our secret, right?"

Duane smirked and continued, "Whatever. Anyway, Teeelaaa dared me to enter a stranger's home with a real Bigfoot and give said Bigfoot a hose down."

"Why the doughnuts?"

"Good question ... as for the doughnuts, well that one's for Lou's deputies. She told me she just can't get them to lay off cakes. Unfortunately for the sheriff's department, I like sneaking into people's homes so much I don't want to stop."

MB was well aware that Duane was the Phantom Bigfoot, now that he'd taken on the mantle as Sergeant Sphincter, but the rest of his story was a bit too hard to swallow. And yet he had no choice but to believe what Duane had told him about the Bigfoot.

MB looked back at Teeelaaa and Maaawooo bonking their brains out for the second time and all around at the other

Bigfoot still dancing to the salsa music. He realized that he was in mild shock. No one was going to believe any of this. No one would believe that he'd witnessed a Bigfoot wedding. He didn't quite believe it himself.

40

THE NEXT DAY, the sheriff's patrol car slowly drove down Big Beaver Avenue displaying an array of detached houses with their white clapboard walls and well-maintained gardens, rimmed in by white wooden fences and small Ponderosa fir trees.

The houses were of a wide variety of designs and sizes, having been built over a period of hundred years. There were no cookie-cutters in Big Beaver. All were very clean and presentable looking, picture-postcard like. Several of the houses displayed Bed and Breakfast signs.

Happy Beaverites were out walking their dogs and going about their day-to-day lives unaware that yet another heinous crime had now been committed in their neighborhood.

As Lou drove around a curve in the road she and Deputy Dwight, seated next to her, could see another patrol car and the Medical Examiner's car outside the Funderburk House.

The Funderburk House was the first to be built on the avenue and backed directly onto the verge of the forest. It had Ponderosa pine trees out front, blocking the house from nosy Beaverites.

Lou parked her patrol car behind the other vehicles and switched the engine off. Lou and Dwight sat in the car for several moments with grim faces.

The sheriff blew out her cheeks and heaved a sigh. She was less than eager to enter the crime scene as she'd seen it all before. She glanced at Deputy Dwight and could tell his gut was churning just like hers.

It occurred to Lou that maybe this was the work of the copycat. So far, the local radio had been told to play it down, and so there had been no mention of a copycat. The mayor wanted the entire Phantom Bigfoot Bather Case to be kept as quiet as possible. But it was still the summer season. Hordes of tourists were descending on their idyllic little town and so word had started to spread. Big Beaver would probably make national headlines and become the laughing stock of the nation. Lou didn't want that to happen to her town.

"Come on, chubby, move it," Lou ordered, as she opened the door of her patrol car and got out. She took in a massive, deep breath of fresh, pine-scented air, as if it would be her last.

Dwight lingered for a moment inside the confines of the sheriff's patrol car. He took a deep breath of the scented magnolia stick that hung from the rear view mirror. He savored the pleasing fragrance for a moment then slowly got out.

As they approached the house they saw the comfy outdoor floral-patterned chairs dotted about the porch. Hanging plants dangled from the veranda's overhang. The bright yellow front door was wide open.

Sheriff Lou and Deputy Dwight heard a dog barking and children playing in a nearby neighbor's garden.

Lou reached the front porch first and muttered to herself, "No fainting, Lou. You're the sheriff . . . got that?"

Just as she was about to place her foot onto the front porch, Deputy Bill burst forth from the open door and jumped down the steps into the front lawn, almost knocking Lou and

Dwight off the veranda. He had a hand to his mouth as if about to puke.

Sheriff Lou and Deputy Dwight turned round to watch in horror as the deputy bent over. Thankfully nothing came up.

Lou swallowed down the need to throw up herself, thinking this is going to be bad.

Dwight patted his rounded stomach and muttered, "I've gotta real bad feeling about this one, Lou."

"Oh yeah," Lou agreed with a grimace.

"Don't go in there. It's the worst one yet," Deputy Bill groaned, gasping for fresh air.

Lou turned away from Bill, and entered the house with Deputy Dwight.

ONCE IN THE HALLWAY, Lou and Dwight heard Deputy Will and the ME's muted voices coming from somewhere upstairs. Throughout the lower part of the house there was the sweet fragrance of Lily of the Valley air freshener mixed with that familiar pungent odor. Lou saw two large sets of muddy Bigfoot prints making their way from the rear kitchen to the stairs.

She gave the neat hallway a cursory glance as she walked towards the stairs with Deputy Dwight in tow.

They paused outside the open living room door. There, seated in a rocking chair, was Ms Mamie Funderburk, quietly watching TV with the sound muted. She was a petite, white-haired, eighty-five-year-old woman. She was quite deaf and more than a little absent-minded.

Ms Mamie's housekeeper had reported the crime before breakfast that day. She had told Lou not to upset Ms Mamie, as she was totally oblivious to anything untoward going on in her home. Apparently the old girl slept downstairs these days due to arthritis that prevented her from climbing the stairs, and as such, had not witnessed the crime.

AT THE TOP of the stairs, Sheriff Lou and Deputy Dwight noticed the plethora of small gilt framed photographs of the bygone years of Ms Mamie and various family members and friends.

They could still hear Deputy Will and the ME talking. Sheriff Lou and Deputy Dwight exchanged anxious glances as they walked down the hallway towards the crime scene, following the muddy footprints.

Lou's nostrils twitched. She could now smell the faint hint of bleach and that all too familiar, pungent stench, that would cling to her senses for days afterwards.

Sheriff Lou and Deputy Dwight took in deep breaths. Slowly, with stomach-churning dread, they tentatively walked down the hallway towards the bathroom.

They reached the open door to the crime scene and peered into the bathroom to see Deputy Will photographing the ME, as he drew a plastic sheet over the bowl. Both had pegs on their noses.

Sheriff Lou and Deputy Dwight could clearly see muddy Bigfoot prints completely covering the linoleum floor. Lou correctly concluded that one perp had used the toilet. The air was now so overpowering that Lou felt dizzy.

Deputy Will and the ME were too involved with the crime scene to notice that the sheriff and Dwight had come in to the small bathroom and were standing quietly behind them.

Lou coughed as the stink burrowed into her brain.

"Smells about the same to me," Lou declared, announcing her presence with a wrinkled nose.

Both Will and Herb jumped almost out of their skins, turning round to look at the sheriff and Dwight who stood a few feet behind them, revealing the toilet bowl with a plastic sheet over it.

From Deputy Will's puce-green pallor and the ME's whiter than normal features, Lou didn't need to know what she was about to see was going to make her feel pretty bad too.

Lou walked over to the toilet with leaden feet while Dwight stood fixed to the spot trying not to breath in the disgusting stench that invaded his nostrils. Lou removed the sheet to see two partially eaten chocolate éclairs floating in the pan.

It had to be Duane, she thought, and he was escalating to a different confection. Not that there weren't other suspects in town, but Duane was the number one. And Duane was smart, which meant the Phantom Bigfoot was smart, for he knew to put plenty of bleach down the toilet bowl and in the bathing facilities.

Lou checked the bath and saw the drain clogged with matted fur, as yet unidentified, although close to being human hair. So the hair could not be Duane's.

"You just going to stand there like a lost turd, Dwight?" Herb remarked somewhat peevishly. "Do you think it's the work of the copycat?" Herb asked Lou.

"Perhaps?" Lou replied, who was now unable to tear her eyes away from the clumps of fur stuck to the sides of the bath and tiles. She dared to sniff the hair and thought the smell was very similar to Duane's Bigfoot suit.

"I've seen enough. Time for the extraction!" Lou pushed Dwight aside and breathed in fresh air at the window.

Dwight fell backwards into the bath, floundering like a beached whale.

From her vantage point, Lou had a clear view of the garden below and of the small group of eager Beaverites now gathered on the lawn.

Deputy Bill was there, telling them, "The Phantom Bigfoot has struck again."

In response to the deputy's declaration, everyone cheered loud and clear for all to hear.

Typical, Lou thought.

Less than fifteen minutes later, Walt Flucker and son arrived at the crime scene. Having received an urgent call from Noreen to get ASAP to Mamie Funderburk's house, Walt wasted no time, and with sirens blazing on his "Dumpster" mobile, as he affectionately called it, arrived ASAP at the crime scene.

THE BRAVE SHERIFF WATCHED the Fluckers standing over the toilet bowl staring at the éclairs. Father and son were dressed in their professional-looking, dark brown jumpsuits with "No dump is too big for a Flucker" emblazoned on their backs in luminous lime green.

It suddenly occurred to Lou that the Fluckers might very well be the copycat Phantom Bigfoot. It wouldn't surprise her if they were, but for now she needed to concentrate on this crime scene.

The Fluckers' faces remained their usual ruddiness. But strangely enough neither held their hands over their mouths to cover up the foul stench. They were professional sewage extraction experts, a job not to be taken lightly.

Walt took in a big breath. "Ah, ambrosia to my nostrils." He started to giggle. "Damn . . . that éclair looks real tasty."

Lou looked with revulsion at Walt.

"Which one?" Beau chuckled, taking a snapshot of the offending items with his cell phone. "That one's mine!" Beau reached for one éclair.

Lou slapped Beau's hand and looked disapprovingly at father and son. "This isn't a laughing matter . . . just get on with the extraction." She turned to Herb, "Bag all the hair in the bath and make castings of the prints in the back garden."

Lou gave Dwight an urgent look for him to do something, indicating Beau's cell phone.

Dwight, still wiping Bigfoot hair from his uniform with his hand, took his cue and made a dash towards Beau in an attempt to grab hold of the cell phone before he decided to mail it off.

Beau quickly raised his cell phone up high out of Dwight's reach.

Deputy Will, the ME and Walt started to snigger.

"You can't take photos of a crime scene," Dwight spluttered excitedly as he tried, with arms raised, to grab hold of the cell phone. He looked like a plump ballerina.

Walt grinned at Dwight then at Lou. "Come on, Lou, leave Beau alone . . . he's been through enough."

"Uh-uh," was Lou's reply. "Hand it over, Beau."

"Shit," Walt mumbled under his breath. He nodded to Beau.

Beau heaved a sigh and handed the cell phone to the deputy, but dropped it into the toilet.

"You did that on purpose, didn't you?" Dwight demanded with as much authority as he could muster.

"Go fetch it if you want it that bad, blubber guts," Beau teased.

Dwight gave a hurt look to Beau before looking down into the toilet.

Walt chuckled at Dwight's discomfort. With a manly swagger he turned his attention back to the toilet bowl. Walt unzipped a chest pocket and removed a pair of heavy duty latex gloves, extra long, which he slowly slipped over his hands with a resounding snap.

Lou heaved a woeful sigh. "Hold it Walt! This time we should keep the crime scene intact. I want you to drain the water from the toilet bowl and unscrew the fixings and bring the toilet intact to the Medical Examiner's lab." She glanced over at the ME who nodded his head in agreement.

Lou rushed from the bathroom with Dwight and Will in tow.

᷾   ᷾   ᷾

A LITTLE OVER TWO HOURS later, the Fluckers staggered out of the Funderburk House with the offending toilet between them, wrapped in a body-bag.

A rapturous cheer came from the large crowd of Beaverites and deputies awaiting the arrival of said toilet.

Walt and son had great difficulty heaving the cumbersome toilet into the back of their Dumpster Mobile.

Both men removed hankies and mopped their sweaty brows.

Grimaces and yucks came from the crowd.

Sheriff Lou hopped into her patrol car and drove off.

Following her were the deputies' cars, the ME's car and Walt's Dumpster Mobile.

Lou's thoughts drifted towards Willis. That's it.

41

A COUPLE OF MONTHS LATER, Lou sat at her desk dressed in a white bridal gown, just one hour before getting hitched to Willis. She had just enough time to tidy up her desk. Deputy Dwight entered her office. She picked up a file marked "Phantom Bigfoot Bather Case" and dropped the file into a drawer then slammed it shut. There had been no new cases since number five, but Lou didn't feel optimistic. She felt sure there would be more. Question was—when?

Dwight hovered with a peculiar look on his face.

She looked at him. "Please don't tell me the Phantom Bather has struck again?"

"Not exactly." He cleared his throat. "Well . . . you're not going to believe this, sheriff?"

"Try me."

"You see . . . it's kinda like this . . . Walt's been abducted, again."

"Little Beaver?"

"Where else?"

"How do you know he was abducted?"

"Go ask Duane, he witnessed the whole thing."

"Where is he?"

"In the outer office." Dwight gave a slight chuckle.

Sheriff Lou sighed heavily and thought whatever Duane would tell her she wouldn't believe. "Until I get back from my honeymoon, it's your case." She stood up.

Dwight admired her wedding dress, "You look absolutely ravishing, Lou."

"Why, thank you, Dwight." With that, Lou stepped out of her office to stare in utter amazement at Duane.

AFTER ALL THESE YEARS Duane-o stood before her looking gorgeous as she knew he could. His clean-shaven face grinned at her. His beautiful blond hair was neatly trimmed. His black tuxedo showed off his muscular body. He was an Adonis with a delicious aroma to match.

Lou's face flushed as she thought what she could do to him, but thoughts of marrying Willis confused her. She became breathless due to the tight bodice she was wearing.

"Are you okay, Lou?" Duane asked.

No she definitely was not alright. She felt light-headed. Lou swooned.

Duane caught her in his strong arms.

Lou looked up and swam in Duane's blue eyes. "Oh Duane . . . you've ruined everything."

WHILE THIS WAS GOING ON, Acting Sheriff Dwight sat at the computer and used the mouse to activate a hidden file.

On the screen appeared the lurid picture of Bigfoot seated on the toilet, eating a doughnut. He used the mouse to activate the printer. Dwight rubbed his hands together with excitement.

"This is going to be so cool."

LATER THAT DAY, the town welcome sign had the same lurid picture taped to it with a desperate plea—

"Has anyone seen this toilet?—If so, please
contact the sheriff's department immediately."

This message was also displayed on every lamppost, telephone pole, electricity pole and on every milk carton in town, as ordered by Acting Sheriff Dwight.

THE END

About the author

Simon Okill turned to writing as therapy after a disability forced him into early retirement. He has written a number of screenplays and has several novels in progress. He lives with his wife, Shirlee Anne and their cat, in a pretty coastal town in South Wales, UK.